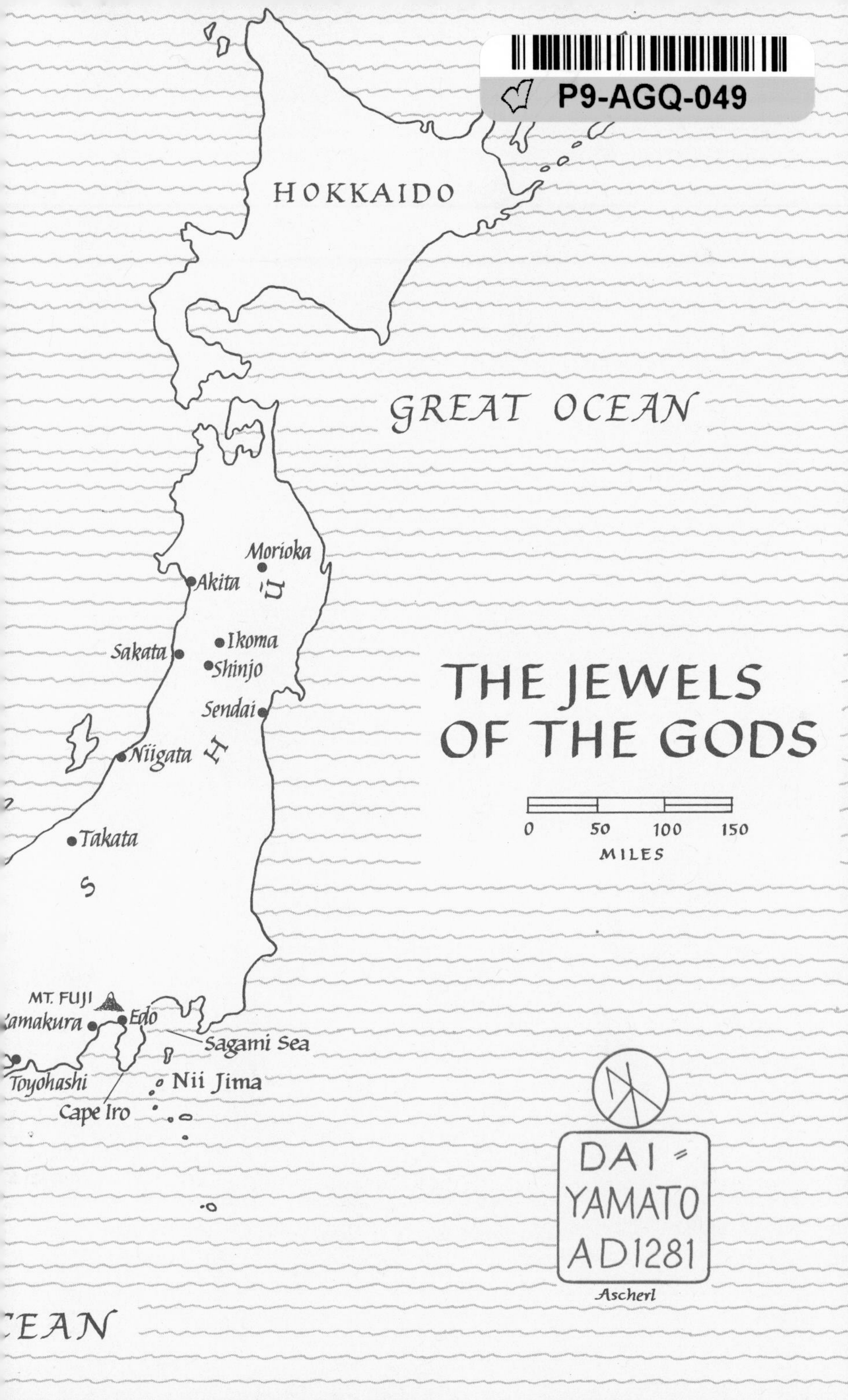
HOKKAIDO
GREAT OCEAN
Morioka
Akita
Ikoma
Sakata
Shinjo
Sendai
Niigata
Takata
THE JEWELS
OF THE GODS
0 50 100 150
MILES
MT. FUJI
amakura
Edo
Sagami Sea
Nii Jima
Toyohashi
Cape Iro
DAI =
YAMATO
AD1281
Ascherl
EAN

Sakuran

Sakuran

A novel of medieval Japan

by Edward Tolosko

•

Farrar Straus Giroux

New York

Published simultaneously in Canada by

McGraw-Hill Ryerson Ltd., Toronto

Printed in the United States of America

Designed by Cynthia Krupat

First edition, 1978

Library of Congress Cataloging in Publication Data

Tolosko, Edward. / Sakuran.

I. Title.

PZ4.T649Sak [PS3570.0429] 813'.5'4 78-6560

For Doreen
These are
the thoughts
that took
your place
in my mind
for a moment

The gods were dying off, and the eldest of them directed the two youngest, Izanagi and Izanami, to create a memorial worthy of their honor.

The two young gods thrust a holy spear into the greatest ocean of the world. Then they held the spear aloft, and the 4,223 jewels that dripped from it became the sacred islands of Yamato.

Izanagi and Izanami mated, founding the Japanese race. The first-born was the goddess Amaterasu, Keeper of the Sun. She was born over the jeweled islands, and the sun rises there as an eternal memorial. But this was just the beginning: from Amaterasu was born the god Ninigi, and from him came all the emperors of Japan, in an unbroken line, to this very day.

Dai-Nippon, or Great Japan, was divided into almost three hundred fiefs, which lasted through the thirteenth century. These daimyōdoms were owned by the shōguns, who were powerful leaders of rich families. In reality, these shōguns ruled the land. The Emperor, the direct descendant of the gods, was the divine ruler.

Above the shogunate was the Bakufu, or supreme military council, composed of the most powerful shōguns, who required of their daimyōs periods of tenure as soldiers of the Bakufu or of its military arm, the Samurai Dokoro.

In their sphere, the daimyōs were lords and masters of their land. They remained daimyōs as long as the taxes were forwarded to the shogunate. Wars between daimyōdoms were not uncommon and were usually overlooked by the shogunate—providing the taxes continued to be collected.

The daimyōs hired and maintained trained soldiers to protect their lands. By the ninth century, great sensei roamed the land, teaching the trade of war to the families of the daimyōs; thus, the samurai were created and developed into a caste long before the twelfth century, possibly as early as the fourth.

A son born to a samurai family was given free rein until the age of six. Then, from that point on, he was trained in the profession of war. By the time he was nineteen years old, he was a fighting machine of precision—not only with the sword but with any weapon of the times, including bare hands.

But the most potent weapon of the samurai, however, was the code bred into him—to put it simply: "Do or die, no matter what." The samurai was capable of incomparable drive and total focus, traits inherent in the Japanese even now.

In contrast, there was another absolute aspect to the nature of the samurai: if necessary, he could be converted into a man of peace to seek his ends. Many samurai became monks or priests—though they always kept their swords. This other, peaceful aspect of the samurai is signified by the cherry blossom.

The samurai sometimes wrote poetry and lectured on his interests other than war. He might even paint or work in other art forms. But the samurai had a disdain for money. He would not touch it. In most cases, he did not require it. There was always someone who needed his talents, and from them he received his koku: measured by the year, about five bushels of rice, and all the tea and saké he could drink.

Until the invention of gunpowder made him obsolete, there were no soldiers in all the world who could equal the samurai.

E.T.

Sakuran

Fragile

petals of

the cherry blossom

rush to

nowhere with

the wind

PRINCIPAL CHARACTERS

THE JUGI HOSHI

Yasumori Fugita—Daimyō of Ikoma
Gokarō Ito—Second-in-command to Yasumori Fugita
Okei Fugita—Wife of Yasumori Fugita
Prince Jujiro Fugita—Son of the daimyō
Tasuke Ito—Son of the gokarō
Keisuke Shishido—Master swordsman and sensei
Hetomi Tajimi—Runner

THE RED TRIANGLE

Kumahatchi Murata—Tōryō, the yatō leader
Kogashira Kozo—Second-in-command to Kumahatchi Murata
Sakura Murata—Daughter of Kumahatchi Murata

FROM MINA

Sanda Taizo—Master swordsman and sensei
Aki Taizo—Daughter of Sanda Taizo
Somiko Sei—Friend and neighbor of Aki

Most of the laborers wore only loincloths, their tanned and sweating bodies glistening like wet gold. Carefully, they stacked the crates on the wagons, while two fully dressed samurai worked on the platform, marking the boxes for the caravan. Prince Jujiro checked the tally by numbering the cases to be loaded. His friend Tasuke then stamped each with the large symbol of the Jugi Hoshi. The stamp he used was carved from a single piece of wood that fit snugly into its holder, which also held the ink supply. Obviously, Tasuke enjoyed the work—he stamped each crate more than was necessary.

"You're making a mess of it," said Jujiro, laughing. "Here's the last box. Just stamp the ends."

"Hai," Tasuke answered with a smile. He stamped as directed. Turning, he pointed toward the manor and yelled: "Chotto!"

When the daimyō's son turned to look, Tasuke stamped the crossed star on his back. The dripping symbol stood out large and vivid on the white cloth. The prince arched his stomach forward as he felt the cold ink soak through his kariginu.

The gokarō's son, still with the stamp in one hand and its holder in the other, jumped from the platform to make his escape, but Prince Jujiro gave chase. He pursued his friend down the path toward the manor gardens.

Smiling, people stepped aside. They had become accustomed to the antics of the leaders' sons. Whenever something unusual was happening in Ikoma, these two were surely the cause.

Around a corner, sensei stood talking. The sound of running feet caught their attention, and most of the teachers scrambled out of the way. One of the sensei looked down at his ink-splattered kimono after the first went by, and realized that he should have jumped with the others. The pursuer plowed into him, sending them both to the ground, but Jujiro managed to escape the angry teacher. The yelling of the sensei spurred the runners on.

Tasuke, aware of the accident and knowing that his friend would eventually catch him, stopped. He replaced the stamp in its holder and flung it into the bushes. Hearing more shouts, though, he took off running again.

When the prince reached the spot, another ink-splotched samurai emerged from the bushes. Somewhere in the garden, a partially dressed woman cried and screamed in anger, but Jujiro did not slow down. Finally he found Tasuke lying under a tree. By then he was too tired to fight and he collapsed near his friend. They looked at each other and broke into howls of laughter.

T*he* sky was clear to the north. What would have been a rare cloudless day was marred in the east by a wide band of smoke that obscured the hilltops across the valley of Ikoma.

Centered in the valley, Ikoma manor commanded the mura from a knoll. A patchwork of rice fields spread in all directions, each field a different color, from dark green—almost black—through the lighter shades to yellow. Some patches were flooded; like mirrors, they reflected the trees, buildings, or hills that were near.

Prince Jujiro Fugita looked down into his valley. He was content, glad to be away from the constant training that had been his routine for as long as he could remember.

A dust cloud rose from the mura and mingled with the smoke. The daimyō's son did not envy the mounted soldiers who rode at full gallop on the powdered earth, practicing with the bow or the soft-nosed spear. Jujiro had his share of it, and relaxing on a hillside in the clear air was a welcome change. Iie, he did not envy the soldiers.

Nearby, Tasuke Ito rested on the ground, his hunting bow across his stomach, his eyes closed. He, too, felt content. It was good to rest after the climb, good to be away from the sensei. Indeed, it was best to be hunting the elusive shika, the deer, whose sense of sight, smell, and hearing greatly exceeded that of the hunters. Yes, it would be much better to shoot at live, moving targets, rather than at the inanimate ones the soldiers below were using.

The hunters on the hillside made a striking picture, with heads shaved in front, the rest of the hair piled into a high bun. These features, along with the swords they wore, were the distinguishing marks of the samurai. Today, though, they did not carry the long sword. Tucked in each sash was the kogatana, a short sword in a lacquered sheath.

Together, these men presented a distinct contrast—Jujiro in white with a dark sash, his friend Tasuke in purple with a white sash. The zōri they wore on their feet were of a tightly woven rice straw that appeared new. Yellow hunting bows and brightly feathered and painted arrows completed the picture. On the back and sleeves of both tunics was the round symbol, the monshō, of a crossed four-pointed star, the Jugi Hoshi.

Of the two, Jujiro was taller, slightly more muscular and with cleaner features, all characteristics of the samurai. Unlike most of the soldiers of the mura, neither of the men bore scars. Though they were highly trained for combat, they had not yet experienced the joy of battle.

In the evenings, while their peers relaxed, Tasuke and Jujiro would continue working with the sensei. Shinobi, yawara, and kendō, the study of the long sword, occupied their spare time. When one method of attack or defense was perfected, another teacher was introduced. They had known many. The sensei Keisuke taught them now—Keisuke Shishido, the sensei that could not be equaled.

Tasuke Ito sat up and clasped his hands around his knees. Following his friend's gaze, he, too, looked into the valley and wondered whether all of Nippon was as beautiful. In the eighteen years of his life, Tasuke knew only these hills and this valley. The older soldiers spoke of the sea and of the people that lived only on ships, but Tasuke loved the beauty of northern Honshū. He did not feel cheated.

The prince turned to his friend and spoke. "Only the smoke of the kilns disturbs the scene, nē?"

"Hai," agreed the other. "The kilns are necessary to Ikoma. Notice, much of the smoke comes from the houses outside the mura. I imagine it is the same in all the villages."

It was true. Jujiro saw thin columns rising from almost every house, becoming faded lines as they joined the band of smoke trapped high above the valley. The low, early-spring temperature and the wind skirting the hilltops kept the smoke level.

Jujiro Fugita was the son of the daimyō, the governor, and because of this he was called a prince. Tasuke Ito, the son of the gokarō, second-in-command, held almost the same prestige. This valley was theirs. It came to them from their forebears, who in turn received the land from the shōgun on the condition that the daimyō collect and forward taxes to the shogunate each year.

Ikoma was almost self-supporting; the finest pottery and ceramics were fired here. Trains of wagons left twice a month with its wares. Ikoma's only dependence was upon a town far to the south, Mina, where fine clays were mined and then shipped north for these kilns. Jujiro's great-grandfather had conquered Mina and moved its industry to Ikoma many years before. Since then, the small daimyō-dom had remained a remote satellite of the Jugi Hoshi, flying the same pennant.

A slight sound caused Jujiro to turn away from the valley. "Tasuke! Chotto! I hear twigs snapping there." The prince pointed to a large grove of oak uphill from them.

Quickly, Tasuke was beside him. As one, they fitted arrows to their bows. Then, parting, they walked soundlessly toward the trees.

The buck left the forest, bouncing swiftly toward the prince, but watching the other man. Realizing his mistake, the shika suddenly changed direction in an attempt to escape between the hunters. Two arrows hit from either side. The big buck fell over his front legs, slid, then lay still. Overwhelmed with their luck, Jujiro and Tasuke stared, wide-eyed. Neither samurai had ever seen such a specimen before. Their kill sported four branches to its antlers.

It was late afternoon by the time the smiling procession reached the narrow road of Ikoma. Jujiro and Tasuke walked proudly beside the animal, which hung from a pole threaded between the bone and tendon of each foot. Protruding from the hide, the broken shafts of the arrows told the story. The two nōmin, the peasants, carrying the load, were also proud; they would have something to talk about tonight. Small children ran ahead of the four men, and their excited talk and shouts heralded the event to others.

At the mura, seasoned men gathered around admiring the animal as it was being skinned. Later some of these soldiers would tell of the size of the shika. Its dimensions would grow larger with each retelling.

The two men were already in their ceremonial robes when the bamboo clapper sounded. They entered a small, spartan room. The woman who had summoned them waited in the hall until the men took their places on the thick rice-straw tatami that covered the floor in geometric rectangles. Then she followed, and knelt facing them.

To the woman's right, a sunken charcoal fireplace forced heat into an iron kettle. At her other side, the lacquered chests kept the utensils of the ceremony: the bowls, the whisk, and the round container of powdered tea. She restored the clapper to its holder, then reached for the large tea bowl.

The men, in the middle of the room, sat back on their heels. They held their hands flat above their knees, their eyes closed in meditation. These men were alike. The ceremonial silk kimonos they wore differed only in the colored designs painted on them. The features of both faces were nearly the same. Those of the older, Yasumori Fugita, showed well-defined lines of wisdom and experience, which had yet to touch the brow of his son, Jujiro.

Neither man spoke when the woman, Okei Fugita, set

before her husband a large but fragile tea bowl. She did this with delicate precision and in silence. It was not until she had mixed the powdered tea that the men opened their eyes. Nodding slightly to each, Okei retreated, sat back on her heels, and watched her men.

Holding the bowl with both hands, Yasumori sipped the tea. When he finished, he made a gratuitous noise. Jujiro followed his father's example. The prince held the bowl in the palm of one hand and with the other hand reached into his kimono for a napkin. He carefully wiped the edge of the bowl, where his lips had touched. Jujiro set the bowl down, then turned it, completing the ceremony. On seeing the men finish, Okei Fugita moved forward, now preparing the tea for herself.

The muffled talk from adjacent buildings, the scuffing of zōri, the miaowing of a cat, and the distant sound of a barking dog drifted into the quiet room through the papered doors.

The daimyō spoke first. "The house of Fugita has no enemies. Our potteries are in demand, and even now we are readying a shipment for Heian-Kyō." As Yasumori directed his talk to Jujiro, Okei busied herself with the hot water and china. She listened to the words of her husband with interest.

"We can be thankful," the daimyō continued, "that our losses to the yatō have lessened since I began sending more samurai with the caravans. Soon you will lead the soldiers on some of these journeys."

"Why can't I go with the caravan to Heian-Kyō?" Jujiro asked.

"No, Jujiro." Okei answered. "It is much too far, and your studies would suffer."

"Hai," added Yasumori. "Your time will come soon

enough." He smiled at his son, seeing the image of himself years ago.

There was a lull in the conversation. Somewhere outside the tearoom, a dog barked. Something nearby fell with a crash. Faraway laughter connected these sounds together.

"Okei, you must know that Jujiro is unhappy here. But listen. Outside, across the compound, they laugh. Those samurai are happy because they are home." Turning toward Jujiro, Yasumori repeated, "Hai, your time will come soon enough." He looked questioningly at the woman, started to speak, but changed his mind. Instead, he turned to his son. "You are no longer a child. On the next mission, you will lead. The gokarō's son will be your second-in-command, but there is a condition—"

"Hai," interrupted the prince, smiling now.

"It is," the daimyō continued, "that you learn about the shipments and about the records that must be kept. Now would be a good time to start." He pointed outside. "A caravan is being prepared."

"Hai," said his son. "Tasuke and I will go to the kilns now. Dōmo, dōmo arigatō." He bowed to his father as he backed from the room.

The large-wheeled wagons appeared to be laden only with straw as they lumbered out of the mura, leaving a bright yellow trail behind them. The crowd that gathered to see the caravan off waved and called to departing relatives. Off to one side, Jujiro and Tasuke looked on, full of excitement.

Earlier there had been talk of Mina. Like all untried young warriors, they had listened intently to the soldiers describing the yatō they might meet. The samurai assigned to the caravan spoke as if eager for a meeting with the bandits, though they knew their protection of the caravan would forestall any such clash.

As the last rider cleared the gate, Tasuke spoke. "Soon it will be our turn, don't you think?"

Jujiro ignored the question. Instead, he pointed to a samurai walking ahead of them. "There's our sensei Keisuke. He nears the dōjō. We should already be there. Hayaku!"

As the two passed the teacher, he gave them a stern look, but smiled after them.

Inside the dōjō, without talking, the two stripped completely and donned the special loincloth that was required. The highly polished floor of the combat room reflected two people where there was one. Here, young samurai trained at yawara, the ability to overcome an opponent by using anything or nothing.

The young men, unarmed and barefoot, paired off with sensei. Unlike their students, these sensei were armed with the naginata, a bamboo stick that could be used as a sword or spear, or even a club. A sensei circled the pair, observing in order to criticize and grade, as each in turn was given the nod to begin.

The prince felt a quake in his chest. The master was pointing at him.

The daimyō's son carefully studied Keisuke, his opponent. He knew the teacher would beat him again. It seemed hopeless. Keisuke, the ablest of the older samurai, the severest sensei, stood expressionless before him, fully clothed, wearing a leather chest plate and shin armor. His coarse-woven zōri could become fearsome weapons.

Jujiro drew in great breaths of air, priming himself for the forthcoming effort. He took a defensive stance, feet apart, then one last deep breath. Keisuke bowed and stalked toward him.

Jujiro dropped to one knee and felt the rush of air as the bamboo sword arced close to his head. Good, he thought, the great sensei has missed. But did he plan it that way? A new sense gave the prince warning. He sprang to one side and felt the knurled stick push into the soft part of his arm. The intended force of the blow did not materialize. He moved with the naginata. So far, so good. But he must not stay on the defensive, he must get past the stick, at the man. Today he must win.

Feinting to the right and dropping to the floor, he managed to elude the sword a second time. Jujiro retreated, but the sword hit both his hands almost at the same time. When this sequence was repeated, he realized the strategy of the man Keisuke. Purposely, with a palm edge, he struck at the sword as it swung toward him. He did not make contact; instead, his other hand turned to fire where the sensei's bamboo struck a solid blow.

The sensei was talking now, but Jujiro did not take his eyes off his opponent. Guarding his aching hands, the prince waited for the man to lunge again— Now!

Keisuke smiled, then screamed, as he drove in for the finish. He would strike from the highest point.

Now! Jujiro dropped to both knees. When the sword struck his back, he knew that finally he had moved past the weapon. The naginata was still on his back when he switched to the offensive. From his kneeling position, and with great force, he slammed a palm edge upward into the man's groin. Keisuke suddenly gave ground. The prince pressed the attack. This time he struck punishing blows into the man's sides, still using the edges of his palms. He felt the sensei's wind in his face. Ah! He had him now! Jujiro hammered a fist to Keisuke's jaw.

Then it happened. Something hit the prince, and his body exploded with searing pain. His arms dropped helplessly to his sides. He was aware of Keisuke still standing, almost bending over him. The pain built up where the handle of the sensei's weapon had hit him. He stumbled forward, the leather armor blurring out of focus as he slumped to the floor.

The daimyō's son became aware of a staccato sound, which turned out to be Tasuke's laughter. His friend led the prince from the floor of the dōjō.

"Don't feel bad, Jujiro. No one has beaten Keisuke yet. He told me just now that you were a kuma with too many claws."

"Well, this kuma is going to hibernate and sharpen his claws," returned Jujiro. "That man is unhuman," he added after a thought. When he looked down at his reddened hands, he felt he had learned something. Ah, sō desu—the hands, the most efficient weapon of all. Keisuke was always the sensei. Jujiro smiled.

When Tasuke and the prince left the dōjō, the sensei approached them. "Kimi, I'm proud of you," he said. "You have come a long way."

Keisuke meant it. Hai, the prince had studied under many teachers, and Keisuke felt Jujiro knew well the best of each of them. It was doubtful if any of these teachers could beat the prince now. It had been an accident in the dōjō. The handle of the naginata had stopped the prince, but at that instant Keisuke had been helpless, he had not struck with it. With his great speed, Jujiro had rammed into it. Sadly, Keisuke now realized his role as sensei to the prince was over.

Hai, Keisuke Shishido was more than proud of his protégé. He had picked the sensei for the prince and thus had helped mold this youth into a man—into a samurai, one with abilities that far exceeded his own. He loved the prince and would miss their close association: Keisuke the sculptor, the prince his clay.

"I am happy we are both of the Jugi Hoshi," he told Jujiro.

"Dōmo, dōmo arigatō gozaimasu."

The three walked toward the baths—the younger two each with an arm over the shoulder of the sensei.

The continual music of water running from the bamboo pipe down the small mountain was not soothing tonight. Prince Jujiro lay restless in his futon. Usually the sound from the garden outside his room lulled him to sleep, but not tonight. Sleep is a thief, he thought. A perfect day like today should be much longer. It had been a beautiful day. He had not missed any of his targets with the bow and the spear, and even in the dōjō he had excelled. Why must the cloak of night obscure these triumphs?

Jujiro rose from the bed. He wore no clothing. In the daytime he was confined and regimented. At night, in the privacy of his apartment, he knew complete freedom. He reveled in it.

Crossing the room, the daimyō's son slid open the shōji, the paper-covered sliding door. Outside, the high, unclouded moon robbed the night of its mantle. To one side of the garden, large rocks took the shape of a small mountain. From its peak, a thin stream of water trickled down over moss. It ran into one edge of the pond without disturbing its surface, and from this natural mirror the moon's double looked up at Jujiro. Suddenly the mirror broke into rings from its center; a glistening red-salmon koi came up

for air. The night sounds of the village outside the mura beckoned.

Closing the shōji, Jujiro crossed the room again. This time he dressed. Tucking the kogatana in his obi, he left the manor by way of the garden.

Tasuke was asleep when Jujiro reached his room. The prince called softly through the shōji; finally he entered the bedroom to awaken his friend. Nearby, a dog barked excitedly at the intruder, and in another part of the building a shōji was opened. The gokarō, Tasuke's father, called to the dog. For a while the dog persisted, then left in obedience to the caller.

"I'm glad you woke me," Tasuke said as he put on his kariginu. "What you suggest is a good idea. The saké is good and the women there are not ugly. We shall have a fine time."

Jujiro sat on the tatami. He crossed his legs, then spoke to his friend. "I couldn't sleep tonight," he said. "I feel that I must talk to someone. I'm getting bored. We train with and without weapons every day. I'm sure I could kill any man with these bare hands." He curled the fingers of both hands before him. "But for what?" he continued. "The caravans leave without us. We do not see the yatō. My sword is thirsty."

Tasuke nodded in agreement. These facts also angered Tasuke, but he did not like to dwell on them. He would change the subject.

"Our time will be. Your father has promised that we shall take the next caravan. Be patient," he said. "Come, I am ready, at the teahouse we can forget our troubles."

The moon was still overhead when they reached the teahouse. It was a stilted building surrounded by lit paper lanterns. A woman stood by the opened shōji, welcoming them.

"We are much honored." The hostess bowed. "Please enter. Ah, Tasuke Ito! I did not expect to see you so soon again." She bowed again to Tasuke, this time more slowly. Then she looked at the daimyō's son and smiled.

The two men stepped onto the porch and removed their zōri. Tasuke's eyes met those of the woman and held them.

"Tonight I have brought my usual appetite, Ko-san; also my friend." He nodded toward Jujiro. "This is Prince Jujiro. I'm sure you know of him. I would like you to join us." He smiled, and without moving his head, his eyes swung toward Jujiro, then back to the woman's. She nodded to Tasuke.

"You are most welcome, my lords. I am Ko-tori," the hostess said. "If you are hungry, I will serve you myself. Ah, most delicate." Her eyes still held Tasuke's.

Ko-tori led the men through the large tearoom. The few customers they passed paid them no heed. From somewhere in the building, muffled by the thick tatami on the floors, came the music of the samisen, mingling with the murmur of voices and the clink of thin china.

Jujiro looked at the woman he followed. Pretty, he thought. Small and fragile, as her name—"little bird"—implied. He smiled. So this was Tasuke's love. Jujiro had not missed the look in their eyes.

The woman pushed back a shōji and motioned the two men into the small room. Except for the wooden lantern near one wall and the tatami on the floor, the room was bare. "Make yourselves comfortable," Ko-tori said. "I will be back very soon."

"You will like it here," Tasuke told his friend after the woman left. "I come here often, and usually stay late." He laughed.

"It's no wonder. Ko-tori is very pretty," Jujiro said.

"You think so? I haven't noticed. She is good company."

The prince broke out laughing. "Kimi, I am your friend, remember. You should know me. I am not naïve."

The shōji opened. Ko-tori returned. She set an ozen, a legged tray, in front of them. Behind her, another woman entered and bowed to the floor.

"I introduce you to my friend," Ko-tori said to the daimyō's son as she poured the wine. "This is Aki Taizo. She is not from Ikoma. Aki, this is—" A moment of panic seized her. She had forgotten the man's name.

"I am Jujiro. It is good to meet you." The prince bowed.

"Aki, this is Jujiro," Ko-tori began again. She had planned a good introduction. She would give it. "Aki can read and write kanji. Her home is samurai, so you will have much in common."

Jujiro looked at Aki, trying to see her face, which was averted. The dim light of the lantern brought out the pearl color of her white skin. As she sat up, a fan spread from her hand, covering her face below her eyes. She did not speak as she walked on her knees toward the ozen.

The prince could not take his eyes off the woman. Her hair, piled high, was flawlessly and artfully set with ornaments which hung from long hairpins, gathering and reflecting the light from the lantern. The fan spread in front of her face bore a picture of a wind-blown pine tree; the same scene was repeated on her kimono. The white obi around her waist was the field of snow from which the pine tree grew. The background of the scene was night, her dark kimono. As she slowly lowered her fan, a faint smile met the prince's gaze.

"I am Jujiro," he said again. "I—" Aki closed her fan. She was beautiful. The daimyō's son searched for something to say. He felt the blood rush to his neck. Why did he feel so decidedly uncomfortable?

Tasuke helped him. "Here, let us drink a toast to this meeting. Who knows what may come of it?"

Jujiro reached for his cup and tried to hide his eyes in it. The woman was beside him now. The wine would help. He took a big gulp. For some reason, he still felt weak.

"You do not live in Ikoma?" Jujiro asked. A moment later he knew it was a silly question. Hadn't Ko-tori just told him that?

"No," said Aki. "I am from Mina. It is many miles to the south. I arrived only this afternoon with my father, the samurai Taizo." She pointed to Ko-tori. "Her family and mine are very close. I came to visit."

Aki refilled Jujiro's cup. The prince took a smaller sip this time. Now he felt better. He looked toward Tasuke. He and Ko-tori were sitting close together, talking in low tones. The prince started to say something but changed his mind. He turned to Aki and met her smile. She was so beautiful. He looked down into his cup. Hai, he felt much better.

"I did not know why I could not sleep tonight," the daimyō's son began. "I am glad that Tasuke brought me here. It is very pleasant."

"Hai."

Jujiro again searched for something to say. Today has been a good day. Ah, yes! "Today the weather has been good. The night is clear and warm and I am happy to meet you." The prince took another sip.

"Dōmo arigatō gozaimasu." Aki smiled. She wanted to say that she was happy to meet him also, but she didn't.

"Where do you stay when you are here?" he asked.

She pointed to Ko-tori. "Tonight I stay with her, tomorrow at the mura, in the house next to the daimyō's. Even now, my father Taizo is with the daimyō." She braved a look straight into Jujiro's eyes. Their gazes met. Quickly she looked down at the closed fan in her hand, and did not see the slight blush on Jujiro's face. They both looked toward the other couple, but they were gone. Neither Jujiro nor Aki had been aware of the others' departure.

"Then I will see you at the mura," said the prince. "For I live in the daimyō's house. He is my father." He reached for the cup again, then continued. "So your father is a samurai. Is he interested in pottery or china?"

"Hai. But that is not why we have come. In Mina we have much trouble with the yatō. The daimyō there sent my father with letters to Ikoma. I do not understand. I am just happy that we finally got here. We have traveled for almost a month." Her fan dropped; Jujiro picked it up and handed it to her. She smiled thank you. He smiled back, and now he felt at ease. He emptied his cup. Aki poured more, and this time, some for herself. They toasted together, their fingers touching as their eyes met.

For a long time, it seemed, neither of them spoke. Each enjoyed the other's closeness, though it would be awkward to admit it.

Aki broke the silence. "Do you know the game of chess?"

"Hai, but I have not sat with the game for a long time. Why do you ask?"

"I thought that you would play the game. It is much like war."

"That is true." He smiled. "That was what interested me in it, but now I am ready for the real thing."

The woman saw his hand clenched as if holding the sword. Suddenly she felt sad, though her face showed no emotion. This man beside her would swing the sword in battle. In turn, he would become fodder for another's sword edge. She must change the subject. "Ikoma is the home of the finest china in Yamato. Are you not interested in this?"

"Hai, I was brought up next to the kilns. My mother is the artist of the finest pieces. I suppose I will always be interested in the pottery that bears the hallmark of the Jugi Hoshi." Jujiro did not want to talk of pottery. "But we were speaking of war."

Aki would have no more talk of war; it saddened her. "And chess," she added. "I have played the game many times with my father. There are just the two of us. My mother is gone." She paused. "I hope you and I may play the game together."

Jujiro was silent for a while. Was she playing the game now? "If that situation could ever be, I would lose to you. I would not want to win." He smiled. She did not answer; she smiled back warmly, instead.

There was a noise in the hall.

"Come in, please."

The missing couple returned. Ko-tori carried another tray with her. The four of them talked as they ate. It pleased Tasuke to see that Jujiro and Aki got along together so well. He could have stayed away longer. Tasuke reached over and patted Ko-tori on the knee. She moved closer to him. The other couple was oblivious to everything except each other.

As the men stepped from the building to leave, Aki bowed deeply to the prince.

"I have enjoyed your company, Jujiro. I will look for you at the mura."

"Dōmo arigatō. I, too, will look for you." He leaned against a pillar as he bent down to replace his zōri.

Later, as they approached the gate of the mura, Tasuke asked, "Did you leave the room after I did?"

"Iie, of course not. Why do you ask?"

"Never mind. It's not important." Tasuke saw that the question had angered his friend. He did not speak again until they reached the manor. There they bid each other good night.

In his futon, the daimyō's son did not think of war. Instead, he thought of the beautiful Aki, until sleep overtook him.

The eastern sky showed daylight. The pots were steaming in the kitchen, and the fragrant odor of the newly made tea pleased Prince Jujiro as he entered the eating room. His mother looked up and smiled.

"Ah, but you are a late sleeper this morning. Your father is already gone. I have waited so that you do not have to eat alone."

"Where did he go? Is something happening?"

"I am not sure," Okei answered. "Yesterday we received letters from my father. The one letter addressed to me from your grandfather assures me that all is well at Mina. However, your father talked most of the night with the samurai who brought the messages. Then the daimyō called for the officers to meet at his court this morning."

Jujiro suspected the reason for the change in routine. Aki had told him last night that her father was with the Ikoma daimyō and that it had something to do with the yatō. Hai, that was what she had said. He would not alarm his mother, though. "I doubt that it is of any importance," he said.

"Well, something of importance is happening," Okei insisted. "Look there." She pointed toward the compound. "It seems every officer of the Jugi Hoshi has been summoned."

"They don't look excited to me," Jujiro said. He held up his bowl while his mother filled it with tea.

"Where were you last night?" She did not wait for an answer, but continued talking. "Jujiro, you need all the rest you can get. I went to your apartment when the messages came. I wanted to tell you what your grandfather had said."

"What did he say?"

"He asked how you were getting along. You know he's concerned about you. He expects that someday you will replace him as the daimyō of Mina. You didn't tell me."

"What?"

"Where you were last night."

Jujiro told Okei of his visit to the teahouse and of the late hour of his return home. He made small mention of Aki.

"You need your sleep, my son." Okei thought for a moment. "Maybe today you will help me in the gardens. I will speak to your father." She waited for her son to agree, but noticing that he was preoccupied, she left the room.

At first, Jujiro could not explain to himself his inner excitement—perhaps something his mother had mentioned, about being assured by her father. That, and what Aki had said about the yatō. Of course! Mina was in trouble. The meeting of the officers could mean only one thing.

Jujiro burst from the room, almost stumbling over the servant kneeling just outside the shōji. He made his way toward the daimyō's court.

Yasumori Fugita, in ceremonial attire, sat cross-legged. He and his aides on either side formed a line. In the courtyard, his retainers, also in formal dress, knelt before him, bowing their heads to the ground. The daimyō looked at these men and knew that each, without exception, would fight and die for him—for the Jugi Hoshi.

Prince Jujiro reached the courtyard and took his place in the front rank. He bowed with the others. One of the aides clapped his hands, indicating the start of the proceedings. Another dipped a brush into the ink plate and started to write on rice paper. He must record everything that would be said.

The daimyō looked at his subjects. He waited until all were looking at him, then cleared his throat and began speaking. "A threat has come to an esteemed ally of the Jugi Hoshi. This is of great concern to us as well. We are bound by oath to all our allies in the event the air is disturbed by the sound of war drums." He paused and looked toward the building where he knew his wife was. Then, in a lower voice, he continued. "At this point, the yatō are attacking Mina. Though the daimyō there requests no aid, I am bound not to ignore the situation. One hundred of our samurai will begin the march toward Mina today."

The gokarō, who sat to the daimyō's right, nodded to him for permission to speak. Yasumori waved him on. "Tomosama," began the gokarō, "the journey under forced march to Mina will take the better part of a month. The samurai who brought us the information rests even now, after this great journey. If Mina is in grave danger, the element of time fights against us. If Mina is in true danger, would not the message have said so?" Gokarō Ito pointed to the soldiers. "Here is but a small part of the samurai of the Jugi Hoshi. The rest protect the caravans—"

"What is your point?" the daimyō asked, showing impatience.

"It is just that we must act quickly, as you suggest—but is it necessary to send a force that large?" The gokarō saw the anger rising on the daimyō's face, but nevertheless continued speaking. "Or, on the other hand, one hundred might not be enough." The anger left the daimyō's face.

Another member of the cabinet begged recognition and received it. "To send one hundred of our samurai would leave Ikoma wide open for the yatō. We need only send a messenger for more information." Other members of the cabinet nodded in agreement.

"It is the consensus, then, that we do nothing?" Yasumori spoke slowly and deliberately, as though shaming the opposition. "These facts I will tell you, and you all must digest them. First, the house of Mina is tied by blood to the house of Fugita. Second, the fine clays, unknown anywhere else, come from Mina. It is our only source, and it must be protected."

Again the gokarō nodded for recognition. The daimyō let him speak. "Tomosama, as I acquaint myself with these truths you speak, I concede that we must send soldiers. It is expected of us by the mere fact that the yatō were mentioned in the daimyō's message. My thought is this: so that we do not leave Ikoma unprotected, let us send, say, fifty. Then, as those that protect the caravans return, we send them on a second mission as soon as possible." The smile on the daimyō's face told the gokarō that he had said the right thing.

Prince Jujiro could not remain silent. He stood up and bowed to his father and the gokarō. "Most honored men"—the prince spoke loudly and clearly—"the yatō are vermin; it is a pity that good swords must be wetted with the urine that the yatō have instead of blood. I have been told, and I know, that ten yatō are no match for one samurai. Send a hundred samurai and keep a handful, or do it the other way around—it makes no difference, the yatō will die."

For a brief moment the daimyō smiled. He waved his son down. "The good gokarō has already said it. Time, too, is our enemy. While we speak, we waste time. Action is needed. A handful will ride. This conference is ended." With that, he rose, motioning the gokarō to follow him.

From a nearby building, Okei Fugita watched the proceedings. She looked at her son and felt sad. Okei could not hear the words that were being spoken at the conference, but when Jujiro stood up and bowed to Yasumori and the cabinet, fear had welled up within her. At this moment, she knew that her son was a man and that he must go with the sword. Yasumori and the gokarō were walking toward her now. She turned and quickly dried her eyes.

"We will have tea," Yasumori told Okei when they entered.

The men talked in low tones, as Okei prepared and served the tea. This time she fixed tea for herself, too. The daimyō pointed to the outside shōji, which Okei opened. Outside, Yasumori saw the samurai talking together in groups. He motioned the gokarō to him, then pointed to the soldiers. "I remember many times, kimi, we waited as they do now. Do you remember?"

"Hai," replied his friend. "You say we will send a handful to Mina. Is it your wish that I lead the soldiers there?"

"No, kimi, this time blood younger than ours will go. I will send my son, Jujiro."

"Then send Tasuke as well. The two are like brothers."

"Hai, as we are. I have not forgotten the many times we have swung our swords back to back. I have these thoughts, kimi. We will send only the best fighters with them, only the very quick and the deadly. That is how it must be."

In the background, Okei missed nothing. She resigned herself to that which she had feared most, and her face showed no emotion. She bowed to the men and backed away as though to leave the room. But Yasumori was aware of her real feelings.

"Stay a moment, Okei-san. I have something that I want you to hear." He clapped his hands, then turned to the gokarō. "One of the samurai must have special orders."

An inner shōji opened, and a servant came in on her knees. She bowed to the daimyō.

"I want the sensei Keisuke Shishido brought here."

"Hai." The servant retreated from the room.

Yasumori toyed with his empty tea bowl and waved Okei away when she came forward to fill it. He smiled at her. "I do not expect the situation to be serious at Mina. The samurai Taizo is of the opinion that any show of Jugi Hoshi soldiers will scare away the yatō. But we will do more—"

A knock in the hall interrupted him. Keisuke entered the room. "My lords?" He bowed to the leaders.

"Prince Jujiro and the gokarō's son, Tasuke Ito, will lead the mission to Mina. You will be their shadow. No harm must come to them. If they die, you must do the same. You will remain their sensei, but the lessons you teach them now will be the most important of all."

"Hai, it will be done."

"Hai, it will be a problem. You must do it without their knowledge."

"It will be as you say, lords."

The gokarō nodded in approval. Some of Okei's anxiety subsided, but only a little. The men continued talking.

Lying on his stomach, the samurai Taizo relaxed, almost asleep, as the young woman massaged his bare back. She beat with both hands in time with the tune she was humming. Shouts from the compound interrupted her rhythmic song, and Aki listened. Though she could not make out the words, she knew the soldiers were being mobilized. Aki had heard these shouts many times before, in Mina. The man stirred beneath her hands, and rolling over, he sat up.

"Relax, my father. This time the calls are not for you. Wasn't the long journey enough?"

"My kimono, kudasai! I cannot lie down while the swords rattle." Aki helped her father put on the clothing. "You do not leave with the soldiers, or do you?"

"Iie, Aki-san. We return to Mina when they come back. I am just going to watch the preparations and help if I can."

"Will you not eat something first? There is gohan ready, and the water is boiling for your tea."

"Ah, Aki. Your way is your mother's way. Hai, if you insist, we will eat first."

Aki smiled at her father, then left the room. She heard him call back to her. "Chotto matte! Some samurai approach. I will call you when I need you."

Taizo studied the two men as they drew near. They were very young, he thought. Ah, surely that one in white is Yasumori's son. Of course, he favors his father.

"Ohayō gozaimasu. Please enter. I am most happy to receive you both as my first visitors." He bowed to them, and the young men returned the greeting.

"May I present Prince Jujiro Fugita. I am Tasuke Ito; the gokarō is my father. We leave soon for Mina."

"Hai," added Jujiro. "The daimyō suggested that we meet and have a talk with you."

"Ah, very good. Please enter, we will be comfortable inside." Taizo waved them into the building.

In another room, the woman looked into a mirror, making certain her hair was in order. She was humming again. Aki listened to the voices of the men as they talked.

"We have just left the leaders," Jujiro explained. "They have gone over in great detail what we should expect on the trip, and at Mina."

"Very good. I spent most of the night with your father. He feels as I do, that the presence of Jugi Hoshi soldiers will take care of any situation. Excuse me." Taizo clapped his hands. "We will have tea, kudasai." He turned to the visitors again. "I have an inrō here that I promised your father I would prepare for you. The maps it contains—you must forgive me, I am not an artist—they are so bad I feel that I must go over them with you. Ah, the tea."

Jujiro almost showed his surprise when Aki entered the room with the tea service. He had taken it for granted that the samurai Taizo had servants assigned to him and his daughter. He could not take his eyes off her, but only once did he catch her eyes. She smiled warmly at him, but did not speak. Her father was busy spreading his maps and had forgotten to introduce her. She left the room.

The three men talked as they sipped their tea. Later, as Taizo and Tasuke talked over the maps, Jujiro excused himself. He would wait in the garden.

Aki called his name. "I did not want you to leave without saying goodbye. I am sorry that you must go so soon after our meeting."

He smiled at her. "I have looked forward to this day, when I would leave as one of the soldiers. Here my time has arrived, and I am excited, but . . ." He felt uncomfortable, much the same as the night before, when they had first met. "I, too, feel sad about leaving just now." He did not want her to misunderstand him. He continued. "My mother, I am certain, also does not want me to leave."

"I am sure she doesn't. What assurances does she have that you will not return cut up and disfigured?"

"Oh, that would not matter. She is proud that the men of her family are samurai. Are not the families of samurai proud when their men die honorably? The scars of the older samurai are marks of honor."

"You are wrong, Jujiro, it would matter to her. You know that well. It would matter to other people also." Aki looked straight into the prince's eyes and watched the half smile appear on his face.

"You?" he asked.

"Hai, if you must know. Please, Jujiro-san, take care of yourself. I would like to see you again as you are now."

"Dōmo arigatō, Aki." He looked behind him. He hoped that Tasuke would not come out right away. He turned again to Aki. How beautiful she was. He noticed, for the first time, how fragile she looked—how small and delicate; how intoxicating her smile was as she talked to him. "Ah, Aki, I could think of no excuse to talk to you when you served the tea."

"I would have been out of place had I spoken."

They were silent for a few moments. The sounds of horses and wagons came to them from the compound. The troops were assembling. Aki and Jujiro heard the shouted orders.

"Oh, Jujiro, they are getting ready."

"They will wait. They cannot go without me. Besides, I have not finished talking to you."

"What are we to talk about?" There was coyness to her smile.

"You pick the subject."

"Well—I noticed the pottery and fine china here in the guesthouse. I will say that the ceramics of Ikoma are the most beautiful."

"It seems to me," said Jujiro, "that we talked of pottery before."

"Must we talk of war?"

"No."

"Well, what shall we speak of, then?"

"I could tell you how beautiful you are."

"Oh, Jujiro! Be serious. Let us talk of your trip."

The prince laughed. "I cannot talk of that, I have not yet left."

She, too, laughed. "Jujiro, there is a place close to Mina that you might see. It is where the river widens into a lake. In the middle of the water is a huge rock like an island. On my way here, I swam out to it, and from there I saw the graceful shika drink from the water's edge. It was very beautiful and peaceful. I did not want to leave."

"If I find the place, Aki-san, I will think of you."

"Only then?" she asked. She reached to her hair, removed a small comb from it, and handed it to the prince. "Keep this with you, Jujiro-san. It is a token. Know always my wishes of good luck are with you. The symbols on it are mine."

"Dōmo arigatō. I will treasure it," he said. "The samurai usually tie things such as this to their sword's hilt, but since you think of the sword as you do, I will tie it instead to my wrist. That way, something of you will be with me even if I should lose my sword."

"Jujiro, why do you honor me so? You must know many others." She said this in a low voice.

"There are no others!" he answered. "I—I don't know."

Aki smiled that intoxicating smile, and the prince was lost.

"Well, I love you," he blurted out. He felt relieved when he had said it, but he did not know what to say next. When he felt his face flush, he said, "I must leave now."

He hesitated, then gently reached for her hand. "Sayonara," he said as he turned to leave.

"Jujiro!" She called him back. "I have something I must tell you."

"Nani o?"

"I will not return to Mina. I did not tell you that I love you, but you must know that before you leave. I do love you, Jujiro-san."

The prince gathered Aki to him and kissed her. He felt her sob. He kissed her again—this time, on the whiteness of her neck.

Jujiro held her hands as he stepped back. He looked into her sad eyes. "Sayonara, my pretty one."

"Until we meet again. Sayonara, my samurai. I shall wait here for you."

Prince Jujiro walked toward the compound. After a while, he looked back. Aki had not moved, she was still in the garden watching him. He waved and she returned his wave.

The samurai rode three abreast, except where the ruggedness of the trail forced them to travel single file. One rider led the rest, maintaining a steady gait and setting the pace for the soldiers. They moved as a unit through the timber along the river. The pennant, which fluttered from the spear of the pacesetter, was large and on it was emblazoned the crossed star of the Jugi Hoshi, the monshō of the house of Fugita.

Prince Jujiro looked about him as he rode; the two who flanked him only looked ahead. The sun, just above the hilltops, was getting close to the west. It was time to stop for the night. The prince spoke to the man on his right, who called ahead to the lead rider. The unit swung near the river's edge, then halted. The animals, unburdened, were hobbled and left to graze. Within a short time, campfires burned before the tents of the small army.

Near the water's edge, the three leaders of the mission talked as they watched some of the soldiers fish. The method that the soldiers used was crude but effective: a lantern was held close to the water, small pieces of bait dangled just above the surface. The fishermen then tried to spear the fish that were attracted by the bait and the light. As often as not, they were successful.

"The men are enjoying themselves," said Keisuke. "They have been at it for over an hour."

"Hai, and they are not doing too badly," added Tasuke. "It looks like some will eat fresh trout in the morning."

Prince Jujiro, the third member of the group, paid no attention to his companions. Though he did not realize it, he was tired from the long march. His eyes were fixed to the river. He was mesmerized by the reflection of the lantern light on the undulating water. Rings of light spread in circles on the black water, endlessly. How much like life, he thought. One goes, another takes its place. It is all unpredictable, that is as close as one can get to a meaning.

"Kimi." Keisuke's voice brought Jujiro back to reality. "Kimi, your tent is ready if you are tired."

"Dōmo, sensei. What makes you think that I might be tired?"

"Well, for one thing, we've been on the march for two weeks. For another, we have spoken to you and you have not answered. And you have not moved from your position for some minutes now. I thought you had fallen asleep sitting up."

"Gomen nasai, I'm sorry. Maybe I am tired. But I will sleep here on the riverbank. Good night, my friends." Jujiro lay back, cradling his head with his palms, looking up at the stars.

"If you don't mind, my prince, I, too, will sleep in the open," the sensei said.

"I think you both are baka," Tasuke said, laughing. "In the morning you'll be soaked with the pee of the gods. I'll see you then." He made his way to his tent, still laughing.

"How many more days until we reach Mina?" the prince asked Keisuke.

"We are halfway there."

"Can't we go any faster?"

"Iie. Go to sleep."

"Hai." But Jujiro did not close his eyes. Though he was tired, he could not sleep. Suddenly the flash of a shooting star streaked across the sky for a brief instant. It was the gods fighting on the other side of night; one of their swords had cut through the darkness. Even the gods lived to fight in battle. Jujiro closed his eyes, and sleep overcame him . . .

A hand pressed over his mouth brought the prince to consciousness. He opened his eyes to the dim early light. Keisuke whispered in his ear. "Kimi, don't make a sound. We are under attack!"

Jujiro sat up and looked around: nothing. He turned to the kneeling sensei. "Where?" Keisuke motioned him to be silent, then pointed to the trees nearby.

The first rays of daylight reflected off the metal of uncovered swords. The yatō were making their way, silently on pine needles, toward the Jugi Hoshi camp. The attackers were unaware of the two men at the riverbank.

"We are unarmed," Jujiro whispered. "I don't even have my tantō, my little knife."

"Nor do I. But we are never unarmed. Come, the others must be warned. We must get to the camp first. This way." Keisuke pointed to a direct route, and they sprinted through the trees side by side. One hundred yards from the camp, they stopped. Ahead, blocking their path, two yatō who had seen the runners were waiting with drawn long swords.

"Listen carefully, kimi," Keisuke whispered. "They are both right-handed swordsmen. We will charge. You, to the man on the right. I, to the other. But at the last instant we both hit your man and keep him in the way of the other. Remember, give me room. Keep far to the right. Now!"

The yatō, who were advancing, halted when the unarmed men began their charge. They smiled. These Jugi Hoshi were nothing. How easy, they charge well apart. There would be plenty of room for two long swords to work at the same time. The two blades were lifted, poised, waiting for their victims.

As Keisuke suddenly changed direction Jujiro twisted to his right. The first swordsman swung his blade, but the prince had already circled out of reach.

Keisuke screamed as he slammed feet first into the yatō. The man went down. The second swordsman swung at Keisuke, but the sensei was rolling, and the blade missed. Keisuke scrambled on hands and knees, crab-fashion, his eyes on the sword. He watched the blade lift again.

Jujiro also shouted when the first yatō went down. When his sensei rolled out of the way, the prince jumped with both feet on the downed yatō's chest. He felt the body snap and give way beneath him. One out of the way; now the other. Jujiro scooped up the sword and turned to aid Keisuke. The sensei was still on the ground. Had he been cut? The second yatō stalked the sensei. He prepared his second swing.

Jujiro screamed as he charged, drawing the yatō's attention. The man on the ground was no threat to the yatō, but this Jugi Hoshi with the sword was. The yatō turned from Keisuke. He readjusted his sword to the defensive position and waited for the prince.

Again, Keisuke struck first—this time with the palm of his hand. He swung upward under the man's nose, raking his hand up the face, shoving the nosebone upward and in. The yatō was dead before his body hit the ground.

The two Jugi Hoshi samurai did not speak. Sounds of fighting came to them from the camp. They ran to help the others.

The entire battle, made up of individual sword fights, appeared to encircle the camp. From somewhere, an occasional arrow flew through the air. On the ground, two men lay dead. They were not of the Jugi Hoshi.

Keisuke pointed to one side. More yatō were pouring into the camp. "You of the yatō," the sensei shouted, "look, it is I, Keisuke Shishido. It is I who have slain your fathers and slept with your mothers. Which three of you are ready to die?" He sprinted toward the yatō. Jujiro stayed close to his side. Keisuke waved him back. "See to the horses. Get someone to the horses."

"Hai." Reluctantly, the prince dropped back.

"Ah, the hare runs frightened from the kuma!" someone shouted.

Jujiro turned around. The man who spoke wore the helmet of a leader. It was much the same as Jujiro's, which had been given to him by Yasumori when he left Ikoma. It bore the same polished black horns of oxen. The yatō leader spit on the ground, then held his sword in challenge to the prince. "Come, come to me," he mocked.

Jujiro took his stance and waited. A wave of excitement passed over him. Suddenly, he was back at the dōjō. The man in front of him threatened only with a wooden sword. Jujiro waited now for his sensei's signal. He held the sword with one hand. It was this that misled the yatō leader.

"No one but I must duel with this child. I need no help. Go, otokonoko, I give you two chances to kill me. I will not strike you."

Jujiro was not listening. He wondered why the man did not start his attack. Why was he smiling? This his sensei never did. But this teacher held no wooden sword.

"Come, kodomo, I am waiting for you."

Holding the sword straight out, still with only one hand, the daimyō's son lunged forward. The blade struck the leather breastplate of the yatō, parting it into two pieces. The man did not seem to be hurt, but if he was, there would be no way to know. The yatō stepped back out of the sword's reach. No longer was there a smile on his face; his boasts were forgotten. He slashed back at Jujiro.

A new feeling—was it panic or fright?—swept over the prince. This sensei was trying to kill him. Jujiro went on the defensive. Blocking and sidestepping, slashing back only when there was a definite opening.

As the fight progressed, his sense of panic left the

prince. He found that he could easily avoid the thrusts and swings of the yatō. Now he played the game of chess: thinking, looking for a pattern in this man's mode of fighting. Each swing the yatō made was different. He, too, Jujiro realized, was looking for a pattern.

A quick motion to one side caused the prince to retreat from the yatō leader. He saw Tasuke, his back to him, fighting his own duel. Farther back, the prince noted, Keisuke was busy with two others. Jujiro was dismayed to see so much blood covering Keisuke's kariginu. Caution brought his eyes back to his opponent.

The yatō leader held his sword straight up. He circled Jujiro, his face showing no emotion. The leather chest plate was parted; the yatō's chest was red with blood.

The daimyō's son charged forward, swinging the sword with one hand. His other hand was clasped on the handle of his kogatana, still in his sash. He was the aggressor now. Sidestepping, he swung the long sword at the other's legs. The man effectively blocked. Three more times Jujiro struck at the man's legs; each time he was blocked. They circled each other. The yatō swung high at Jujiro, and the prince slashed again at his feet. This time Jujiro's kogatana was free and in his left hand. When the yatō blocked his long sword again, the short sword plunged into the unprotected throat of the bandit leader. The surprised man dropped his weapon. His chest became redder still. The prince ended the yatō's life with one more fast swing of the long sword.

The sight of so much blood suddenly made Jujiro sick. When he turned from the body he felt relieved. He saw that the entire battle was over and that the last of the yatō had disappeared into the forest.

Looking once more at the dead leader, Jujiro saw that

the man's face held an expression of surprise, even in death. He looked away again. It all seemed so easy, unreal, as though he were only an onlooker. Where was the great thrill he had expected? He had heard others speak of battle, and listening, he had experienced a thrill. In reality, there was no time for it. The actions and reactions were automatic. Was it this which made it seem so easy? Or was it the many years he had spent training? Somehow, nothing made sense. He felt let down and exhausted, but he tried to fight it off, thinking he could still go on. He became aware of his sword hanging like lead from his arm. A hand touched his shoulder.

"Kimi, are you all right? Do you have any wounds?"

The prince shook his head. He stared at the blood covering the sensei's kariginu.

"It is not my blood," Keisuke assured him. "Only Tasuke is wounded, but it is not serious."

The gokarō's son displayed a small cut on his leg. "You won't believe this, I did it myself when I tried to hold the sword with one hand as you did. You made it look easy. But believe me, from now on I keep both hands locked to the handle." He joined his friends in laughter.

Suddenly Jujiro turned to the sensei. "I don't know about you," he said with a smile. "First you use me as bait for the first two yatō. Then you arrange it so that I have to cross swords with the yatō leader. Are you trying to take my place?"

Keisuke put his arms around the prince. "What came about was not in my plans. But you did well, very well." He reached out and pulled Tasuke toward them. "You both did well. To be honest, I had hoped that neither of you would have to fight. I shouldn't have worried."

They counted twelve enemy dead. Two of the yatō

were samurai. Their swords were returned to their dead hands.

The samurai of the Jugi Hoshi did not break camp. The day was lost rounding up the horses that the yatō had scattered just before the attack. They could not find them all, though. No doubt, some had headed back to their stalls in Ikoma.

When night came, the samurai sat around small campfires, relating events of the morning's battle. Laughter occasionally broke from one group or another. Saké was poured. Toasts and solemn oaths were made with each raised cup.

At the prince's tent, Jujiro lay in his futon, his swords at his side. He thought of Aki back at Ikoma. In his hand, he held her comb.

As she had done so many times before, Okei Fugita opened the lacquered box and removed the fine china and the tea whisk to prepare tea for her husband and guests.

This time, she also prepared tea for herself. At Yasumori's right sat the samurai Taizo. The place at the daimyō's left was reserved for Okei, who at this moment was stirring the tea in the large bowl.

"I am happy to talk to someone who has an interest in pottery," Okei said to Aki. "Some months ago, our son and the son of the gokarō brought in the largest shika ever seen in Ikoma. To commemorate that feat, we are firing some delicate tea-service ware. Would you like to see it?"

"Oh, yes, I would be happy to." Aki smiled, her eyes sparkling.

Okei could not help but think how beautiful this young woman was. This Aki, she thought, is the daughter of a highborn samurai. Aki's manners and bearing proved that no sensei had been negligent in her rearing. She was healthy and would no doubt bear healthy children. She must mention this to the daimyō. "After our tea, you and I will go to the finishing kilns. I am going to put you to work."

"I am sure I will enjoy it. I have seen much fine pottery in Mina, but I have read your name on the bottoms of only the finest. If I could work with you, I would be greatly honored."

As the women talked, so did the men. Presently, all were quiet as they went through the ritual of the tea drinking. When that was over, Yasumori watched Aki as she helped Okei. Yes, Aki would be a good wife for Jujiro. Tonight Yasumori would tell Okei of the decision he and Taizo had reached. Aki would bear good sons for the Jugi Hoshi.

At the kilns, Aki watched the deft strokes of Okei's brush. She marveled at the detail of the pictures of the two hunters carrying the trussed shika. Okei's skill brought life to the figures. Aki was amazed to recognize Jujiro and the purple-clad Tasuke in miniature. After she was shown how, Aki picked up and held each tea bowl by spreading her fingers inside, so that the artist could brush the kanji on the bottoms.

"It is not right," Okei said, "that you do so much of the work and do not reap any of the glory. The kanji Aki must appear in your own kanji along with mine on the bottom of these bowls."

Aki protested, but, at the stern insistence of the older woman, finally agreed. Now Okei held the bowls while the younger woman wrote her name on each.

When the bowls were ready, a workman tested the heat of the kiln. He counted the time it took for a small piece of wood to burst into flames. He cautiously placed the bowls in the kiln, then rebanked the fires below.

"Now they are in the hands of the gods," said Okei. "In three days we will see what we have done."

"So this is how your pottery is made."

"Ah, yes," replied the artist. "But the bowls will look completely different when they come out. The colors will change. With luck, only a few will be destroyed in the oven." She changed the subject. "My son, Jujiro, has been gone almost a month. Will you still be here when he gets back? I wanted you to meet him."

"But I already have, my lady." Aki blushed. "I have talked with him twice." She told the older woman of her meetings with the prince. It was a relief to have someone to share her secret with.

"I've wondered about your interest whenever I spoke of my son," Okei said. "I am happy for both of you. You have my blessings. I should have known he would like you."

"Oh, I hope so. To be honest, I think of him often."

"Chotto! Just a minute." Okei turned her head toward the manor. She had heard a shout. The low rumble of running horses came to the two women. This was a natural sound to hear on the practice fields, but the practice fields were empty now.

"What is it?" asked Aki.

"I don't know."

The two women hurried from the kilns. When they reached the compound, Okei and Aki saw the horses being led away. "They have been driven hard, these horses," Okei said. "They are well-foamed and completely soaked." She turned to her young friend. "Aki, I must find out what is happening." Without another word, Okei made her way to the daimyō's court. There she saw the haggard soldiers standing in the courtyard. They did not wear the smile of the homecoming samurai. Many times Okei had seen returning soldiers, but this time it was different. She entered the court.

The tired sergeant knelt and bowed low before Yasumori and the gokarō, his head touching the tatami.

"My lords," the soldier began, "two days ago, near Kofu, our caravan was ambushed, and as far as I know, it is no more. Only nine of us have returned. We nine live because we were the advance guard and because of the orders we were given."

"What orders do you speak of?" broke in the daimyō.

"These, my lord." The sergeant produced a paper from his inrō. "These orders," the soldier continued, "were handed to me by a runner from the main column."

Yasumori read the paper, then handed it to Gokarō Ito.

"These orders speak of a sealed scroll. Where is it?"

"It is here, my daimyō."

The sergeant handed over the clay-sealed bamboo cylinder, and the daimyō opened it. The scroll was unrolled and read by both Yasumori and the gokarō.

The daimyō shook his head. It did not make sense; this particular caravan had been well protected. Yasumori rested his chin on his fist and stared at the tatami. The gokarō pointed to the soldier. "Your men of the advance guard, are any of them hurt?"

"Iie, my lord. After my orders were received, we did not try to fight. My orders forbade it, as you have read. We were followed and attacked once. An arrow found its mark, and one of our samurai died. Our final contact with the yatō was last night. We forced the horses on, as we were ordered."

"That is all." Yasumori waved. "You are excused."

The sergeant left the room.

"What do you make of it, kimi?" asked Gokarō Ito.

"It is beyond me," said the daimyō. "There were thirty samurai with them. Hai, something is happening. We should call the officers."

"Hai." The gokarō left the court.

When Taizo and the other samurai officers arrived, Yasumori motioned to Okei to leave the room. She took up a position just outside the shōji and waited. Here she could hear every word. The daimyō came out and spoke to her: "I do not want you here. Go to the apartments. I will tell you what I want you to know."

"Hai." She bowed to her husband, then left the court.

Over two hours passed before Okei heard the scuff of Yasumori's zōri. Seeing his look of preoccupation and concern, Okei did not speak to him. She knew that, whatever the problem was, or grew to be, the daimyō could and would take care of it. Later, as they lay in their futons, she slept. Her husband nearby could not.

The following day brought a change in the regular routine of Ikoma. Hastily built lookout towers were put up along the mura's walls. Long lines of wagons made their way in and out of the fort. Supplies were being stockpiled in the long warehouse. Today the training areas were again empty. Soldiers carried weapons different from those they used in training. Blacksmiths busied themselves grinding and honing the utensils of war.

A second meeting was called. The samurai Taizo sat with the leaders of Ikoma. This time, besides the officers, others of lesser rank filled the room. Along one wall sat the soldiers who were trained as runners. They differed from other samurai in that they were dressed in black, and carried no long swords. The tantō and the kogatana in each runner's sash made them look almost identical.

Yasumori called for silence by holding up his hand.

"Those of you who were not here yesterday," he began, "I say this for your information. The yatō prepares to knock on our gates. We know this from the fact that two of our heavily protected caravans have been wiped out. This time, they were not robbed, they were slaughtered by superior forces. From one caravan, only nine survive; from the other, only one. He arrived this morning." Yasumori hesitated, then continued. "They are killing off our soldiers for one reason, nē?"

"They plan to be here soon," the gokarō answered for all.

"Hai," returned Yasumori, "and we must be ready for them. What is our strength, as of this moment?"

"We muster about seventy samurai in all," Gokarō Ito said, "and that includes those that have not yet finished their first level of training. At this very moment they are being instructed in the duties that will be required of them."

"Can we expect more samurai to return soon?" the daimyō asked.

The gokarō could not answer. He looked inquiringly at one of the other officers.

"I have listed about twenty who will arrive within three days," answered the officer. "In two weeks, another twenty. Only one contingent will not return for another month. That is the one to the south, at Mina, led by the prince and Tasuke Ito—"

"The first twenty," interrupted the daimyō, "from where do they come?"

"My lord, they come from the south, but they must get through the yatō to reach us."

"There are no others?"

"Only one mission, my lord." The officer checked his figures again. "They number five samurai. They come from the west."

Yasumori turned to Gokarō Ito. "Kimi, send a runner to those in the south. Warn them of what lies before them. They should circle back to us."

"Hai."

The daimyō looked at the people assembled in his court. He noticed Okei kneeling by the shōji. He spoke now for her benefit. "The yatō that approach Ikoma are not samurai, and they are unwise in the ways of war. Though we will conscript the men from the villages, it does not mean that we are preparing for a full-scale war. It is not so. Instead, we will teach the yatō a lesson. My orders are simple: we will take no prisoners, only the heads of the leaders will be brought into Ikoma."

The runners left. The three leaders—Yasumori, Gokarō Ito, and the samurai Taizo—analyzed the information as it was brought back. The picture became clearer with each returning runner. Though they numbered half a thousand, the yatō appeared to be bypassing Ikoma.

"Kimi, do not be deceived," said Taizo. "An army cannot survive if they ignore the rice bowl. We will be at war very soon."

"Those are true words," replied the daimyō. "We do not have many options, but one thing must be done. I want runners sent to Akita and Morioka in the north, and to Takata in the south. Prepare dispatches for those daimyō. It would be better to warn them that we may need their help."

"Hai, I will see to it." The gokarō motioned to three runners to follow him, and they hurried out of the room.

"Is it your intention to bring the war to the yatō?" asked Taizo. "Or do we wait for more of our samurai?"

"Iie," answered the daimyō. "We cannot hesitate. Otherwise, Ikoma will burn. We will fight outside the walls."

A crude chart was set up in the court room. The positions of the yatō and Ikoma's returning samurai were sketched on it. The five samurai returning from the west had been warned. Hours later, word came that the twenty coming from the south had also been warned. Both groups were marching toward Ikoma.

A new report brought great concern to the leaders in the mura. This report located the yatō in two positions at once, both to the south and to the north. Campfires had been sighted on the nearby mountains. Later reports confirmed this, along with the information that liaison had been set up between the separated yatō troops. Their purpose was obvious: Ikoma was completely surrounded.

The cattle and other livestock were herded into the walled mura. They wandered loose, soon destroying the beautiful gardens around the manor.

Two days later, the runners stopped returning. Yasumori's early plan of attack had been abandoned under the threat of the overwhelming odds. The three leaders resigned themselves to the coming siege. They were sure that time would bring aid.

The last rays of the setting sun topping the western hills of Ikoma turned the clouds to blood. The shrill whistle of an arrow arcing over the walls broke the stillness. The samurai, waiting in the towers, looked to the trees outside the walls. The war drums began.

Okei heard these sounds from deep within the manor. She tried to ignore them and continued talking to Aki. The women did not speak of war, but of someone they both loved, someone who made Aki's eyes sparkle again.

K*eisuke Shishido* pulled his horse to a stop. He did not dismount. He waited for the prince and Tasuke to reach him. "In one more day we will be at Mina," he told them as they approached. "Ahead, there is a perfect place for our final camp. We will rest there for the balance of the day. Tomorrow we can enter Mina fresh."

"Ah, sō desu, I agree," said the prince. "I feel that I have become a part of this horse, and just as dirty."

"I see the resemblance, now that you mention it," said Tasuke with a laugh.

Jujiro gave him a wry look. "You have progressed further than I—I speak only of the dimension of smell."

Tasuke burst out laughing. He pointed to Keisuke. "What about him?"

"Don't get me involved," said the sensei. "If I started to look like my horse, I would consider it an improvement." He patted his mount on the neck. "She is a beautiful animal, nē?"

Keisuke signaled for a runner. "Tell the lead man we will camp at the lake."

"Hai." The runner spurred his mount ahead.

"There is a lake near here?" said Jujiro.

"Not really," replied Keisuke. "It is just that the river is very wide for a short distance and it looks like a lake."

"There is a large rock in the center, nē?"

"Hai," said the sensei, with a questioning look.

"I know of this place," said the prince. "It is where the shika live."

"I remember the last time that we hunted the shika. We must do it again together," Tasuke said.

"That is a good thought, kimi. It would be good if we brought a shika to Mina for the daimyō's table. It is hours before night. Hai, Tasuke and I will try to outsmart the shika."

The shika stood back in the brush, allowing his doe to approach the water with their fawns. The scent of man was heavy in the air. The buck sniffed upwind, then turned to the opposite direction. The scent was stronger there. The animal looked directly at Jujiro, but did not see him. The deer snorted, producing a whistling sound. The men did not move. The shika tried another tack by stamping one of its front hoofs. This usually made the enemy betray himself. Still, the men did not move. The shika turned its head slightly as it searched the brush in front of it. Slowly, imperceptibly, the men brought their bows forward.

The deer searched again, taking in great breaths of air. This time the animal saw the men. The shika stood transfixed for a moment, until the sudden motion and sound of the released arrows caused the buck to spring upward. The fawns froze. The doe bounced off, away from her frightened mate.

The arrows had hit, but the animal bolted with springing leaps away from the hunters. It would soon be out of sight among the trees. The prince held up his hand, signaling to Tasuke for silence. Neither man moved. Jujiro and Tasuke listened. They tried to distinguish between the sounds of the two running deer as they crashed through the brush.

To the right, the doe stopped. The men could still hear the sound of the buck. Then that sound stopped. The men began to track the shika, pausing only to search for fresh-snapped twigs or turned leaves.

The bright color of the broken arrow caught Tasuke's eye, and the men hurried forward. Here the wounded animal had pushed itself against the pine to get rid of the offending projectile. Farther on, the hunters found the first drop of blood. As they progressed, the drops became more numerous. Finally they found the blood-smeared tree where the shika had applied pressure to the wound. The hunters knew they were close now. Their bows held ready, they continued the tracking, which had become much easier.

Suddenly the buck leaped before them. Both men released their arrows as one. For a few hundred yards, the shika continued its run, then it collapsed. This was like old times. The hunters were proud of themselves.

If these men were tired from the day's journey, they were even more so now. They carried the trussed animal into the camp.

"The daimyō will be pleased, kimi," Keisuke said as he came closer to look at the shika. "This is a rabbit compared to the other," he added, laughing, "but it will do."

As the day darkened into night, the leaders sat together and ate their evening meal. Tasuke held his ohashi sticks midway to his mouth. "I am happy this journey is over," he said. "Perhaps our services are no longer even needed."

"We will know tomorrow," said Jujiro. "One thing is certain. The samurai at Mina are no different from those at Ikoma. It would take many yatō to kill one samurai."

"You've said that before," Tasuke said with a laugh. "Now I'm beginning to believe it."

"It is true there is no urgency for our appearance in Mina, but shouldn't we send a runner to announce us?"

"Hai, it has been taken care of," replied the prince. "The runner Hetomi Tajimi is making ready to go. Tasuke has seen to it."

As Jujiro spoke, a samurai clad in black approached them. The horse he led was also black. There was no metal or leather on the animal. All the trappings were fashioned of dyed black cloth. Attached to the saddle of the horse were the crude straw woven hoof covers the rider might need to use. Hetomi Tajimi had received special training as a runner, whose primary purpose was the gathering of information. For his skill, the runner held a position that was envied.

"I am sorry, Hetomi," said the prince. "It is not enough that you have ridden all day. Now you must ride most of the night."

"I am happy to be of service."

"Keisuke will give you your orders, he has been through this before." Jujiro nodded to the sensei.

"It is possible, though I doubt it, that there is trouble at the mura." Keisuke spoke slowly. "If all is well, announce us. Whatever you find, we must know of it before the sun is on the horizon. That is our wish."

"It will be as you say, my captain. I will be at this spot before the sun."

"One thing more, Hetomi." Jujiro smiled. "Tell the daimyō that his grandson comes tomorrow."

"Hai." The runner bowed. He mounted his horse, waved to his superiors, and rode off, melting into the shadows.

The prince excused himself, leaving the company of the other leaders. He walked to the river's edge, disrobed, and swam to the rock island. Out of the water, Jujiro lay on his back and looked at the stars. The night was clear. A large, bright moon rose from the close hills. Could Aki see this moon, too? For a long time his thoughts remained with her, but he felt sad when he remembered that his future had been planned by his parents and that Aki could not be a part of it. But Jujiro would find a way, he'd see to it somehow. When he returned to Ikoma, she would be there.

Jujiro stood and looked across to the camp. The bright moon, now high overhead, made the scene clear, almost like daylight. The call of the night bird, the splash of a trout, he had heard these sounds many times before, at Ikoma. But here these peaceful sounds were deceptive. He was far from home. Troubled, the prince dove into the water and swam back to camp.

Hetomi Tajimi guided his horse through the trees at a steady pace. Purposely, he kept off the road that paralleled the river. Several times he stopped, holding the horse's ears gently, listening. To his right, he could just make out the sound of the river. Even though the bright moon was directly overhead, he felt secure. He knew he reflected no light. The only thing that could give him away were the sounds he might make, but as long as he kept to the trees, he would not have to cover the horse's feet.

Two hours later, Hetomi stopped again. He cupped his ears with his hands. He heard the barking of a dog. Mina was close. From here he could walk. He dismounted and tied the animal. Minutes later, he sprinted in the semi-darkness.

The runner stopped once more. He became aware of an odor carried to him by the slight breeze: the smell of putrid flesh, death's strong remainder, assailed him. The smell grew stronger the closer he drew to Mina.

Hetomi broke into a dogtrot until he reached the edge

of the forest and the clearing that surrounded the mura. These fields were kept tilled for more than one reason.

Crossing the clearing would pose a problem for the runner. Undoubtedly, there were lookouts posted on the catwalks of the wall, and it would be almost an hour before the moon dipped. But he could not wait, he needed all the time there was until dawn to complete his mission.

The odor of decay was overpowering. Hetomi looked about him and saw bodies scattered against the trees around the perimeter of the clearing. There were hundreds; he felt sick.

Keeping to the shadows, Hetomi examined the dead. Most were the samurai of Mina. They were mutilated, headless, and stripped. Those not molested bore the insignia of a simple red triangle, a new sign to Hetomi. Not all the dead were soldiers. Many were old men and women, and here and there he saw the small bodies of children.

Sudden shouting made Hetomi look toward the open gate of the mura. A horseman galloped out into the clearing. The accompanying dust cloud enveloped another body. Hetomi stood motionless as the soldier untied his burden and returned to the mura.

Hetomi circled the clearing, staying within the trees. He noted that there were at least four lookouts on the catwalks. He looked up at the moon, then down on the gray earth of the clearing. If only his kariginu were white! Iie, he could not cross the clearing now.

Hetomi Tajimi trotted back to his tethered horse, calling quietly as he approached it. The animal neighed in recognition. Untying the horse, he did not mount, but instead he turned the animal in the direction of his Jugi Hoshi comrades. He slapped the horse on its flank and sent it on its way.

With a stick, the runner scratched a long line in the

pine needles, then a circle. Tearing a piece of cloth from his tunic, he placed it in the circle.

An hour later, Hetomi was back at the clearing around the mura. Now the moon was gone and he blended with the tilled earth of the clearing. Crawling on his stomach, he inched himself forward toward the open gate. He thought of those who waited behind in the forest. They expected him back with the sun, but he knew he would need more time for his mission.

Tōryō Kumahatchi Murata looked out from the crude tree-branch shelter, a blanket pulled tight around him. He stared down into the black valley. The few lights he could make out in the darkness came from the torches set up within the mura. These lights, less bright than the stars, held the yatō leader's attention.

Lean-tos sheltered Kumahatchi's small army. Across the valley, on other hilltops, the tōryō knew that other yatō forces awaited his commands. Together, they would devour the rich prize that lay below them. Within the next three days, many others would join them. With so many of the yatō banded together, Ikoma's fate was sealed. Kumahatchi felt good. He turned to a sleeping figure and spoke in a soft voice. "You sleep in the forest now, Sakura-san, but soon you will sleep in a daimyō's manor."

The woman slept on, oblivious to her father's voice. Kumahatchi reached over and adjusted her blanket. Rising, he pulled his own blanket to him and walked to the next lean-to.

"Ah, Kozo," Kumahatchi said as he approached, "you are also awake, I see."

The tōryō's lieutenant stood and bowed to his leader. "Hai," Kozo said. "I have many thoughts which drive sleep from me. Soon many more yatō will join us. Then we will rule this land, nē?" His hand waved over the valley.

The tōryō smiled. "Hai, in three days we are to begin. The yatō flock to us, all eager to enrich themselves. But to wait so long is not in our best interests. First, the spoils will have to be spread thinner. And second, too many yatō make me uncomfortable. I fear they think as we do and therefore cannot be trusted."

Kozo nodded in agreement. The tōryō continued. "We already outnumber the Jugi Hoshi many times over. Their samurai are everywhere but at home. Three days from now, it may be different, nē? I'm sure that by now they are aware of us. True, the samurai that are left in the mura will be no easy chore. The badger fighting from within its nest fights with four times its strength. But, as I said, we can overwhelm them if we attack now. What do you think, Kozo? We will not wait for the others. Tomorrow, when night falls, we will bring down the walls."

Kozo looked at his leader with surprise. "But if we wait as we agreed, there is no question that we will crush the Jugi Hoshi. It will be very easy if we wait."

Kumahatchi's face showed his anger, then became expressionless as he stared at his lieutenant. "Kozo, you carry many scars of the kogatana and the long sword. The other yatō fear you because of them. These scars are an asset to you, and because of them, you are in command of my samurai under me. You tell them my wishes. I have two questions for you to think about. Do those who see you think you got those scars by sitting back and letting others fight for you? And then, too, does anyone know how you received those scars?"

Kozo sputtered. His face could not conceal his anger.

His subconscious mind would not allow his hand to come near the handle of his kogatana. He forced a smile. "My lord, you misinterpret me, you did not let me finish my statement. I tried to say it would be easier if we waited, but it would be better if we did it on our own. I will, if you permit me, be the first to enter Ikoma's walls." Kozo's forced smile grew wider.

Kumahatchi smiled in return. "My friend," he began, "if I misinterpret you, I am sorry, we will speak no more of it. We have much to do. Listen carefully. We will attack the Jugi Hoshi at dusk tomorrow, as I have said, but you must carry these orders to *my* soldiers. All groups of yatō that have joined us I want separated into new groups, each led by one of our own samurai. That way, no one will know that I am the only commander. After Ikoma is ours, we must rid ourselves of the yatō that ally with us—by any means."

Kozo held up his hand to interrupt. His smile was now a distorted grin. "I understand, kimi, you are right. At the moment the battle is decided, we will turn on the other yatō, nē?"

"Hai," Kumahatchi agreed, laughing. "You understand. You follow me well, Kozo. It is up to you to bring this about. Between now and before dusk tomorrow, it will be your task to see that only our samurai and our soldiers understand this. And, Kozo, if you do your job well, I will reward you with that which you seek most. Do you understand?"

"Hai, tomosama, I will treat her well."

The tōryō's smile faded. "What are you talking about?"

"Why, I am speaking of Sakura. I will be a good husband for her."

Kumahatchi did not try to conceal his anger. He spat out his next words. "I was not speaking of Sakura as a reward, Kozo. That is the furthest thought from my mind. I picked you as my lieutenant because of your size, because you are a samurai, and because you follow my orders. When first you came to me, I saw your interest in Sakura. When we practiced with the sword, I put most of the scars on your face. They were not accidents. I put them there to keep Sakura from you. I have other plans for her. Know this, Kozo, at any time I could have cut you down. Even now. Know this also: the pride of the samurai is to know that he will die with his sword in his hand. How do you want to die? Would you rather die tied to the slaughter T as an oxen before the victory feast? To die on the slaughter T is the lowest form of death a bushi could think of. This is my plan for you, should you not read my wishes well." Kumahatchi shook his head as if in disgust, then continued. "The reward I meant was this. If you do your job, you shall serve me as my gokarō when I become Ikoma's daimyō. What have you to say now, Kozo?"

Kozo's face still held the hint of a grin. He bowed low to the tōryō. "True, tomosama, I have wanted Sakura, but that is past. I will be a loyal gokarō. Forgive me." He knelt and bowed again. This time his face touched the dirt.

The sun was well up when the three leaders held their conference. Near them, the soldiers gathered, waiting for their orders.

Tasuke started the conversation. "We have no way of knowing what we are riding into. Should we send another runner?"

"Iie, we must wait until night," replied Keisuke.

"We have erred," Jujiro said. "The full moon must have given Hetomi away. We know now that the manor is held by the yatō, but we are not equipped to fight from outside the walls of the mura."

"I don't know if I agree with you, my lord," said Keisuke. "Mina is small, it could not hold a large army. I believe our best chance is to try to draw the yatō out."

"I see no way of bringing them from the safety of the mura," argued Tasuke. "We must force the gates."

"It would be like moving a mountain," said the prince, "but I feel you are right. We are a small number, only fifty, counting the three of us, and we do not carry many arrows. The gates must be opened, as Tasuke says. Only then can we use our swords. If we outnumber the yatō, they will never come out."

"Then, my lord, the plan should be simple. Suppose we show only a few samurai? This has been done before."

"Hai, but that plan has flaws. A few outside the gates are no threat. If these few are ignored, we are back where we started."

As Jujiro spoke, a samurai approached, waiting to be recognized. The prince nodded to him.

"My lord, the runner's horse grazes with the others. He is still bridled."

The leaders rose and followed the soldier to the hobbled horses. The saddled horse continued eating as the men approached.

Jujiro noticed first. "Ah, Hetomi still lives. Only he would know our way to tie the reins. They are fixed so that they will not foul as the animal runs."

"Hai, you are right," broke in Keisuke. He reached into the saddlebag. "But there is no message."

"There is a message, or at least a sign," replied the prince. "It means to me that the yatō are there. He did not have time to return. The freed horse is his sign."

"That is so," agreed Keisuke. "Then we march and camp as close as possible to Mina. Hai, our runner is still working."

Jujiro held up his hands. "This is it. We will march. We will wait close to Mina for Hetomi. If our runner does not appear, we will storm the gates in the darkness. Our course will work out by itself. Pass the orders, we ride in one hour, and we wear our armor, prepared for battle."

It was less than an hour later that Jujiro climbed onto his horse. He wore the full dress of the samurai warrior. Cradled in one arm, he held the helmet with the black-polished horns. His wrists were protected by long leather cuffs studded with hammered gold and brass nails. Shoulder pads and a chest shield were worn over his white kariginu. The Jugi Hoshi monshō appeared large on his back and small beneath the shoulder pads at his front. A quiver, well filled with arrows, hung on his back with his long sword. A bow was tied to the saddle and could be released with one pull of a leather thong. Donning his helmet, Jujiro accepted the spear which a soldier held for him.

Keisuke Shishido wore no helmet. A leather chest plate was his only protection. His tunic was the same as Jujiro's. Tasuke Ito wore complete armor. His kariginu was purple; he did not own one of any other color. All three men carried the same weapons.

The small Jugi Hoshi army marched toward Mina. The sun had passed overhead before they found the long mark scratched through the pine needles. Keisuke dismounted and picked up the small piece of black cloth, holding it up for the others to see. "Hetomi talks to us," he said. "He shows us his path and the one we must follow. The line points to it." He remounted, and the small army followed the prescribed trail. The path was well selected—there were no obstacles, the trail was wide, and the pine-needle carpet was thick beneath the horses' feet. Every so often, it was necessary for a rider to dismount to find the next marker. Sometimes the path almost reversed direction. It was Hetomi's attempt to bring in the small army without a sound. Jujiro understood the meaning of Hetomi's caution, but he tried to keep it from his mind.

The Jugi Hoshi army had drawn close to the mura when the trail came to an end. It was a large but tree-shielded clearing. In its center, marked in the pine needles, was the kanji symbol for night. Hetomi's message was clear. It confirmed what the leaders had guessed all along: Mina's trouble was grave.

Anticipating his superiors, Keisuke gave the necessary orders to the samurai. The horses were hobbled and pastured, still saddled, within a lush roped-off area. The rich forage would keep the animals quiet. The soldiers spent the remainder of the day preparing for battle.

Jujiro Fugita felt uneasy. Not because he would soon fight, but because of the delays. Tonight the moon would be full and bright again. It would be hours yet before it would arc down behind the hills. The prince wanted the complete blackness of night as an ally.

The leaders met again. Another decision was made. When the moon flooded the encampment, another black-clad runner bowed to the leaders and received his instructions.

"The walls of the mura are not far," the prince told him. "I can hear the barking of the dogs. You will walk, for a horse is useless now. The scent of other horses will make him call out and betray you."

"I understand," said the runner.

"You know what we must have," continued Jujiro. "Without information, we are helpless. We want you back here, with your report, in two hours. Then we will march, with or without information."

"Hai, tomosama, it will be as you say." Turning, the runner disappeared in the blackness of the trees toward the sounds of the dogs and the smell of death.

Yasumori Fugita held council. Before him, sitting cross-legged, the officers of the Jugi Hoshi were attentive to their daimyō. Each listened to the cadenced booms of the challenging war drums outside the mura.

Yasumori's face showed the signs of a sleepless night. He raised his head to speak. "The enemy is brave today. They outnumber us by at least one thousand men. At this moment they are sacking the town at our door. The people of Ikoma have done well. They have left nothing for the yatō. Where are our samurai?"

An officer held up his hand, asking for recognition. The daimyō nodded as the officer bowed. "My lord, some of our samurai have returned. But their number is small. I am sorry to report that all liaison with the others has been broken."

The daimyō listened to the drums before he spoke. "The drums of the Red Triangle moan only for the death of the yatō. This you must remember and tell to the other soldiers. The drums of war are meant to demoralize the Jugi Hoshi. Instead, they will inflame our samurai and make them quicker. Iie, we shall not perish."

Gokarō Ito turned to his friend. He spoke softly so only the daimyō could hear. "Kimi," he said, "soon we will don our armor and fight side by side again, nē?"

Daimyō Fugita's only answer was a faint smile. He turned to the other officers. "Go to your men and inspire them. Especially those that have not trained, for they will die first. The arts of the yawara cannot protect them."

As Yasumori's retainers moved to rise, he spoke once again. "I have only one more thought for you to relay to my samurai. We must be deadly with every strike, with every swing, and with every arrow, deadly and swift. Go now."

"Hai," the men shouted as one. They vacated the court, leaving only Yasumori and the gokarō.

"Iie, kimi," the daimyō told his gokarō. "This time we will not fight side by side. The samurai Taizo will command the armies. You and I must protect our women and prepare to go through the final rites together."

"Hai."

"The girl Aki is with my Okei. The task before us is grim. The timing of our actions is delicate. Soon I will go to these women and prepare their minds for what must be."

"I will not leave your side, my friend."

"Dōmo, dōmo arigatō."

Okei Fugita knelt on the tatami and poured the boiling water into the bowl. Her face was expressionless, only a hint of worry lingered in her eyes. Though she was concerned about the impending battle, she had made up her mind that her anxieties would not be transmitted to her young companion.

"There is nothing to worry about," Okei began. "Many times the yatō have knocked on the gates of Ikoma, but the samurai of the Jugi Hoshi have no equal. All will be well again."

Aki looked at the mother of the man she loved. "I know of our samurai at home in Mina. The best there have trained here. In Ikoma and in Mina, my father taught the sword. Even now, he stands first among the soldiers. If the yatō enter, I am not afraid.'' Aki was trying to soothe her friend. She continued talking. ''Please, Okei-san, do not think for one minute that I am frightened. I am happier here with you.''

''You have not noticed the bowls we are using,'' Okei said, changing the subject. ''Look, do you not recognize them?''

''Oh, they're beautiful. It is he—Jujiro. And here is Tasuke. The purple one. These are the bowls we made together. They are so fine. I thought they had been lost in the kiln.''

''Six came out whole. Maybe soon we'll add more to them.'' Okei whisked the powdered tea in the bowls. The women went through the age-old routine of the tea ceremony in silence, each enjoying the company of the other.

After Okei closed the lacquered box, she broke the silence. ''Aki, I have something I am honored to tell you.''

''Hai.'' Aki held her breath.

''The daimyō and Taizo have spoken together.'' Okei smiled at the tense girl beside her. ''You know,'' she continued, ''they sometimes talk of other things besides business.'' She was teasing Aki now.

''Hai,'' Aki repeated.

''This time Yasumori told me they talked of you, Aki.''

The younger woman was frightened. ''Why would the great daimyō ever bother to talk of me? I would think he would talk of his son, the prince, nē?''

''Ah, but he talked of both of you, and what they spoke of pleased me very much.''

''Oh, tell me, tell me.'' Aki put her hand imploringly on the woman's shoulder.

"It is that your father and the daimyō deem that the wife of Prince Jujiro shall be you, Aki. I had hoped to tell Jujiro first, but I cannot. So it is something that you and I can speak of and share."

"Oh," uttered Aki. The word was almost a whisper. Tears rolled from the young woman's eyes, and she turned her head to hide them.

"Is that all the comment you have? Just oh?" said Okei. She heard the young woman sob. She gathered her close and felt Aki shudder as she cried. "I'm sorry," Okei comforted Aki. "I'm sure now I should have waited and let Taizo tell you."

Aki turned her wet face up to the older woman. "Oh, Okei-san, I am so happy."

When Yasumori approached the tearoom, his hand already on the shōji, he heard the two women laughing. For the first time in days, he felt relieved. The sounds of laughter drowned out the dull beat of the war drums.

The daimyō did not open the shōji. Instead, he returned to his court room.

Ikoma's air vibrated with the monotonous sound of war drums. The sound grew louder and reached a crescendo of thunder before it stopped altogether. Then, suddenly, the shouts of many voices filled the air—the yatō charged.

The defenders in the towers and on the catwalks fired their weapons into the invaders. Arrows flew over the wall from both directions. Many in the forward lines of the yatō disappeared, felled by the rocks and lead pellets thrown or propelled by a sling.

The yatō line faltered, drew back for less than a minute, then charged forward again. This time, some carried torches, which were slung up onto the catwalks. Heavy straw mats, first used as shields, burned furiously at the heavy gate.

For only a short time, the warriors of the Jugi Hoshi shot on command. Soon a steady shower of missiles rained into the invaders. The archers of Ikoma stopped shooting long enough to replenish their supply from below by pulling up cords tied to more ammunition. The fighting only slowed down when an archer drew up an empty cord.

The assault on the walls began. Makeshift ladders appeared on one side of the mura, and some of the yatō reached the top, to become the first to die within the walls. But this was just a diversion. Yatō bowmen concentrated their arrows on the catwalks near the gate, where the battering rams had started to hammer.

The warriors inside the mura did not attempt to keep the gates from falling, they waited in their ranks for what appeared to be inevitable. Immediately above the gates, huge buckets waited for the intruders, held taut by trip ropes.

Finally the gates fell in. Those yatō who manned the battering ram did not escape the arrows that came to them from both directions. The Jugi Hoshi held their ground, shooting the last of their arrows through the opening.

The yatō, seeing the small number of their enemy, charged confidently toward them. But quickly the buckets were tripped, spilling hot lye on the charging yatō. They faltered, and were trampled by their own hordes.

The invaders spread out into groups of fighting swordsmen. Horses came charging through the opening. One rider, Kumahatchi Murata, the yatō leader, shouted commands as he raced forward to the Jugi Hoshi, spurring his heavy horse into an enemy. Methodically, the tōryō went from group to group, using his horse and his kogatana. Each time, he was successful in cutting down an overwhelmed Jugi Hoshi samurai.

Kumahatchi's horse became wounded on both sides, but the tōryō continued to use him as a shield. The animal glared, wild-eyed; desperately, it backed away from the cutting swords. His rider jumped clear, realizing that the fear-crazed horse was useless. The tōryō's lieutenants immediately gathered to his sides and together they attacked, but only when they could outnumber.

Cheers and shouts erupted from the victorious yatō, as one by one the Ikoma samurai dropped lifeless to the bloody ground. The yatō spread out, working their way toward the manor. All about them, arrows and other missiles still flew through the smoke-filled air. The heat from burning buildings scorched nearby trees and bushes until they too were burning.

One last group of samurai, wearing the monshō of the Jugi Hoshi, protected the manor. This last line of defense pushed forward, at times fighting on top of the bodies they had slain. But soon they, too, fell to the ground, exhausted and overwhelmed.

Within the manor, the daimyō and the gokarō knelt, each before a small cabinet altar. In front of them, white towels hid the tantō that lay on small cushions. Standing to one side and behind the kneeling men, two samurai waited for the ritual to begin. Each of the standing men held his long sword unsheathed, point down on the tatami.

The daimyō nodded to his gokarō beside him, and these two bowed forward, their hands finding the small sharp knives under the towels. For a moment they stayed in this position and prayed to the altars. When they sat back on their heels, they held the knives with both hands above their heads. The samurai behind them readied their long swords.

The incense on the small altars smoked, the scent mingling with the smell of oil that had been spilled on the tatami.

For scarcely a minute, the leaders held the small knives aloft, poised. Swiftly, together, the blades descended. The tantō cut deep and were pushed hard sideways, reaching for the spinal cords of the daimyō and the gokarō. The daimyō achieved it first.

"Sayonara, kimi," said Gokarō Ito.

Yasumori said nothing. He could no longer hold the towel against his stomach, the tatami beneath him was crimson. He bowed his head forward, inviting the long sword of the samurai. A second later, Gokarō Ito bowed his head also. The two long swords swung at once, and the sound of the blades in the closed room broke the silence with a whoosh.

Carefully and unemotionally, the samurai, specially honored to aid their leaders' seppuku, dressed Yasumori Fugita and his friend Gokarō Ito and laid them on futons, as though preparing them for a peaceful sleep. This was as tradition dictated. When their honored chore was completed, the soldiers poured more oil on the bodies, then ignited the room. Soon the room was a blazing inferno, a funeral pyre for the rulers of the house of Fugita.

Kogashira Kozo stayed astride his horse. He was not yet ready to meet the Jugi Hoshi on the ground. So far, he had been more than successful, fighting from the saddle. His horse seemed to have the instinct to move the right way at the right time in close battle. Kozo worked his way to the manor. Although by now it was burning, the resistance there was greatest. These last Jugi Hoshi defenders defied the odds, and Kozo's soldiers seemed unable to press farther. Kozo shouted at his men and urged them forward, only to watch them fall. He would have to breach the line himself. Suddenly Kozo pulled back on his reins. He looked with disbelief at one enemy warrior, one who chopped down all yatō that came against him.

Kozo's eyes met those of the Jugi Hoshi warrior, full of hate. He heard the man shout at him: "What is it, yatō? Are you frightened of me? I am Taizo, an old man. Will you dismount and join me, or must I slay your animal first?" Taizo spat at the horseman and laughed.

"Bowman, bowman!" Kozo bellowed. "Get him."

A single arrow sped true toward Taizo, who with ease deflected it with his sword. Seeing this, Kozo decided not to dismount; being on a horse would be his advantage. He would make the Jugi Hoshi come to him.

"You have reason to fear me," Taizo taunted. "All who have come to me have died. Now it is your turn."

With one hand, Taizo pointed his sword at Kozo. Then he lunged under the horse's head, grabbing the bit with his free hand. Under the horse he was shielded from Kozo's swings. With the momentum of his forward motion, Taizo pulled the horse's head down and back, bringing the animal to its knees. Kozo landed on his feet. Fear kept his sword down, he could not defend himself. As though in a trance, helpless, Kozo faced his executioner.

"You are almost graceful, yatō," Taizo told him. "But now you die!" The samurai Taizo shifted his body to initiate his swing, but suddenly he halted, his head jerking unnaturally, his sword crashing to the ground. Taizo wheeled slowly, uncontrolled, his knees buckling underneath him. The warrior fell.

Kozo looked into the lifeless eyes that stared up at him. The man was dead, but how? He looked away from the body. Kumahatchi and a soldier ran to him.

"He is my kill!" the soldier shouted at Kozo. "He is mine."

Kumahatchi pushed the soldier away. "Quiet!" he commanded. He knelt by the fallen samurai, gathering the dead man to him, and put his ear to Taizo's heart. Kozo's amazement grew. The tōryō looked at his lieutenant. "He was my friend," he explained simply. "How did he die?"

Kozo shook his head. He did not know.

"I killed him," said the soldier, "with this rock to his temple. I am a thrower. It is seldom that Hitari misses." The soldier showed a toothy grin to the tōryō. "Because I killed him," he continued, "his clothes and his swords are mine." Hitari's eyes pleaded with Kumahatchi.

"Iie," said the leader, "this samurai will not be defiled. He will keep his head." Kumahatchi paused, then added as an afterthought, "Hai, you can keep his swords, he should not have raised them against me. But these are special swords, do not sell them. Do you understand, Hitari?"

"Hai."

"My lord," Kozo interrupted. "These are the swords of a samurai. Hitari is a simple peasant. He does not even know which end to hold. I recognize them as Masamune swords, and I led the soldiers. I should have these swords. The nōmin will have mine instead."

"Iie," said the leader. "Had you beaten him, they would be yours. But had you stood up against him, you would have been dead in a second. Believe me, I know.

Hitari, be proud, you deserve the spoils. No man but I myself could have bested this man with the sword. It is ironic that he should die by the hand of a peasant. I am sad, I was his friend and I loved him. He was a true bushi, but I will deny him his weapons in death because he raised them against me. The swords are yours, Hitari. I will not avenge my friend, I will let you live. The spirit of Taizo must know that he cut all bonds between us with his swords. Now a nōmin will carry his revered weapons." Kumahatchi's laughter became mixed with cries of grief.

Kozo reached for his horse's reins, then led the animal away. At the gate, Kozo stopped but did not turn. The insane laughter of his leader frightened him.

When it had ceased, Kozo looked back and saw Kumahatchi carrying the body of the samurai toward the burning manor. Hitari was tying his new swords to his back, but now Kozo did not care, they were unlucky. He aimed for a better prize: Sakura. Kozo motioned for Hitari to join him, they had a job to do. Now they must turn on their allies.

Smoke and the smell of spilled oil had reached the far corner of the manor where Okei and Aki were hiding. Both women cried silently, but openly. They waited in what was once Jujiro's room. The shōji to the garden was partially open. The water still ran into the pond, but now the surface of the water was heavily covered with ashes. Okei noticed the grim absence of reflection.

The shōji to the hall slid open, and a samurai entered and knelt before the women. "They are gone," he said. "They left us as gods would. You must be proud."

The older woman did not speak. Firmly, she set her mouth and held Aki to her. The soldier spoke again.

"Come, follow me, the daimyō's last wish was for your safety." The soldier pointed to the garden. "We must go this way."

Okei hesitated, remembering something. "You will have to wait." She left the room, returning a few minutes later with a small package. "They are the bowls we made," she said to Aki.

The three left the building by way of the garden. The women followed the samurai, who walked directly to the large pile of rocks at one end of the pond. With little effort, he slid one of the rocks aside, exposing an opening. He motioned the women inside.

"Tonight, someone will come for you," said the samurai. "If not, there is a way to the outside of the mura through these rocks. But be careful, wait until all is quiet. Sayonara."

Inside the damp sanctuary, the women heard the man tamp down the earth after pushing the rock back into place. Then they heard him unsheath his sword as he walked away. The light from the burning manor flickered through the spaces between the rocks. The shouting and the fighting drew near, then slowly subsided into silence.

The fire died. Hours passed, yet no one came. Together, the women made their way in the darkness of the tunnel to the wall. Finally they found the swinging balanced rock. They crawled through and stood up. Behind them was the wall of the mura, before them the clearing. Clutching each other's hands, they ran straight out, away from the mura of Ikoma.

At first, the horseman was not aware of the women. But the horse he rode alerted him with a snort. Something white was moving fast in the darkness. The kimonos of the women had given them away. The rider pulled his kogatana from his belt, swung his mount toward the fleeing figures, and gave pursuit. He knew he could get to them before they could reach the safety of the trees.

The moon was low, and dimmed by a moving cloud. In the darkness, Hetomi Tajimi sprinted to Mina's mura. He was less than ten yards from the walls when he stopped and fell prone. Then, straining his eyes, he again searched the top of the walls for the sentries he knew would be there. Whispered voices above the gate showed Hetomi their positions. Slowly, a bit at a time, the runner pulled himself along the ground. Soon he was against the wall, just under the sentries, where he could clearly distinguish their voices. For a while he listened; the guards complained about watching for an enemy that did not exist, while their friends enjoyed the fruits of Mina.

Undetected by the sentries above him, Hetomi noiselessly passed through the gates. Making his way along the wall on the inside, he listened intently for other sounds. The moon was gone now. To one side, he saw the bare timbers of the burned framework that was once the Mina manor.

Around the central area of the mura, small tents and lean-tos showed Hetomi where the soldiers slept. Unobtrusively, he walked to the manor, at times barely a foot away from the sleepers. As Hetomi passed one tent, a sleepless soldier noticed him. When the runner bid him a peaceful night, the soldier bowed, lay down, and tried again to sleep.

Hetomi made his way toward a fire that burned to one side of the manor. The light revealed a group of men who did not sleep. Because of their dress, the runner guessed these to be the yatō leaders. He crept as close as he dared, then concealed himself.

From his vantage point, the runner could see only three of the four who talked before the fire. Carefully, he studied them. The hanchō was an old man; the two at his side, who bore a resemblance to him, were probably his sons. The fine kimonos they wore looked out of place. The youngest of the two sons fondled a jewel-handled kogatana. On a blanket beside them were four swords, their polished lacquered cases reflecting the light from the fire.

The old man was talking. "By now we should be hearing from the others. We have done as Kumahatchi has ordered, but we have lost many soldiers."

"It is just as well," said the oldest son. "We have lost only those who could not fight. Besides, there is more for us who are left, nē?"

"The harvest here is small," the old man retorted. "Kumahatchi goes after the richer prize. But he will have no easy chore of it. Their chore will not be easy," he repeated. "The samurai of the Jugi Hoshi are like the nighthawk. They do not sleep."

For a while they remained silent. Then the oldest son spoke. "Ah, little brother, otōto, I am surprised you are here with us. The women of Mina must not be to your liking."

"I have no time for them, I know that soon the Jugi Hoshi will come, this is what I think of."

"It sounds as if you fear them. Is that so, otōto?"

The second son looked angrily at his brother. "You'll see when they get here. I will not stand back as we did before."

The old man interrupted. "That is enough; all three of

you will do as I say. You will stay back again, I will lead the battle. Only I among all of us have trained in the yawara. The Jugi Hoshi, if they come, will be small. Most of them will die before they pass the open gate. I have no fear. I did not even replace the gate."

"It is so," the oldest son added. "The Jugi Hoshi do not have a chance. Even now, our soldiers wait with taut bows. We are ready. Maybe tomorrow night it will all be over and I will be the gokarō of Mina. If you fall, Father, I will be daimyō of Mina."

The leader looked at his first son, shaking his head. "Maybe soon, yes, but not now. I do not believe it is my time to die yet. We should be sleeping. Good night, my sons."

As the group around the fire made their preparations for sleeping, Hetomi moved from his cramped position and made his way back to the wall of the mura. He would have to guess at the number of soldiers from the number of tents and shelters. If he could leave the mura now, he would be back at his camp with the sun.

When Hetomi spotted two yatō walking toward him, he scrambled under a wagon. But they did not see the runner. When they reached the wagon, they stopped and talked quietly together. Others were coming to join them. In the darkness, the trained eyes of Hetomi could make out five yatō.

On his guard, Hetomi tried to crawl away, relying on the darkness of his clothing. But, as two more yatō approached the line of his escape route, he retreated again beneath the wagon.

The soldiers seemed to talk endlessly. When they finally left as a group, hours had slipped by and the eastern sky began to show the gray color of dawn. Time had run out on Hetomi. Now it would be impossible to cross the clearing undetected.

The runner slipped out of his black robes, rolled them into a bundle with his kogatana, and crawled from his hiding place. Wearing only a loincloth, he was not dressed very differently from most of the awakening soldiers. With his bundle in one hand, he walked toward the ravaged houses of Mina.

The first house he approached, though half demolished by fire, sheltered at least half a dozen soldiers. All the houses he checked contained soldiers. Finally he found what he was looking for: a collapsed remnant of a burned building. By now, the sun was visible and sounds of activity increased.

After looking about him, Hetomi quickly slipped into the rubble, sliding and pulling himself along in the darkness. After careful maneuvering, the runner lay quiet and tried to sleep, but a sound close by startled him: the sudden scurry of a rat caught his eye. Relieved, he closed his eyes again. This time, sleep overtook him.

When Hetomi awoke, he knew the sun had traveled through most of its arc. A voice, barely audible, was speaking to him. Silently, Hetomi withdrew his kogatana from the bundle, all too aware that it would be useless in the confined space.

"Sire, are you all right?" The words came in a whisper.

Hetomi looked into the semi-darkness. The question was repeated. It was the voice of a woman. In the dim light, he could see only a hand on the ground where the filtered light entered. For a moment Hetomi remained silent, then: "Hai, who are you? Why are you here?"

A whisper came back. "I hide here from the soldiers. You too, yes?"

"Hai, until tonight, then I will be gone."

Someone walked nearby, the two under the fallen roof remained quiet. When the footsteps departed, the woman spoke again. "You are not a yatō, I can see you well. Your head is shaved high. You are a samurai, yes?"

"Hai, I am a samurai. I am a runner for the Jugi Hoshi. How long have you been hiding?"

"Four days now, since the yatō entered Mina. All in my family are dead. The yatō came at night. I hid in a clay pit. After the fires died down, I came here."

Hetomi thought about her story. "When did you eat last?" he asked.

"I have some food with me. At night, it is no trouble. Last night I even found some wine," she said. The woman slid toward him, dragging a small bag with her. "I will share my food with you before the rats get all of it."

Now the man could see her clearly. He guessed she was not yet thirty, though her hair, scraggly and matted, made her appear older.

Lying prone near him, the woman opened the cloth container and from it produced two hardened small cakes. Hetomi was hungry, he ate slowly, relishing the taste. As they ate, the woman did not take her eyes from him. She handed him a ceramic bottle. It was good wine, not to be wasted. Hetomi took only one sip, holding it in his mouth for a long time before swallowing.

"Dōmo." Hetomi spoke now. "It clears my head. Dōmo."

The woman gave him a weak smile. "I had more food, but the rats—" She showed him the chewed part of the knapsack.

"Tell me," began the runner, "what is your name?"

"I am Somiko Sei. And you?"

"Hetomi Tajimi," he answered. "Tell me, what happened here in Mina?"

The smile left the woman's face. For a moment she was silent. "I will start from the beginning. Two months ago, the arrows flew over the walls and our samurai went outside and killed many yatō. It happened again last month. Soon it was feared that we were under siege, for none of our supply wagons returned. We stopped working in the clay pits, and all the men practiced for war. Outside the walls each night, we saw fires and knew that the farmers were under attack. Our samurai would go and fight the yatō, and for a while a few wagons would get in. Then—" She stopped talking, her eyes wet with tears.

"Go on," prodded Hetomi.

Somiko wiped her eyes with her wrist. "Then," she continued, "we saw many of our samurai return and we were happy. But it was only the yatō wearing our clothes. My father was in the tub when they walked into our house. They killed him with the kogatana. The water that spilled from the tub was all red—my father's blood." Somiko was sobbing now, but she went on. "My mother pushed me outside. Then I heard her scream and the soldiers laugh. I ran to the clay pits and covered myself with mud. Last night I came here. This was our house."

"I am sorry, Somiko-san, I am very sorry. Now it is almost over. I will get you away from Mina."

"There is no way out," she told him.

"Hai, you will see. I came in, and together we will leave the same way. Tell me, how many yatō are here?"

"I do not know. I cannot even guess."

Hetomi thought this over, then asked, "What can you tell me of the yatō? Anything you can think of might be of some help."

"Not very much," she answered. "Only that they do not fight like the samurai. Only a few of those I saw had swords. I think there must be more rock throwers than swordsmen. Last night, when I looked for water, I saw many soldiers, but few swords. If I had to guess, I would say maybe there are—maybe one hundred yatō. I do not know—" A loud thump on the roof of their hiding place interrupted Somiko.

Protectively, Hetomi pulled the woman to him. The voices outside were uncomfortably close.

"There must be bodies here. The smell is terrible," one of the soldiers said.

Hetomi and Somiko could see the legs of two soldiers now. They were barefoot; this was why the runner had not heard them approach.

The second soldier spoke. "How can we get inside? Maybe it would be better if we just burned it all. Hai, that is what we should do."

The runner felt the woman quiver with fright.

"We will burn this one tonight," said the first yatō. "That way, it will warm us later when it is cold."

"Should we search it anyway? There may be something of value."

"I doubt it. Besides, it looks too hard. Do you want to crawl under and see?" asked the first, laughing as they walked away.

For a while, neither the runner nor Somiko spoke. Hetomi was conscious of the caked clay on her robe beneath his fingers.

"I do not know whether to trust you. You still hold me, yet you wear no clothes," said Somiko.

Hetomi quickly pulled his arm from the woman. For the first time for as long as he could remember, he felt embarrassed. He did not want to show it, yet it angered him. He was conscious of the many scars on his body. He began to put on his clothing, which was next to impossible in the cramped space. Somiko helped him. The touch of her hand on his body felt warm.

"I need no help, ojōsan!"

"Yes, you do, my otoko," Somiko replied. Now she was smiling. "It is better to have your clothes on, not just because of the cold."

Hetomi forgot his anger; he, too, was smiling.

When night came, but before the moon had risen, the two made their way in the darkness to the wall. Hetomi held Somiko's hand and pulled her with him. Finally they reached the wall. Fires burned again in the mura, so Hetomi kept Somiko between him and the wall. He, with his dark clothing, shielded the woman and made them both invisible within the shadows. Soon they were at the gate. They could not hear the sentries.

The sound of an arrow being fitted to a bow made Hetomi lie on top of his companion. He looked up and saw only the black edge of the wall against the lightening sky.

The arrow was released. Shouts broke the stillness, as soldiers from the inside ran out the open gate. When they returned, a black-clad prisoner stumbled before them. The yatō prodded the prisoner with their kogatana. The dim light from the fires made the wet blood glisten on their sword points.

Hetomi recognized the yatō's prisoner, but it would be foolhardy to try to aid him. The runner was expendable, the information the Jugi Hoshi needed was not.

While the two sentries argued on the catwalk, Hetomi and Somiko slipped undetected across the clearing.

In the far distance, the old man watched the smoke as it rose, then faded in the sky. For days, he had noticed the smoke, and now he could smell it. There, in the west, a town was burning. This worried him, since it was the direction he was headed for.

The man was not so old. He still had the walk of a much younger man, though not the swagger of a samurai. In each hand he held a bag; on his back he carried a traveling box. A cloth band around his forehead, tied to the box, helped balance his load.

His head was balding, and his lean face was deeply lined and tanned. He wore no sword or tantō, but the round red spot on the left shoulder of his tunic revealed his identity: he was an oishasan, a doctor.

Isha Koan walked steadily, making good time. He had traveled this path before, and he knew that soon he would reach the river. He was eager to get there; the traveling would be easier, the food better. For a week, Isha Koan had not seen another human being.

Every year, Koan Tachibana made the long trek from coast to coast. Along the way he plied his trade, gathered herbs, gave advice, but mostly enjoyed simply being free.

Koan was expert at almost everything he tried, except women. Though he had never married in all his fifty-five years, he still experimented whenever the occasion arose. Children, whom he loved, marveled at his sleight of hand, as did the old people he tended. He was usually successful with his treatments, and because of this, he was often referred to as the "isha who talks with the gods."

Yes, Isha Koan, though he never gave it a thought, was

appreciated as a special healer. When he first noticed this, he tended to take advantage of it: he ate the best foods and drank the best wines. When he found that his privileged life was getting the better of him, he abruptly changed. Now he only collected the bare necessities as his pay. He did not have to worry about carrying too many things when he moved on.

Because of his extensive travels, people looked to Isha Koan for news of the distant towns. When he reached a new destination, he would usually see the local daimyō first. If he didn't, he knew he would be brought to the daimyō's presence without ceremony, and this would be beneath his dignity.

On the whole, Koan Tachibana was a good isha: he knew his herbs, he knew what they could do, and he knew where to find them. He even dabbled in surgery.

The smoke in the west bothered Koan. He was sure it came from the village of Mina. His plans were to go to Takata, far to the north, but if he bypassed Mina now, it would be a long time before he would come to another village.

Koan stopped and set up camp for the night. First he checked the skies for signs of changing weather. Then he checked the vegetation to be sure. Hai, tonight he would need a lean-to. Koan built his shelter, making sure the roof extended high over the campfire in front.

Later, as the rain rolled off his makeshift house, Koan continued to argue with himself about his destination. And before he slept, he made a decision: in the morning he would not change his direction, he would head west for Mina, then follow the river north to Takata. Koan had never been to Takata, but he was sure they had heard of him there. "If not, they will," he said aloud. Soon Isha Koan slept.

Morning came early for the isha. Something pulled on the boughs of his lean-to, waking him. It was a shika. The deer was nibbling on the cut branches. Koan remained still so as not to frighten the animal, and watched the doe eat as the skies turned brighter. When a second visitor arrived, the shika bounded away.

A kuma had smelled the strange scent of man and now prowled in search of food. The bear stood upright and surveyed the lean-to. When Koan spotted the bear, he reached into one of his bags, keeping his eye on the animal. Finally his fingers found what they had been searching for—a small earthen jar. Opening it, Koan poured some of the contents into his hand, then waited, watching for the bear's next move. The bear, on all fours now, braved the smoke and approached, stretching its huge head forward toward the human.

When the kuma reached the opening, Koan threw the powder into the hot coals near the bear. As the powder erupted, it created a dazzling flash, a muffled roar, and thick white smoke, which obscured the bear from Koan. When the isha vacated the smoke-filled lean-to, he saw only the rear of the kuma as it crashed through the underbrush, running for its life.

Later the isha sat in the middle of a small stream, scrubbing himself. His kimono, soaking wet, was draped over the bushes near him. Koan's attention focused on a large trout that lay motionless in the water nearby. Carefully and slowly, Koan reached for the fish. He tried many times, but with no success. Yes, with the carp it was easy, no trouble at all, but with the trout or the salmon, it was another game.

Koan gave up. Still nude, he left the stream and gathered large buckeye nuts from nearby trees. When he had collected almost more than he could carry, he tied them in a cloth bag. He smashed the contents of the bag with a rock, and when the pulp of the buckeyes soaked the bag all around, Koan took it back to the stream and threw the bag in. Minutes later, and a little downstream, the isha gathered his breakfast of large fresh trout.

Koan Tachibana felt good today. He had not seen the stars last night, but his sense of direction told him that he was on the right path to Mina. Topping the next rise should verify this, and by noon he would be in the village.

Kumahatchi Murata sat cross-legged on the tatami, looking through the open doors of the dōjō at the landscape of Ikoma. A pennant in view bore his emblem, the Red Triangle. The new daimyō's eyes shifted to the high walls of Ikoma's mura, walls that had almost kept him from his great victory. Now these same walls held his powerful army.

Daimyō Murata had come a long way since he had decided not to hire out his sword to lesser daimyō. At first, he was just another yatō of the forest, but when, one by one, samurai soldiers of fortune had joined him, he had been able to form an army. It was an army without roots, constantly moving all through the land. Kumahatchi had become rich and today he was a daimyō, his daughter a princess, and a new manor was being built for them.

Most of the activity within the mura of Ikoma centered on the dōjō, which now served as the temporary manor. Much had been added to the building: the highly polished floor was crisscrossed with walls and sliding doors; the room in which Kumahatchi was sitting had become his court room.

Kumahatchi was tired. The efforts of the past half year—a gamble that he could conquer Ikoma—were over. It had taken months, the plan had been crude: if the yatō harassed Mina, the Jugi Hoshi would be forced to scatter their army. By lying to the other yatō forces, Kumahatchi had been able to gather the superior numbers it finally took to crush the Jugi Hoshi. The few Ikoma samurai who had left for Mina were still unaccounted for, but it was just a matter of time, he would see to that.

Kogashira Kozo appeared in front of Kumahatchi. "Ohayō gozaimasu," said the new gokarō as he bowed to the daimyō inside.

"Ohayō," returned Kumahatchi. "It is good that you are here. I wanted to talk with you about the Jugi Hoshi who are still alive."

Kozo entered, then sat facing his leader.

Kumahatchi spoke again. "I am worried about the Jugi Hoshi we decoyed to the south. From our prisoners we have learned that those that went to Mina were the most loyal to the Fugita clan. They were sent mainly to protect the prince and the gokarō's son. It has been some time, we have not heard a word from the soldiers we left for bait at Mina. I have no trust in them." The daimyō picked up a rolled paper from the chodai beside him. He unrolled and glanced at the paper before he continued. "We have about fifty samurai to account for who have sworn the oath of junshi to the names Fugita and Ito. These names are all listed on this paper. The name on the top is Jujiro Fugita. This is what I want done. You will send enough men to annihilate all that is left of the Jugi Hoshi. Those that straggle in here, we will continue to send to the slaughter T. This way we will be finished with the Jugi Hoshi, and then we will be able to reduce the number of soldiers we must keep here. Kimi, it is essential that you bring back the heads of the two pampered otoko."

"Hai, my lord," the gokarō answered. His scarred face beamed. Ah, indeed, this was good news. This could be the answer Kozo had been looking for. It was perfect. "I will see to it now, tomosama," said the gokarō as he rose to his feet. He backed from the room, bowing to the daimyō. Hai, the answer had come at last. Kozo would do as he was told. He would send the soldiers to Mina, but only those who were most loyal to Kumahatchi. Those that were loyal to himself, he would keep here—to protect Ikoma. Kozo's scarred face formed a twisted smile.

As Gokarō Kozo left the daimyō's court room, Kumahatchi noted that his lieutenant walked with a faster pace than was his custom. The daimyō knew that Kozo was a good soldier. He had studied the shinobi and the yawara, and both Kozo and he had been sensei of the long sword. Kozo bore scars; Kumahatchi did not. Kozo was a good swordsman, but not one tenth as good as the daimyō. Kumahatchi had proved this many times.

The daimyō had promised Kozo that he would become the gokarō of Ikoma. Kumahatchi kept that promise because he knew that Kozo feared him and could be trusted since, as gokarō, he would be distracted by his own self-importance. To be on the safe side, though, Kumahatchi would not let him control the army that would leave for Mina. He would retain Kozo here, where he could keep an eye on him.

The gokarō walked swiftly to the practice fields. The soldiers were mustering already. They stood in straight lines.

Kozo faced them and shouted for order. "As I walk down the lines, each man whose chest I touch will prepare to march. Tomorrow you will leave for the south."

Kozo walked down the long lines, passing those he knew, tapping those he did not. He selected carefully; he would make no mistakes. It took him the better part of an hour.

Much later, Kogashira Kozo walked to the kiln area. Maybe it was time for the stubborn one to be prodded again. The woman held prisoner in the cell was a paradox. It would not be good if her spirit was broken completely. But the dark cell might have done the job. She would have to do, if other matters did not work out as Kozo planned.

Hai, this woman in the cell was a paradox. Not only did she not speak, but she was Sakura's double. Each was a copy of the other: their actions, their forms, the same curves. Hai, the one in the cell was a twin to Sakura, there could be no doubt of it. When she had been brought to him as a prisoner, the gokarō had thought at first that it was Sakura. Kozo did well to hide the prisoner in the cells. Ah, the time would come when he would keep both women in his apartment.

Kozo reached the kilns. Most of the low buildings in the area were vacant. One structure was boarded up as a blockhouse. Two monban lounged before it, talking. When they saw the gokarō approach, they quickly stood up and bowed to him.

"Open," Kozo commanded. Once inside, the gokarō walked purposefully to one cell. He ignored the pleas that the prisoners, mostly women, called out to him.

He stopped at the farthest cell and looked in at the pitiful creature. "Are you ready to come out?" he barked.

Aki Taizo looked up at the fearful man, but said nothing.

Kozo smiled. The smile only masked the anger within.

"I could make you speak, but I have patience. Do I not keep you away from the others? Do you not eat better?"

Still, Aki did not answer. She put her chin down, her arms around her knees, and ignored him.

For a long while Kozo looked at the woman. He knew it was a waste of time to try to get her to speak, but he could not continue to hold his patience. Turning, he left the cell block.

Aki felt some of her fear leave with the man's departure, but the fear of the unknown stayed with her. What was it that was in store for her? This was the tōryō's second visit to her cell. The first time, he had knocked her unconscious in a fit of rage. She had expected worse this time, but she told herself that she did not care what happened, she would not give in to the yatō. She would kill herself first, somehow.

Aki's uppermost thought now was escape. She listened to the other prisoners at night when they talked, hoping some plan would come to her. She had learned much from their conversations. It would be easy to dig out of the cell block, but it would be next to impossible to escape from the mura. Then she remembered the small rock mountain in the garden with the pond. Aki did not speak to anyone; she would trust no one.

Something moved nearby. She stared in the semi-darkness. A rat was drinking her water. She shooed it away; she did not want the jug broken. The rat looked thin. It, too, was not getting enough to eat.

True, Aki did eat better than the other prisoners, which, at best, was barely enough, and her small jug was kept full of water. As each day passed, Aki scratched another line on the wall, marking the weeks since she and Okei had been taken prisoner.

If the goddess Aki prayed to heard, Aki knew she

would soon be free. Her once long fingernails were gone, worn down by the determined digging in the darkness each night. Her only tool was a pointed piece of pottery.

Each night, Aki pulled the loose dirt from the hole, then dug at the exposed hard earth. Before morning, she would push the loose dirt back into the excavation and cover it with the straw she slept on. Her digging was almost over. She had no idea what might await her on the other side of the wall, but tonight she would know.

Aki's plan was simple. She knew that she was in the kiln area. All she had to do was make it to the manor. Then, as she did months ago with Jujiro's mother, she could escape through the rocks. Aki's main worry was whether the escape route by the pond had been discovered.

The food the monban brought Aki that night consisted of a lump of rice, but she did not eat even that. Instead, she wrapped the food in a bit of cloth from her torn kimono. As she did this, she felt the eyes that watched her. The guard did not leave. He stood glaring through the slatted door. "You do not eat," he said. "You save it. Why?"

Aki had hardly spoken since her capture. Now she must talk to mislead him. "I do not get enough to eat. I save it so that I can eat it all at once," she said.

"So you do talk. They told me that you had no voice. You will talk to me now, yes? I will be here all night."

Aki hesitated, then: "I cannot, I must sleep. Tomorrow night I will talk with you." Though the guard frightened her, Aki tried to sound friendly.

The tone of the woman caught the guard unaware; his smile became sincere. "It is good for you to have a friend here. I am very powerful among the monbans, I am aide to the gokarō. You will not tell anyone that I am talking to you?"

"No," said Aki.

"Good. I will be back later. I am called Hitari." The man departed.

Aki was defeated. The word "later" meant she dare not risk digging. She tried to sleep, but could not. She thought of her samurai, Jujiro. With his parents dead and Ikoma gone, the prince would not return, he could not. She herself must find him. Again she prayed to Amaterasu, the goddess who lights the sky, to watch over the prince and lead her to him.

The other prisoners were quiet now. Outside, Aki could hear the movements of the guards as their feet passed over the gravel. She could position them by this sound. She must sleep, she thought; most of the night before had been spent in digging and it was almost impossible to sleep through the noise of the day. But footsteps pushed sleep further away.

"Psst, are you awake?" Hitari had returned.

The straw rustled as Aki got up from it. "Hai," she replied.

"Take this," Hitari said, pushing something through the opening under the door. "This will prove to you that I am your friend. You said that you must sleep. I will come again tomorrow night. Sayonara."

Aki did not move. She listened, and followed Hitari's footsteps until she heard them on the gravel outside. Then she opened the package Hitari had left. It was food and, with it, something that felt like a round stick. A tantō? Hai, a thin sharp knife slipped out of its wooden case. Aki was overwhelmed with gratitude.

Sliding the straw aside, Aki worked quickly. She began scooping the loose dirt out of the hole. With the aid of the tantō, the digging was easier in the hard earth. As she dug, the pile of dirt in the cell grew. Soon the work became much easier. She had reached the moistened earth outside the wall. When the surface collapsed, she pulled the dirt into the cell. She enjoyed the smell of this new earth.

Before leaving the cell, Aki made preparations. She undid her clothing and bound the knife to the small of her back with strips of cloth. When all was in order, she slipped into the hole.

For the first time in months, Aki saw the stars. Her breath, she felt, was noisy; she thought her heart was pounding much too loud. Aki looked about her, but there was no one. After praying to Amaterasu again, Aki climbed out of the hole and slowly made her way to the next building. She could afford no mistakes. Fearfully, she tried not to hurry her flight.

Because of Aki's confinement in almost total darkness, her eyes worked now as if it were daylight. Keeping to the trees, bushes, and buildings, Aki headed for the manor. She prayed she would not mistake the direction. Yes, ahead she saw the slight rise: the framework of a new structure had taken the place of the burned manor. She circled a group of buildings near the dōjō where guards were posted. Until now she had not realized the effect of the long inactivity of her confinement.

Aki reached the top of the rise. Materials for the new building were everywhere. At first, this made it difficult for her to locate the pond and the rocks that ran from it to the wall. When she found the pond, she discovered that tall weeds had almost covered the small rock mountain. It all looked much different from the last time she had been there.

At first, the rock wouldn't budge. Aki was tired, but she was also desperate. Finally she pried the rock loose and crawled inside the tunnel. She reached up behind her, pulled on the metal ring set in the rock, and swung the door closed with ease. Only a rat was watching her, but Aki gave it a weak smile. She had become used to them. With the adrenaline gone from her body, exhaustion took over and in less than a minute Aki Taizo was asleep.

Hours later, sounds outside the rock tunnel woke her. Aki recognized these sounds: a workman sawing wood, another chopping steadily, smoothing a timber with an adze. During her confinement, Aki had heard only the shouts of the angry or the cries and moans of the anguished. These new sounds were a comfort.

Here and there, the new sun shone through the spaces between the rocks, giving a smooth, even light within. Aki would remain in her damp hiding place until night. Knowing that the worst was behind her, this would be easy.

Aki took stock. She removed the treasures from her sleeves. The food she had saved consisted of six small crackers and two balls of rice. This was more than enough, she thought; she would surely find things to eat in the forest. Aki placed her knife with her supply of food. On its lacquered case was a symbol. Holding it to the light, Aki saw the four-pointed star inscribed on it.

The woman remembered the guard who had given her the knife. Could it be that he was not a yatō? Or, as she first thought, just one of those who at night would enter to satisfy himself with one of the women? Aki's cell had been kept locked and could be opened, she had assumed, only by the tōryō. If the guard was not of the Jugi Hoshi, why would he help her?

Aki's outer kimono was in shreds, but now it served to keep her warm; she would discard it later. The inner kimono was still in good condition after all these weeks. If she could only bathe and wear clean clothes again. She looked forward to the first stream she would find—she might even spend a day in it! Near her, within her rock sanctuary, water seeped down from the split bamboo pipe above. This would do for now.

Aki's thoughts wandered to the night that she and Jujiro's mother had attempted an escape from this same place. They had been captured in the clearing just outside and taken before one of the tōryō of the yatō. Tears welled in her eyes as she thought of Okei, remembering her clutching the precious package of pottery. Okei's arrogant posture and defiant refusal to talk was no different than asking to be killed.

"Slay the obāsan!" This command still rang in Aki's ears. She had not seen or heard the sword as it cut through her friend, but Okei's screams were still with Aki. She would hear them forever.

For the first month, Aki had been kept isolated. A monban was assigned to her and never left her side. She soon discovered she was given almost everything she wished for, except freedom. When she complained of the eternal darkness, a lamp was supplied, then a bath, and clean attire.

One day, the tōryō Kozo had appeared. Unlocking the cell, he had entered, a smile distorting his scarred face. "You are happy you do not live as the others do here?" he asked.

Frightened, Aki did not answer.

"You will speak!" he commanded.

Aki remained silent, her head bowed.

The smile left the tōryō's face. He made no effort to shield his anger. "You live only because I let you live," he snarled. "I keep you as I have, to show that I am good. I can take you as I take the others, but I want you to be willing—" He hesitated. "Or, not willing, I want you dead. Think about that," he shouted.

The woman did not move or speak, her eyes still lowered. Something struck her head, throwing her off her feet into a corner. She tried to stand as Kozo left the cell, slamming and locking the door behind him, but her legs would not support her and she fell, lapsing into unconsciousness. When she awoke, she reached for the lamp. She could not find it; everything had been removed from the room.

So it had been until she left. But that was now the past. For the present, she was safe, and she had hope for the future. Amaterasu, the goddess she prayed to, would leave signs for her to follow.

A few hours remained before Aki could attempt to slip away from the mura. She prepared for her escape: she massaged and exercised her cramped legs until they felt normal; she tore strips of cloth from her outer kimono, and used the strips to make padded makeshift zōri, which she would need in the forest. Though her outer kimono was almost gone, the sleeves were still good. They would carry her treasures—her food and her tantō. Aki picked up the knife and tested its blade. She had dulled it by digging with it in the hard earth the night before. Finding a damp, smooth surface on one of the rocks, Aki methodically sharpened the blade.

In the darkness, Hetomi pulled Somiko behind him. They ran the last half of the clearing. When they reached the trees, Hetomi stopped, letting the woman catch her breath. He sat down on the ground beside her. A close sound alerted the runner. He rolled, ready to spring. A glint of the fire from the mura reflected off polished steel.

"You have returned too soon, why did you alarm them?"

Hetomi recognized the voice of Tasuke.

"My lord," the runner began, "I am Hetomi. The man you just sent to the mura is dying. Because of him, I am able to be here now."

"Forgive me, Hetomi, I thought you were he." Pointing to the woman, he asked, "And her?"

"She is of Mina."

Minutes later, these three met with the other leaders. Hetomi knelt before them and began his report. "My lords, as you already know, Mina is in the hands of the yatō. These yatō wear the symbol of a red triangle. I am sorry that I could not return before dawn—"

The prince interrupted. "It is no matter," he assured the runner.

Hetomi continued. "Few if any of Mina still live. The daimyō and his family are dead."

Anger swept over Jujiro. The loss of a grandfather and a grandmother—relatives he had never met—made him grieve for his own mother. How could he tell her? "How do you know they are dead?" Jujiro asked.

Hetomi pointed into the darkness. "Their bodies are over there with the others. When I got here, I found them first. I am sorry, kimi."

"Tell me about the yatō. What is it that we must know?" asked Jujiro, now in a hurry.

"The tōryō of the yatō is an old man, but he is a samurai. He controls the yatō with his sons."

"How many yatō?"

"About one hundred, my lord," answered Hetomi.

"Ah, good," broke in Tasuke. "It will be a small matter."

The runner continued. "The yatō know of us. Even now, they prepare for us. But they cannot lock us out, they did not replace the gates."

"You say that we can expect no help from inside?" It was the sensei Keisuke who asked this question.

"That is true, sire. The yatō have executed all, except the young women. Here are other facts I discovered in the mura: they have few swords, their army consists mostly of archers and throwers; they expect us, as I have said; they are alert. Listen, they are extremely quiet now, they are inviting us in." Hetomi sat back on his heels.

"You have done well, Hetomi," said Jujiro. "Is there anything else that you can remember?"

"Just one more thing, my lord," the runner answered. "I listened to them talk about attacking Ikoma. Either they have by now or it is being planned. This is all that I was able to find out."

"Dōmo arigatō," said the prince as he turned to the woman. "What can you tell me of the yatō?"

For a long time the leaders questioned the woman, who answered clearly and directly. She told them all she had related to Hetomi before.

The leaders excused the runner and the woman. When the two were gone, Jujiro spoke. "It won't be bad, as Tasuke says. They have only throwers and bows, and no swords; it should be easy."

"Hai, I agree," Tasuke chimed in. The two young men turned to the older one for his opinion. Keisuke was quiet, but when pressed for his thoughts, he spoke. "There is something that bothers me, kimi. Maybe I am getting old. Help me. I will number the points in order, then maybe together we can make sense of them. One: there were samurai in Mina. But where are their swords? Two: these yatō who call themselves the Red Triangle, where are their swords? Three: we are sure there is one samurai, the tōryō, and he is an old man. Four: they have not bothered to replace the gates they stormed. Why? Five: they managed to capture Mina despite the few swords. And six: the planned attack of Ikoma. Something is wrong. What is it?" Keisuke was definitely worried.

"My sensei," said the prince, bowing to his teacher. "I must apologize for not thinking. You are not old. You have that which Tasuke and I will take a long time to acquire—wisdom. You are right. It does not add up."

Tasuke pondered the points, then spoke. "I, too, apologize. I can find no answer, except if we attribute it to coincidence."

For a long time they were silent as each tried to solve the riddle.

The prince held up his hand. "I have a fear, but it does not concern us. Two of your points do add up: the open gates of Mina and the attack of Ikoma. Could it be that the yatō have no fear of the Jugi Hoshi? I add one more point: as there are few Red Triangle dead near here, and they must have attacked Mina with many in order to win, where are they now? Wherever they are, you can be sure the missing swords are with them."

"You have something," Keisuke said quietly. "It is one of two things. The open gates of Mina, with few yatō inside, is an invitation. I am sure the missing yatō are nearby. The second, which I doubt, is that they march on Ikoma."

"I am inclined to agree with you," said the prince. "The yatō would have had to pass us on their way to Ikoma. The few we saw and battled with by the river could have been no threat to anyone. Hai, if there are more yatō involved, they must be here. Ikoma and Mina are too far apart for tactical strategy. What do you think?" the prince asked of Keisuke.

Tasuke spoke first. "Permit me," he said, as he placed his hand on Keisuke's shoulder. "This reminds me of one of the problems put to us by our sensei. So let us figure it in Keisuke's way. Let us assume it is that they mean to attack Ikoma. What is for it and what against?"

"For one," said the sensei, "for the yatō to organize is unlikely. And, as Jujiro says, the distance between the two mura would involve logistics enough to tax any general's mind. But assume, too, that the yatō did organize. Ikoma has too much traffic, too many samurai go in and out. Morioka's daimyō has as many samurai as Ikoma, and they would protect each other. We are wasting time."

"This is what we must do," said the daimyō's son. "If the mura of Mina is meant as a trap for us, we must be the kitsune, the fox. Send runners to search all around us while it is still dark. We must know their position. It will take a little time. If they mean to trap us, they cannot be far. If they are not around, we will attack as soon as we are sure. We need the mura. One more idea: Hetomi will ride to Ikoma with the woman for testimony. Give him four horses, the best. I want him to ride fast. Do it now."

"Hai." Keisuke bowed, leaving the two others alone.

"It is another delay, kimi, nē?" said Tasuke.

"Hai, but the delay will not be long," returned the prince. "They would have to be hiding behind the next tree to keep me out of that mura. Listen, Tasuke. If there are no swords in that mura, we can take it easily. There aren't even any samurai in there. Kimi, go see that the runners get out and back. Have them search for two hours. If they find nothing, we war at dawn."

When Tasuke returned, he found the prince asleep, still wearing his armor, his helmet a pillow. The black horns encircled his face. A sword, uncovered, lay to one side of the prince, an arm rested on the handle.

Tasuke smiled. It was a good idea to rest before battle. He lay down at his friend's side, but he found that he could not sleep.

All the runners returned with the same information: there were no other yatō nearby!

"We know now what happened here at Mina," Keisuke explained to the prince and Tasuke. "The samurai were lured from the mura a few at a time. Many signs show that Mina's wagons were not allowed to return. They were under siege for at least three months, since we last heard from them."

"But what of the swords? Where are they?" asked Jujiro.

"Their absence can be explained," answered the sensei. "I have seen it many times. A good sword is a valuable commodity, but these yatō do not know how to use them. You can be sure that the swords they captured are in a wagon on their way to a large village to be sold. That can be the only answer."

Just before dawn, the Jugi Hoshi samurai assembled. No longer were there any cautions about silence. Jujiro spoke in a loud, clear voice. "We have friends to avenge. As my father the daimyō said, the blood of Mina is also that of the Jugi Hoshi. The yatō number about one hundred, twice our own. Each of us must try to account quickly for three yatō. That way, there will not be enough for all of us. But do not miss your share. This I command: all of them must die. Come, we ride."

A drum tied to one of the horses began its hollow call. The pennant of the Jugi Hoshi waved in the first early light of morning. Jujiro wore the black-horned helmet. He rode at the point of the phalanx as it crossed the clearing, pointing to the open gates of Mina.

On either side, but slightly behind the prince, rode

Keisuke and the purple-clad Tasuke. The formation moved slowly, the horses keeping cadence with the war drum. The men noticed the women waving at them from the walls.

The phalanx stopped. The drum continued. Ten archers advanced before the point and formed a line. Then, as one, the Jugi Hoshi resumed the slow march into battle.

A wave from the prince, then it began: the dreadful sound of a whistling arrow, arcing from the Jugi Hoshi into the mura.

Jujiro noticed that the women still held their positions on the catwalks, they did not take cover. They must be there under force. He knew his samurai would also realize this. Meanwhile, Tasuke shouted warnings to the others. Keisuke spoke quickly to the prince and waved the men into a spread position. The phalanx opened at its point, only the forward archers and the prince held their positions. Tasuke was shouting again. He pointed ahead. "The enemy, they come!"

The yatō charged first. Shouting and screaming, soldiers on horseback sped from the gates of the mura. They used spears, bows, but few swords. The forward archers of the Jugi Hoshi fired point-blank at the yatō before dispersing. The phalanx opened wider to form a funnel for the yatō to ride through.

Arrows filled the air from both directions. Those from the wall were falling short. The Jugi Hoshi held their position, shooting as their horses cantered almost in place. Their first arrows hit; the yatō dropped before them. Wounded and riderless horses hampered what remained of the yatō charge.

Keisuke, close to Jujiro, told him what to expect at each second. "These first are only fodder they feed us." As he spoke, he released an arrow. "Remember," he shouted, "save some shafts! They will try to disarm us!"

The yatō charge died. Those that tried to escape back into the mura lay dead at its threshold. The yatō horses still milled in the funnel formed by the Jugi Hoshi. The samurai, keeping these horses as a unit, full-charged them back into the mura. They would use the horses as a buffer.

On entering, the Jugi Hoshi again tried to form a V, spreading from the gate. They were pelted with arrows and rocks. The first of the Jugi Hoshi began to fall.

As he fought, the prince noticed Tasuke leading men on the opposite side into yatō forces. Then Tasuke disappeared from view.

Keisuke was trying to stay ahead of Prince Jujiro. The sensei hurled insults at the enemy, trying to draw their fire. There was no formation now. Already some of the Jugi Hoshi had left their horses, so as to use their long swords more freely. Jujiro sent his last arrow; it was a good one. A rock thrower on the catwalk plummeted to the ground. The prince turned to see Keisuke dueling with two of the yatō.

The passion of hate that had first propelled Jujiro into battle was gone. He felt nothing, but he knew automatically what he must do. When he missed a yatō, it was because his horse, wet with blood, was dropping beneath him. Now on his feet, Jujiro pressed forward, joined by the sensei.

Ahead of Jujiro and Keisuke, a sword-swinging mounted warrior guided his horse toward them. Keisuke tried, as before, to intercept the yatō leader. But two yatō soldiers stood in Keisuke's path. Keisuke screamed at them. Yet they did not move. They waited for the sensei to strike. With dismay, Keisuke watched the prince and the tōryō come together. He himself charged into the yatō who waited before him.

An arrow whizzed by Jujiro, penetrating the leather armor of the tōryō. Still, the old man came on, his wild-eyed horse towering above the prince. Jujiro held his long sword back and above his head. He jammed the weapon forward like a spear, aiming for the yatō's chest, but the sword was torn from his grasp. For an instant, the prince saw the face above him—the wide-open mouth shouting with no sound, the blank glassy eyes. The dead man rode past the Jugi Hoshi prince before toppling from his crazed horse. Both hands still clutched the raw edge of the blade that had felled him. Jujiro retrieved his sword.

With the yatō leader gone, the prince joined Keisuke. Together, they concentrated on the throwers. There were no longer any swords opposing them.

Suddenly the fighting stopped. The samurai of the Jugi Hoshi became hunters, seeking out and slaying the yatō who still lived. In this cleanup, they found the women of the catwalks. They had been butchered by the yatō. Jujiro shook his head slowly. Of all those that had lived in Mina, only the one woman Hetomi brought out had survived.

W*hile* Kogashira Kozo sat in the steaming tub, the almost nude woman beat a steady tattoo on his back with the sides of her closed fists. Kozo, his eyes partially closed, felt better. Once he was just a yatō tōryō; now he was a gokarō. But still there was one more step to go. Two short weeks should do it. Kumahatchi had approved the list of the soldiers who would ride to Mina. Kumahatchi had balked at the number but in the end agreed, at Kozo's insistence, that eight hundred soldiers would do the job once and for all.

"You feel better, master?" the woman asked.

"Hai," the man replied.

"After your bath, I will make you feel even better, nē?"

"I do not have time, woman, not today. I will let you know." The gokarō was tiring of this one. Now, if it were Sakura, or even her double, the stubborn one— Well, first things first. In two weeks, three at the most, both women would be in the manor. Sooner or later, they would both come around.

"My clothes, woman," Kozo suddenly shouted to the servant, "the soldiers are leaving today, and the daimyō is waiting for me."

Kumahatchi looked up as Kozo approached. "Ah, kimi," he said. "I was going to call you. Have you prepared the soldiers?"

"It is taken care of, my lord," Kozo replied. "The soldiers will ride today. When the sun is setting, they will leave."

"Good. And you, do you expect to ride with them?"

"Iie, my lord. I have much to take care of here."

"Ah, good, very good," said Kumahatchi. "As gokarō, you should take care of everything. Very good." The daimyō waved the gokarō away. Ah, what a puppet, Kozo. And to think he had dared to look at Sakura.

The daimyō rose to his feet, crossed the room, and opened the shōji. "Sakura-san," he called.

From another part of the building, a female voice answered. On hearing her father's call, Sakura Murata did not stop what she was doing. "Hai, otōsan," she called back, her voice carrying easily to her father through the paper walls. She did not rise from the tatami or take her eyes from the drawings in front of her. Again, Sakura dipped the writing brush into the ink stone and added another line to the drawing. "Otōsan, it is almost finished," she called again. "Come, you must see."

Kumahatchi smiled as he slid open the shōji and looked at his daughter. Her back was to him. All about her on the tatami were paper drawings and sketches. Sakura's hands were on her waist, as she surveyed her accomplishment. She was the perfect princess, Kumahatchi thought. Even before he became daimyō of Ikoma, he had thought of her as a princess. The daimyō frowned. Soon she must marry, but nowhere in his new daimyōdom was there one good enough for her, and she must be bred to the best. Only the highest-caste samurai, one who lived the Bushidō, would be good enough. Hai, there was still time. Maybe two, maybe three more years, then he would worry about it. "Sakura, princess," he said, "what changes have you made today?"

Turning, Sakura looked at her father, her flawless oval face alight with excitement. "Come, get on your knees. Let me show you what I have added to one end of the manor." She held the drawing before him. "See here, where the pond is, we will not change it, but we will put a wall—so." She pointed with the brush, then continued. "My apartment will face it. Around the pond will be a garden. Now, your rooms will be on this end, see?"

Kumahatchi did not listen to the young woman. What did he know of manors? If this manor in the drawings pleased his princess, that was the way the manor would be. "Ah, it is good, Sakura-san," he said. "A garden here would be beautiful, and it would be private, it would be for you only."

"Iie, otōsan," Sakura said, scowling at him. "It will be for both of us." She hesitated, laughed, then added, "Also for your lady friends."

"My lady friends do not bother you?"

"Otōsan, I am not a child," she said, smiling.

"Hai, I know. You are a beautiful, grownup princess."

Rising from the tatami, Sakura hugged her father.

Kumahatchi patted his daughter's shoulder. "I will see

that the workers make these changes. Or you could go up there and direct them. Soon it will be finished, and this"—he swung his hand around—"will be a dōjō again."

Sakura rolled up the drawings. "I will see to it now, otōsan. I am eager to move."

"Hai," he agreed. He embraced his daughter, then left, closing the shōji behind him.

Sakura sat on her heels again and straightened the remaining papers. She was more than happy now. She had once lived in a pretty house, her father had told her, but she couldn't remember it. All she could recall were old houses in little villages and branch shelters in the forest, and even, one time, a cave had been their home. Now she could have anything. Why not a manor? Her dream prince would come later. Amaterasu would see to it.

That Sakura Murata was beautiful was not just prejudice on her father's part. Before coming to Ikoma, her beauty was kept hidden beneath cloth, her hair was never dressed as now, her nails were never groomed. But now Oumi, her servant and companion, worked hours combing her luxuriant hair each day. These preparations bored the princess, but she pretended to enjoy them. She liked Oumi, even though she hovered over Sakura, trying to make her flawless.

Sakura clapped her hands. A shōji opened, and Oumi appeared. "I am going to the workers at the manor," the princess told the servant, "but I do not wish to go there in this kimono. Get me something else."

"Hai," Oumi said, bowing, then departed from the room.

At the manor site, Sakura walked among the workers, inspecting the progress of her new home. The raised platform, now completed, looked much too small to her. It was not as she had pictured it in her mind and her drawings. She mentioned this to the prefect who directed the carpenters.

"Ah, little girl," answered the old man, laughing, "it is always the same. See, look at the plans. It is exactly what you asked for." He motioned to the drawings, which were cemented to a paddle-shaped board hanging nearby.

Sakura felt chided, as if her importance had been questioned. "Refer to me as 'your lady,' hereafter. Not as 'little girl,' " she snapped.

The expression on the prefect's face changed, and Sakura instantly regretted her words. "I am sorry," she said to him, "this is new to me." She bowed to the old man. "You are doing good work." Sakura handed the man the drawings. "This is the way I want the garden fixed."

The prefect bowed as he accepted the papers. "Dōmo, my lady, dōmo arigatō gozaimasu."

Sakura walked through the tall weeds toward the pond, surveying the scene carefully. It was pretty, she thought, except for the weeds. Sakura noticed where the water once ran down into the pond. Hai, it would flow again. She tried to imagine the garden completed, but the weeds made it difficult. Sakura began pulling them out.

Suddenly she became aware of a metallic scraping noise which seemed to come from within the pile of rocks nearby. The princess cocked her head. There was no mistaking the source of the sound. Sakura went over to the rock pile and looked into a space between two rocks. She was shocked to see the rag-clad figure of a girl crouched within. For a moment, she simply stared, then Sakura called: "Sumin asen'."

The metallic sound ceased. The woman inside turned a face of terror toward Sakura.

The ship off Cape Iro was a Chinese junk. With its sails ull-spread, it sped north. To starboard, the islands of Nii nd To were only faint dots on the horizon.

Young Prince Sayada Hojo sat on the high roof of the orward cabin and stared down into the passing sea. The olor of the water was changing again. Now it was the color f dark turquoise, then it changed to green. The loud crack verhead caused the prince to look up. The sails were winging to a new position. The *Sea Carp* changed course. and that had lain to port all day was now straight head. The *Sea Carp* entered the Sagami Sea. In two more ours, Prince Sayada would be home.

Sayada Hojo did not look like a prince; he was dressed n a fudangi. He differed from the Chinese, who made up he crew, only by the style of his hair. A purple band tied round his forehead covered most of his shaved pate. He vore a wide-spaced mustache and a small triangular beard. On his feet were rice-straw zōri. And he wore a kogatana.

The sails caught more wind, causing the junk to cleave leeper at the bow. The ship plowed forward at much greater speed with the wind behind it. Sayada felt and asted the salt as the mist sprayed from the bow.

Prince Sayada looked ahead to land. There it was: penciled in light blue, almost washed out against the white sky, he snow-mantled wedge of Fujiyama swooped upward to he gods. Sayada bowed his head to the great mountain even times. For this, his ancestors, the gods, would look kindly on him.

Prince Sayada Hojo reached to his side, then ran his and over the inrō tied to his sash. The purse contained what he knew would change the lives of all the inhabitants of Yamato. The information had taken almost three years to accumulate, and its significance was frightening.

Sayada's ports of call had ranged from China's Wenchow in the south to the towns bordering the China Sea. The *Sea Carp* had then sailed around Chōsen to Seishin in the north, and finally south again.

By the time they reached Fusan, the pieces had fit together, making an ominous picture. Yamato was the target of the greatest sea invasion the world would ever know—almost ten times that of seven years ago. Kublai Khan was sharpening his ax. The *Sea Carp* raced home with the news.

Pulleys creaked, a pennant was being hoisted to the top of the mast. The purple Imperial flag talked to the wind. The ribbed sails of the ship relaxed and folded like the wings of a bat. The *Sea Carp* was home.

Small boats made their way to the ship as it drifted unaided into the harbor. A sledge wielded by a Chinese sailor pounded out the pin, and the large wood and stone anchor splashed into the bay. The junk swung slowly around its hook.

Sayada glanced at the familiar shoreline of the bay. Nothing had changed. Below, small boats were being tied to the *Sea Carp*. Prince Sayada recognized the heavy form of Baron Kamo in one of them.

The baron shouted up to him. "Welcome home, welcome home, Sayada-san. It has not been the same here without you."

"Dōmo, Baron. It is good to be home after so many months. Is everyone well? No, stay where you are, I will join you in the boat. We must hurry to the Bakufu."

"What is it?" asked the baron.

Prince Sayada climbed over the side and, when he was seated in the small boat, answered. "The news I bring is grim, Kamo-san. We will soon be at war with the Mongols."

"So they will come again." Kamo shook his head in disbelief. "How much time do we have?"

"A little. But I do not know what must be done to prepare for them. I am sure of only one thing, Kamo-san—they are coming."

K*oan Tachibana* topped the last rise. Below, he could see the heavy green growth that snaked up the valley, marking the river. Nearby were most of Mina's houses and farms; the mura stood in the center of the widest part of the valley.

Koan sat on one of his bags and rested. The climb up had been long. He watched the mura, noticing wagons and people, like ants, going to and from the gate. Someday Mina would be a city. It was much too busy for an average village of its size. And even when there had been a war here, Mina had not become a ghost town. Koan stood up, picked up his bag, and proceeded down to the valley.

It was late afternoon by the time the isha reached the main road that led to the mura. Soldiers blocked his path. "Hold it, ojiisan," one of the soldiers commanded. "What business brings you here?"

Koan studied the samurai before him and was not impressed. The great sword tied across the back of the bushi, and the kogatana on which the samurai's hand rested, brought no fear to the isha.

"Speak up, ojiisan, you have a tongue, do you not?"

Koan Tachibana, oishasan, drew himself up to full importance. "I will have an audience with the daimyō. I have much to do and many places to go. You delay me; step aside!"

The bushi showed no anger. Instead, he was amused, and laughing, he asked, "Ojiisan, I am amazed. How have you lived so long?"

Koan did not answer. He walked past the laughing guard. The bushi made no move to stop the old man. He motioned the other samurai to let him go, too. The ojiisan looked harmless enough.

As he walked toward the gates of the mura, the isha noted again the amount of activity. Many wagons rolled along the narrow roads. Buildings were being put up over the rubble. On one of the new buildings, a sign was being painted.

At the new gate of the mura, Koan was stopped again. The guard pointed to the line of people who waited. "We will talk to you when it is your turn," he said, in a tone that did not encourage argument.

The line moved quickly. Some were turned away, others allowed to pass through the small door cut within the heavy new gate. The guard spoke to Koan. "You are an oishasan, I see. What have you in your bags?"

"They are my medicines and tools. I am here to see the daimyō. He will not be kept waiting."

"I know, I know," replied the guard. "But you will have to stand aside here." He pointed, then nodded to another soldier.

The bags and the traveling box were searched, while the isha berated the guard and the soldier with threats of the daimyō's wrath. When their search was over, Koan was escorted through the gate.

"You will take me to the daimyō now?" asked the isha.

"Iie," answered the young soldier. "I will take you to the armory. The prince will speak to you. Let me warn you now. Nothing but the greatest respect will be expected from you."

When he was ushered into the room, the isha knelt and bowed to the young samurai seated near the far wall.

"My lord, as you desired, this is the first oishasan to come to Mina," said the escort.

"Dōmo arigatō," said the prince. He waved the escort out. For a time, Jujiro looked at the man bowed before him. "What kind of an isha are you?" he asked. "Do you work with the magic of fire and signs?"

Surely, thought Koan, this must be the daimyō. He has the manner of a shōgun. Remembering the warning of the escort, he would take no chances. He looked up, then bowed again. "Great one," Koan began, "I have no magic. I do only what I can with the herbs and medicines that are available to me. I cannot deny that sometimes the gods favor me."

Jujiro noted the alert look in the man's tanned face. "Your name," he asked, "and where are you from?"

"I am Koan Tachibana, my lord, perhaps you have heard of me?" The prince made no sign. Koan continued talking. "I live as a traveling isha. My home is in the forest most of the time. I have been to all of the islands that make up Yamato. At one time, years ago, I even tended the Empress Masako in Heian-Kyo."

"That speaks well for you, ojiisan. But what do you know of the cuts of the sword?"

Koan made a wry face. "It is a shame what the steel does to the flesh and bone. I have tended to many, a few with some success. With most, I am not quick enough, or they come to me too late."

Jujiro clapped his hands. A samurai entered. "Bring the

daimyō here now!" the prince commanded. "Tell him I wish his presence."

"Hai." The man bowed and left.

Koan was puzzled. No one ordered the daimyō around. Who was this man he knelt before? Unconsciously, the isha bowed again.

Jujiro spoke. "Two weeks ago, we battled here. Only thirty of my samurai are still alive. Those who live suffered many infirmities. Our victory was not a good one. I myself have tended to these wounded. There are many who were hurt with the arrow and the sword. You will correct my mistakes, and you will show me what must be done in each case."

"My lord, I will do whatever is asked of me. But please believe me, if the cuts of the sword are not new, there is little I can do for them."

Jujiro rested his chin on his fist and studied the old man. "I have heard of an oishasan who sews the wounds as though they were torn cloth. This I have tried to do. Of the twelve wounds I have sewn, only one shows that my work was good." The prince hesitated, then asked, "What do you know of this?"

So this great man has heard of Koan Tachibana after all, thought Koan. "Hai, it is I you speak of, my lord. But this surgery is not a science. Something within the body rebels at the flesh being treated as cloth. But I have had some successes and I feel that the effort should not be abandoned."

Someone entered the room behind the isha. "Konnichi wa, Tasuke," the prince greeted the newcomer.

The acting daimyō bowed to his friend, then seated himself at his side. "Dōmo, kimi, what have we here?"

Koan's head was on the tatami again. His hands were flat down in respect to the daimyō.

"This man here is Koan Tachibana. It is he who knows about sewing wounds; it is his procedure I tried to follow in caring for you. Please expose your wound, perhaps my stitches can be corrected."

Tasuke disrobed in front of them. A long wound followed a dark red path down his thigh. Koan inspected it closely. "Hmm," he said. "How old is this?"

"Two weeks now," replied the daimyō. "Why does it not heal?"

"Hmm." The isha prodded the wound."It tries to heal, but that within fights against it—this must be nullified. Much hot water must be applied continuously, but mind you, not too hot. It will draw all the inhibitors out. Hmm, this one stitch must be cut." He took a tantō from one of his bags and cut the tight thread. "Go now, you must live in the baths. The wound will heal."

After the daimyō left, Jujiro and the isha talked.

"I have found," began Koan, "that the intestine of the hare, when heated, makes a thread that is not rejected." Jujiro asked him to explain. "I found it by accident. I was cutting up a hare for food when I slashed myself with the tantō, here above my knee. It was a terrible cut, and I knew it had to be closed. The only thing on hand was the entrails of the animal. I heated and stretched its intestines, then bound my leg with it. Two days later I found that the only place where the wound was healing was where it had touched the wrap. Now I always carry some in my bag."

Hours slipped by, and Koan and the prince talked of the work of the isha. The questions the prince asked were good ones, Koan thought. This young man would make an excellent isha. When Koan told Jujiro this, the prince laughed. "Aside from the fact that it is beneath any good samurai, I must admit something. During battle I've often wondered if I could undo some of the wounds I've inflicted. Is this not strange?"

Koan thought before answering. "You are born a samurai, but you must be trained to be one. It is the same with the isha. But to be born both, a samurai and an isha, is godly. You could take a life or give it back. This should not dishonor your dignity, nē?"

"But the isha," the prince said coldly, "is little better than a nōmin. Is this not true?"

"So it is thought," responded Koan, "so it is thought. The peasants are illiterate, and so are all the tradesmen, but not the isha. As I said, he can give back life or take it, without the sword and with little effort. I have two names, I have trained with the kogatana but now I do not need it. I know the Bushidō well. Listen, the way of the isha is secret and comes to us from our fathers who were isha before us. I could talk of this for many hours."

"I see your point," said Jujiro. "We will talk more of this. Now you must come to my house. You will be my first guest."

"I am much honored, my lord."

As Daimyō Tasuke Ito sat in his bath, the pressure of his wound lessened. Hai, he thought, the old man knew what he was talking about. This oishasan would have to stay.

Mina had been a surprise to Tasuke: from rubble to a boom town in just two weeks. Because of the many things that the prince had to involve himself in personally, Tasuke had been made the acting daimyō. For the time being, little strenuous work was required, and Jujiro could be assured that his friend would sit and recuperate from his injury. The prince, on the other hand, had no end of work—

obtaining supplies, equipping a standing army, and training the lesser soldiers. Meanwhile, Keisuke Shishido worked outside the walls of the mura. He hired a samurai and a young nōmin who showed promise of becoming good soldiers.

Word passed that the Jugi Hoshi would bestow a title or two, and the daily number of samurai appearing at the gate increased. Others also headed for Mina: whole families, farmers, nōmin, rich and poor. All were lured by the offer of free land. Mina soon exceeded its original population.

Tasuke Ito had his hands full. He and his aides had to sit and listen to all the newcomers, each pleading for the land that every day became more difficult to dole out. The daimyō's problem was basic: he must balance the trades allowed, and divide the land outside the mura accordingly. Barter and trade were to be regulated and taxed.

Daimyō Ito enjoyed his work. He had thought at first that his wound would incapacitate him, but it did not bother him that much. Now, in his bath, he had forgotten about it.

When the servant woman entered the room with the towels and kimono, Tasuke emerged from the bath.

"Your leg does not look so bad now," she said to him.

"Hai, my leg is better, little one." He pushed the kimono away. "Come, let me show you that it will not hinder us."

The servant woman laughed. "Ah, my lord, that makes me very happy." She pulled herself to his wet body.

As Sakura Murata looked at the frightened young woman hidden under the rocks, she saw her cut at the hem of her ragged kimono with the tantō. Aki ripped the cloth into a long strip. It was evident to Sakura what the young woman planned to do. "Iie! Iie!" the princess called out. "You must not!" Sakura looked back toward the building. The workmen were gone.

Aki, sitting now, began binding her ankles together with the strip of cloth. She would end her life with jigai. It was the woman's version of seppuku. Instead of disemboweling themselves, highborn women cut the jugular vein in their necks with one hooking stroke. They tied their ankles so they would not be found in a degrading position.

"For what reason?" Sakura pleaded. "You must not, I am no threat to you!" The woman within tied the knot, unmindful of the voice behind her. Panic seized the princess. "Listen, listen to me, can't you hear?" Tears were in Sakura's eyes as she shouted.

Aki turned her head and looked at the face again. The young woman outside spoke in a low voice now. "You must not. I will not betray you, believe me. I am of the samurai and live by my word."

This last, Aki heard. Her mind raced; it reasoned, weighed, and balanced the information her eyes and ears brought to it. "Who—who are you?" Aki asked.

"I am Sakura Murata. I will not betray you. Let me come in with you so we can talk."

"No," Aki said, her face impassive. "I do not yet know who you are. Your name means nothing to me." Aki's mind was reaching, questioning, as she realized that the woman outside was not of the Jugi Hoshi.

"I am the princess of Ik—" Sakura stopped herself. The woman before her, hidden in these rocks, must be the rightful princess of Ikoma. Sakura saw the wooden case of the tantō which lay on the ground beside Aki. The monshō of the Jugi Hoshi inscribed on the case was clear. "I know who you are," said Sakura, "and I'm sorry. Let me—"

Aki was no longer listening. Her mind raced again, planning the actions and alternatives ahead. Aki knew she was safe within the rocks. There was no way her jigai could be taken from her, it would be over before anyone could reach her. But was it necessary, her mind asked. Not for the moment. Wait, wait a bit. Let it depend on the woman outside. She thinks you are the princess. Maybe it will help. Let it be.

"Will you talk with me?" Sakura asked.

"Hai," answered Aki. "But what is there we can speak of?"

The princess studied the woman inside. Sakura saw that, despite the rags the woman wore, her beauty rivaled her own.

"What is your name?"

"It is Aki."

"Aki," the princess repeated. "What has happened to both of us was written before we were born, we can do nothing to change it. This is my belief, and because of this I cannot stop you. I feel, instead, that I must help you, or we would not have met."

For a moment, Aki did not understand, but her mind made her seek the truth. "You say you are of the samurai. I am also. Do you know the Bushidō?"

"Hai, I live by that code," said Sakura. "You must believe me, I see no reason for your life to end. It will be as I say. The fact that I do not know you does not mean that I must choose another enemy today. I much prefer friends." She was smiling.

"I believe you," Aki lied. The code commanded unswerving faithfulness to a goal, or if that was impossible, death. Aki, too, lived the Bushidō. She held death in her fingers. Her goal—to somehow reach Jujiro—was not yet completely cut off. For the moment, she would live. She untied her ankles.

"First, I must do something to prove my word," Sakura said. "Tell me, what can I do for you?"

Aki was caught by surprise, she had no ready answer. "Do as you say, do not betray me. If I am left alone, I will be gone. If I am betrayed, it will be this." She held the knife to view.

"I see that you need clothing. I will bring it. Do you want me to get you through the gates?"

"Iie, that I can manage," said Aki, feeling that the risk was too great. "But I am unable to pay for the clothes."

"I spoke of no pay," the princess said. "But I will ask you a favor in return. Now tell me, what else will you need?"

Aki thought for a long moment, keeping the princess silent with an upraised finger. "What I desire most is soap and a comb."

"It will be so," said Sakura. "What kind of a comb do you desire?"

Aki laughed, for the first time in months. "It seems funny to me," she said, "that we are here, discussing a small matter like a comb. I once had a comb, so big." Aki held up her hands to show the size. "I gave it to someone I loved. Now I want it back."

Sakura smiled, sharing her new friend's humor. "Aki, tell me your full name. I have an idea I can help you even more."

"It is Aki Fugita." It was only a half lie, thought Aki. Okei had told her this would be her name.

"Aki, it is getting dark now. I must go. I will return

when all is quiet. Tell me one more thing. Where will you travel?"

"I will go to the south."

"Good, that will be easy. I am going to help you in exchange for your promise that you and I will be friends if we ever meet again."

"Sakura, I believe you to be a friend," Aki said with sincerity. "You spoke of a favor?"

Sakura still smiled. "Tonight, when I return, I will ask it. Aki, please be here until then."

"I will. Sayonara."

"Sayonara. Until later," said the princess.

Aki listened to Sakura walk away through the tall weeds. There was nothing to do now but wait. The light in her hiding place had diminished to almost total darkness. Aki thought about the recent encounter. Hai, the woman Sakura was sincere. This new princess was lonely, she sought someone of her own station to befriend.

Time went by slowly for Aki. She crawled the length of the tunnel to the wall and pushed on the balanced stone, swinging it open. Even in the darkness, she could make out the trees. High grass covered the clearing, and for this she thanked her goddess. But Aki did not leave. Closing the exit, she returned to the other end of the tunnel and waited for her new friend.

The grass rustled again.

"Gomen kudasai, Aki-san," Princess Sakura called.

This time Aki answered.

"I have brought you several things. Will you come out?" asked the princess.

Aki hesitated, then: "Sakura, I do trust you, but it is better if I am not exposed. Do you understand?"

"Hai. But would you trust me inside?"

Aki reached for the knife within her sleeve. With one hand, she pushed on the rock door. Sakura was alone, at her side was a large bundle. Aki helped the princess down, then pulled the rock door closed behind them.

"I cannot see you," Sakura began. "I have a light. May I use it?"

"Wait," said Aki. "We must crawl this way where the ceiling is higher. There the grass has not been disturbed, and the light cannot be seen from outside. Give it to me."

It became apparent that the princess could see nothing. Aki watched the newcomer groping with the bundle in front of her. Presently, a small shell lamp was produced; next, the bottle and wadding. Aki took these from Sakura, poured the oil, set the wick, and ignited it with the flint.

For a minute, the two women looked at each other. Aki held out her hand. "Sakura-san, I'm happy to meet you," she said, smiling.

"Dōmo arigatō, and I you. See what I have for you!"

One by one, the princess produced the articles she thought necessary for a traveling princess. "Here. First is the soap. This flask is water, you can tie it to you. And your comb, is this not the same one?"

Aki smiled. Joking, she said, "Where did you meet my lover? Surely this is my comb." Together, they laughed.

Sakura set a sealed earthen jar on the ground between them. "Here is a surprise, one of two I brought you." She broke the seal of the jar, then opened it. Steam climbed upward to mix with the smoke from the lamp. The aroma of the hot tea was almost too much for Aki. Sakura set and filled two small bowls. As Aki drank the green tea, she felt the strength of it support her. "Dōmo arigatō, Sakura-san. I have not had tea such as this in weeks. Dōmo arigatō gozaimasu."

They were quiet again, as though they were at the tea

ceremony. Every so often, they would look at each other and smile.

"Tell me," said Sakura, "I would like to know of the one who keeps your comb."

Aki smiled again. "He is a baron and a samurai, very handsome and very powerful. His name is Jujiro. I am sorry to tell you that he is a Jugi Hoshi. Hai, it is he I seek."

Sakura broke out laughing. "Forgive me, Princess Aki, but you are a sight. Would your Jujiro be happy to see you now?" Sakura held a small mirror before her new friend. Again they laughed.

They talked back and forth. At every lull, Sakura brought forth a new item from the bundle: hairpins, makeup powder, more combs, zōri, underclothing, a kimono for traveling, an obi, and finally the lacquered carrying case it would all fit into. As Aki looked at these treasures spread before her, tears appeared at the corners of her eyes.

"What is the matter?" asked Sakura. "Did I forget—"

Aki interrupted. "You have forgotten nothing, my dear friend. But I cannot take all this from you, it is too much."

Sakura spoke firmly. "Aki-san, listen to me and don't interrupt. It is true that I am the daughter of the daimyō here. I am your age, and I am smart enough to know, as I have said, that what is written is written. Throughout my life, as yours, there have been events and changes we knew nothing of in advance. It will always be that way. I am the princess of Ikoma now. But you once were. Who knows what is written for tomorrow? Our roles at this moment could easily have been the other way around."

At this, Aki felt guilty, but she held her tongue, not wanting to hurt her benefactress.

Princess Sakura continued. "I spoke before of a favor I would ask of you. It is this: you have been the princess of

Ikoma, but I must be the princess now. Aki-san, I know nothing of being a princess. You must tell me how; how I must act, how I must talk, what I must do to be a proper princess."

Aki loved the open honesty of her new-found friend. Taking both of Sakura's hands in her own she said, "Sakura-san, please try to understand and believe this. You have always been a princess, you were born one. Only this can I add to help you. The code of the samurai was not written for the male alone. Only slight changes of the Bushidō make it applicable to us. Keep this in mind: just be you, as you are. I have learned one more thing this day. A proper princess needs good friends. Always look for them. There is no more to it."

"Dōmo, Aki-san," said Sakura, "dōmo arigatō gozaimasu. It is all clear to me." Princess Sakura bowed to the ragged Aki. "I have one more present for you. It is this paper." Sakura took a document from her sleeve. "It is a safe-conduct pass marked by the daimyō and myself. It states that you are an agent of the daimyō. You will not be questioned wherever this is shown. With it you can walk out of this mura, but you must keep it tied with this marked string, only that way is it not counterfeit. I ask only that you do not use it against us."

Aki thanked the princess as she accepted the roll, then added: "My promise is that when it is no longer needed, I will destroy it, in respect to you." Aki shook her head slowly. "I am a pauper. I have nothing to give you in return."

"The time spent with you more than repays my small effort. I will conduct you through the gates."

"Iie," said Aki, "it is not necessary." And then it dawned on her. "Sakura-san, listen, I do have something for you. This hiding place we are in is not as it appears.

Somehow you must see to it that it is never disturbed. As you say, our fates are written. But should you be as I am now, you must come here. This cave leads to the outside through a balanced rock in the wall, its exit cannot be observed even from the catwalks. You must keep this secret to yourself alone. Come, let me show you."

Together, they crawled to the exit, opening and closing the pivoted door. Back near the lamp again, Sakura spoke. "Aki-san, you are very special to me. This is a wonderful present. Not for one second did I suspect this hiding place was here. It will never be changed. Oh, Aki-san, I will miss you."

"And I you," answered Aki.

They were silent, both women with tears in their eyes. Finally Sakura spoke. "There is one more thing. A convoy left for Mina this evening, and this document will permit you to join it. You say you are going south. Well, this mission does also, all the way to a place called Mina. Come, Aki-san, you must change, I will comb your hair. See, the lamp flickers. I must not use up your oil."

Aki stripped to nakedness. With the soap and the water from the rocks, she washed her hair first, then her body. Sakura surveyed the results. "Aki, you are more beautiful than anyone I have ever seen."

Aki stared into the mirror, then at her friend. "Iie, it is not true." Aki handed the mirror to the princess. "Look carefully in the mirror. Tell me what you see."

Sakura did as she was bid. "I see me," she said, laughing. Suddenly her smile left her face. "I also see you. We could—could we be twins? We are! But it is impossible!"

Two hours later, Aki had crossed the clearing and was in the forest. She made her way south to the river road to join the wagon convoy. Something in her sleeve felt heavy. It was not her knife, that was packed in the traveling box. She stopped and removed a small bag from her sleeve. She poured the bag's contents into her palm. The morning's sun made the gems and coins dazzle Aki's eyes.

Hetomi lay prone on the crest of the hill, listening to the clatter of wagon wheels and the sounds of horses and men. The runner could not read the pennants of the army, he would have to move closer. Hetomi descended the hill and knelt hidden near the road, watching the army as it passed. When he saw the last pennant, his heart sank.

Hetomi Tajimi estimated the number of the troops that marched by him. In the fore were the mounted samurai, at least two hundred. Then the foot soldiers, and finally the wagons. In all, about eight hundred men marched under the Red Triangle banner.

The runner noticed a beautiful woman seated in the straw in the last wagon. In her hand she held a mirror. As the woman moved, the flash of the sun reflected off the mirror to Hetomi's face. Distracted, Hetomi brought up his arm to shield his eyes. The woman saw the movement. When the runner looked at her again, he knew that he had been discovered. She was staring at him now, but she did not alarm the driver, which puzzled Hetomi. Keeping hidden, the runner followed the wagon for a short while. Still, the woman did not speak to the wagon driver. Hetomi returned to join Somiko, who waited with their horses on the other side of the hill. The wagons continued.

When Somiko saw Hetomi, she knew that something was wrong. "They are not the Jugi Hoshi?" she asked.

"Iie," he answered, "they are of the Red Triangle. I am sure the last of the Jugi Hoshi are at Mina—that is, if they have not been defeated already. I must think of what we should do."

Somiko remained quiet as the runner sat before her. At length, he spoke again. "It has been exactly twenty days since we left Mina. With two horses I can get back, maybe in ten days."

Worry crept into Somiko's eyes. "But I must go with you!"

"No, Somiko, I must ride hard." Hetomi looked into her eyes and saw them fill with tears. He realized how much he had grown to love the woman. "I still must go to the mura at Ikoma. I have a plan. We will camp here tonight while I see what is happening at Ikoma, and in the morning I will ride fast to the south. I will beat the yatō there by many days. The village of Takata is midway to Mina. You will go there and wait, with our provisions and the other two horses I am leaving. Later I will come for you. I will find you if you mark where you are staying with a small black cloth. The horses I am giving you are sound of wind and much hardened to the tasks of a warrior. They should bring a very good price. If the Jugi Hoshi still live, I will meet you in Takata in twenty days."

Tears ran freely down Somiko's cheeks. "And if there is no Jugi Hoshi," she asked, "must you die?"

Hetomi did not answer immediately. He must tell the woman the truth. There was no reason to tell her otherwise. "Hai, I have pledged the oath of junshi to the Prince Jujiro. I live only as long as he does. There is no other way."

"I understand, Hetomi. Then we will speak no more of it."

The runner bowed his head in agreement. "Hai. Now I

will ride to Ikoma. I will be back before the night is over. Then we will talk some more."

"Iie," said the woman, "you will eat first." Somiko did not speak as she prepared the food. When Hetomi tried to help, she waved him away.

"Are you angry?" he asked.

"No," she stated simply. This last night with Hetomi would not be lost in talk. She wanted only to enjoy his closeness. This she had learned to love on their journey north.

They ate in silence, then Hetomi stood. "I will go now. Keep this small knife at your side. I will twice sound the call of the small owl when I return. Until then, sayonara." Mounting one of the horses, Hetomi rode into the dusk.

Somiko checked the hobbles on the horses. Then she pushed the fire apart with a stick until the flames were gone. Picking up her worn sack, she made her way downhill toward the stream. She disrobed and entered the water. Her cold bath would be refreshing. Somiko scooped the mud from the shallow water and scrubbed her hair and body with it. Soon she felt this coarse soap burn into her skin. She rinsed herself in deeper water.

An hour later, she was back in camp. It was no trouble starting the fire again, and the next hour she spent drying and combing her hair. After tying it behind her head, Chinese-style, Somiko felt human again. She sat before the fire and waited for Hetomi's return.

As Somiko sat looking into the fire, the tongues of flames brought her back to Mina. She felt sad as she remembered her last days there. Everyone she knew and loved was gone, and soon Hetomi would also be of the past. Only the barest chance might prove otherwise. She must live for that chance. Twenty days from now, she would know.

How unpredictable everything was. The man she always thought she would fall in love with was unlike Hetomi in many ways. Hetomi should have been a baron of the court, instead of a kerai in service to a daimyō. He should have been almost twice as large as he was. His power should radiate out from him so that all women who saw him would be jealous and would say Hetomi is like a god.

But Hetomi was not like this. True, he was fast and agile, and undoubtedly he carried a mighty sword or he would not hold the position he did. Somiko had felt the strongness of his arms one day when they had been forced to ford a river. The current had caught her, but Hetomi had pulled her to safety. Since then, as they traveled, Somiko had watched him. He did not miss with the bow. He moved with the grace of a dancer. Even in the driest woods, he made no sound when he walked. He saw in the dark, and was aware of most things by sound alone. He was more than a baron, Somiko thought; indeed, he was a god!

The call of the owl broke the stillness.

After settling his horse with the others, Hetomi returned to the camp. The light from the campfire filled the small clearing, painting gold the trees that sheltered the camp. The smiling woman looked in his direction, but Hetomi knew that she could not see him in the darkness. "It is I," he said.

"I know," Somiko replied. "Where there is no sound, you are there. Come, you are tired. I will fix you some tea."

Hetomi sat down. "You have changed your hair," he said. "It is good. When I am gone, I will remember you so. This light has changed you to gold; it makes a pretty picture." He handed her a leather bag. "This I bring from Ikoma. It will replace your torn bag. When first I met you, you gave me wine. It is fitting I do the same now. Let the tea be, pour this instead."

Somiko opened the bag, took out the bottle, and poured the saké into a single cup. "Tell me of Ikoma," she said.

"It is as I thought. Only the Red Triangle are there. Many soldiers have left for the south, but many still remain. The Red Triangle is most powerful. I talked to many nōmin in the village. Not one of the Jugi Hoshi live; all were destroyed." He sipped the wine, then handed the cup to her. "It is strange, I have known nothing but war or preparing for it. There is talk of a great war that might start far to the south of Mina. These soldiers that passed us today go to Mina, so my plan to beat them there is a good one. Somiko, I have enjoyed these days with you, even though we had to hurry. Has it been hard for you?"

The woman did not respond. When Hetomi looked at her, she poured more wine in the cup. He could see no answer in her face. "Why are you silent?" he asked.

"I am thinking of Mina," Somiko said. "The Jugi Hoshi there did not number half the yatō in the mura. You will not return." She looked into his eyes.

The runner put his hand on her shoulder. "We do not yet know what has happened at Mina, but let me tell you of the sensei Keisuke Shishido. He has one duty above all else. He, too, is bound by an oath of junshi to the name Fugita, and Keisuke Shishido is the greatest swordsman of all time. Whatever happened at Mina, Prince Jujiro Fugita still lives; this I know. I will be in Takata in twenty days. Whatever happens, I will live that long, if only to see you again."

Somiko drew herself to him. "We will talk no more of this. The night flies too swiftly from us, Hetomi-san. I—I have loved no man before you. I want only that you stay a part of me."

He kissed her forehead. The faint scent of her powder mixed with the scent of the pine needles they lay back on. He felt the softness of her breasts against him. His mouth found hers. Was he hurting her? He tried to lift the weight of his body from her. She pulled him back.

"Lie perfectly still," Somiko whispered close to his ear. "Our love will be perfect and you must remember it so." A moment later their bodies moved together in flowing rhythm.

The golden bower dimmed to red, then to the silver of moonlight. The fire died to a thin column of smoke that reached upward through the pines.

The twittering of a bush bird close to Hetomi's ear woke him. Already, the new sun sent light beams through the branches. Hetomi reached for Somiko and drew her close again.

After they had eaten, Hetomi emptied one set of saddlebags. He replaced only the few things he would require on the fast journey to Mina. "I will leave you with the bow, can you use it?"

"Hai," Somiko said, "but I am more at home with the naginata, the fighting stick. It was beaten on me until I learned to use it well," she said, smiling.

"Good," he said. "I suggest you remove the sign of the Jugi Hoshi from the quiver. And if you use the bow, remember to retrieve the arrow if you can. They are a full count of twenty-four, and because they are fletched with the falcon feather, they, too, will bring a good piece of silver. I am sorry, Somiko, that I must talk so, but I will worry if I do not tell you to be careful. Follow the river south, but stay in the woods until you near Takata. Wear the black noragi as I do. I cannot think of anything more."

"Ah, Hetomi-san, you worry as much as my mother did. I will be all right. You will find me in Takata. A small black cloth will tell you where."

"Hai, in twenty days, maybe sooner, nē?"

"I love you, Hetomi-san. Sayonara. I will always know you are with me."

Hetomi kissed Somiko, then took the tantō from her sash. He cut a small strand from her hair, then from his own. He mixed them together, giving her half. "These strands are of each of us and they are together. Sakuran cannot keep the rest apart. Sayonara."

Somiko held the lead rope as the warrior mounted. They locked their fingers together for only a moment, then he took the rope from her and swung the animal away. Seconds later, the woman heard the departing horses break into a fast gallop. Hetomi was gone. Somiko lay in the pine-bough bed they had shared together and wept.

For over an hour, she lay there. Somiko watched the blue patch of sky, visible through the treetops above, turn to gray. A cloud moved like a curtain across an opening.

Another sound disturbed her reverie. It was not the bush bird who insisted on being nearby. Again she heard the sound. Someone was walking in the woods, coming toward her. Somiko shifted to her feet, at the same time picking up the bow. As she backed from the approaching footsteps, she fitted an arrow to the bow. It could not be Hetomi, she would never have heard him. Somiko tried to kneel, but the length of the bow would not permit it. She moved sideways, shielding most of her body with a tree.

A woman stepped into the clearing. The clothes she wore and the traveling box she carried made her seem completely out of place. Somiko slowly relaxed the tension of the bowstring. Dumfounded, she stared at the newcomer.

The young woman with the box looked around the camp. She saw no one. The fire was still going strong. Saddlebags lay near. Whoever had been here, she thought, must still be close.

"Moshi moshi," the young woman called.

Somiko did not answer. Instead, she laughed as she stepped into the clearing. The two studied each other. Somiko spoke first. "Ohayō gozaimasu, forgive me for laughing, but I thought you to be someone I must kill. Don't be frightened of my bow; I will not use it. How did you ever get here?"

"All morning I have been searching for the black-clad one. I saw him climb this hill. Is he here with you?"

Somiko thought for a moment before answering. "What do you want of him?"

"I saw the runner yesterday," the young woman answered, "when I passed in a wagon. I—" She hesitated, noticing the tantō at Somiko's waist. The symbol of the Jugi Hoshi stood out bold in the sunlight. She looked at the older woman's face. "I know you. You are of Mina."

"Hai," answered Somiko. "I have talked to you before. You are Aki Taizo. Do you not remember me, Aki? I am Somiko Sei."

The two former neighbors fell into each other's arms.

W*hen* the Imperial Prince Sayada Hojo was ushered into the court of the Bakufu, he noted that the upper shōgun and his administrative council were already in attendance.

The shōgun bowed with the others and spoke. "Your

excellency, this court feels humbled by your presence. I am Lord Hakoi. I have been appointed seii-taishōgun by your father the Emperor. He is at the summer palace in Heian-Kyō and I know that he will be happy to know of your return. Again, let me say that I am much honored." He made a deep bow to the prince.

"Dōmo arigatō, Lord Hakoi. It is I who am honored. I have heard only goodness and greatness of you." Sayada lowered his voice to just above a whisper. "Sire," he continued, "though I know most of the officers here, the words I bring are meant only for you and for the cabinet of the Bakufu."

Lord Hakoi nodded. "My prince, Baron Kamo has told me briefly what you bring. Only the members of the cabinet are present. The scribes will leave if we have no need for them."

Sayada looked along the line of officers. He caught the smile of his friend Kamo and nodded to him. The prince spoke now so all could hear. "For the time being, we have no need of the scribes. But they should stay within call. Everyone else, please be seated, there is much to be accomplished."

As the scribes retired from the room, Lord Hakoi took his place in the center of the assembly. Prince Sayada sat in the front of the line, facing the assembly.

"Sires," Lord Hakoi began, "you will please excuse the omission of formality and protocol at this time. The seriousness of Prince Sayada's information precludes formality in favor of the speed of action that will be required of us." He bowed and waved his hand to Sayada. "If you please, Prince."

All eyes were on the prince as he paused to arrange the thoughts he wished to convey to the assembly. "As you are aware, we have been expecting to hear again from the Khan of the Mongols. Seven years ago, he dared to set barbarian feet on this holy earth. The samurai of Dai-Yamato and the Divine Wind pushed these barbarians into the sea. Gentlemen, the Khan is preparing to try again!" Sayada's listeners froze. The prince went on. "I have just returned from the Khan's land. Ten thousand, this many times"—Sayada held up his spread fingers—"is the number of barbarians that sit in the closest Chinese ports. They will all be here. They wait only for the ships to be readied for them. At Fusan I have seen the ways, with hundreds of vessels being fitted for this journey."

Sayada rose, then walked to the ozen at one end of the room. He poured himself some water. There was silence in the room as he took a sip, then put the bowl down on the low table. Sayada returned to the center of the room, but this time he knelt. He placed both hands on his knees, sat back on his heels, then continued. "Kublai Khan has leveled the forests of south Chōsen for timber for these ships. They have done the same in the Mongol land south of Soochow."

Sayada detached the inrō from his waist, emptying its contents on the tatami before him. He pointed to the papers. "I have maps of the departure points of the enemy. Also, here are papers stating the battle plans of the Mongols. These were obtained by us in Tientsin, a port near the manor of the Khan. Most of what you should know is contained in these papers. The drawings that accompany them are of large machines being constructed at Fusan, the closest port. Undoubtedly, they are weapons of war. But what kind will have to be determined."

Lord Hakoi asked the question that each member of the assembly pondered: "How much time do we have to prepare?"

"Sire," the prince replied, "I saw new keels on the ways at Fusan the day the *Sea Carp* left to bring me here. The winds have been good to us. I left Fusan three days ago."

"I see," said Hakoi. "These battle plans, how much can we learn from them?"

Sayada looked apologetic. "The plans are not brushed in the kanji that I am familiar with. I can make out very little, but it will not be difficult for us to decipher this Mongol script. In the reports I wrote, I vouched for more than one thousand ships that are already finished. Twice that many are being constructed in two places—at least six hundred on the mainland, and the others at Fusan. But we must hurry on to our task, gentlemen. May I suggest that we start to assess these papers now? I will try to answer any questions that might be on your minds as we work—that is, if I can."

The papers were spread on the long ozen that was moved to the center of the room. Initially, there was chaos in the room as each man attempted to fathom the information spread before him. When experts were needed, they were sent for. As the day progressed, the data began to fit together. The council labored doggedly on, the work spread to other rooms and buildings.

Occasionally, a council member called to the prince to ask questions of him. A model of the large Fusan machine was hastily constructed. The artisan who built it brought it to the court, setting it up on the low ozen. After winding the small windlass that was part of the machine, they succeeded in hurling a pebble across the room. The nobles became impressed only after the artisan explained that the sling in its proper size could take the place of a thousand throwers. This fact added to the mounting worries of the council.

The day turned to night, and when morning approached, the seii-taishōgun called the administration together again. This time the prince sat at his side.

Hakoi quieted the talking noblemen, then began reading from the paper he held in his hand.

For the eyes of the gods and of the Imperial Majesty Tenshi Basho Hojo II. Your Military Court of the Bakufu, Kamakura, has in its possession the following urgent information: the Khan of the Mongols is readying to attack the sacred collections of the Jewels of the Gods that make up Dai-Yamato. It will be attempted within thirty days from the time this paper is placed in your hands. The plan for this invasion is held by the Bakufu. There is no doubt of the plan's authenticity.

Please refer to map as you read.

1. The capture of our islands of Iki and Tsushima is to be used as a primary base by the fleet from Chōsen.

2. A second fleet will leave the Mongol's mainland and directly attack the southwest shores of Kyūshū.

3. The first fleet mentioned will attack the northwest shores of Kyūshū at the same time.

4. On a day not named, Kyūshū will be the main base of the Mongols, and two fleets, of five thousand (5,000) each, will be assembled there.

5. On a day not named, each fleet will proceed up each side of Honshū. The west fleet will strike at Yonago. The east fleet will split to encircle Shikoku, then strike Ōsaka and Kochi simultaneously.

6. On a day not named, each fleet will strike Fukui on the west and Toyohashi on the east.

7. At this point, also on a day not named, it is estimated the last resistance to the Mongols will crumble. If not, the Khan's fleets must strike Sakata in the northwest and Sendai on the east.

The above is authentic in every detail. It is reiterated by the Bakufu that this information is for your eyes alone. Therefore, the attached edict bearing your sign and that of the Bakufu is now being delivered to each of our daimyōdoms.

Signed: (the stamp of the Bakufu)

Shōgun Hakoi waved the papers to his assembly. "Gentlemen, I think that we have done a monumental task. All that remains at this session is to select emissaries, and the runners to deliver the edicts. The court of the Samurai Dokoro meets at this very minute. I know some of you must be there, so you are free to leave at once. You may tell the senior shōgun they will have my orders within minutes."

About half of the assembly left the room after bowing to both the seii-taishōgun and Prince Sayada. The prince spoke to those still in the room. "It is my idea to lead a group of runners inland to Ashio, then to the daimyōs north. My ship, meanwhile, can leave here for Hokkaido and Aniwa. At the same time, most of you will do the same as I, but to the south. We will all carry the Imperial pennant. It is the belief of both Lord Hakoi and myself that the samurai of Yamato can assemble at Kyūshū with the necessary supplies for war in thirty days. As we have estimated, the barbarians cannot attack in less than that time."

The dry spell had turned the road to heavy dust, which rose and fell fast as the three riders galloped over it. Not far ahead was Mina. Knowing this, the three horses seemed to enjoy the almost free reins.

Keisuke Shishido pulled his horse to a slow walk. He

was in the part of the woods he loved best. The other riders pulled ahead, still holding their horses to an easy gallop. When the riders slowed for Keisuke, he waved them on. He was tired and had much to think about. The animal he rode tried to grab the bit, to hurry its rider, but Keisuke insisted. He brought the animal to a stop.

For a while Keisuke sat there, looking around him at the trees. The heat of the day was lessening. The insects sounded a steady tone that, now and then, was punctuated by the call of the quail. It was beautiful. Keisuke felt a part of the scene. He was especially fond of this spot. Just a bit off the road was a large, flat, wooded area. It was not visible from the road because of the tightly packed pines. One day Keisuke had followed a small stream into the woods and discovered the area. Since then, this land was marked on the maps as the land of Shishido. It was Keisuke's land and he would return to it. His tenure with the Jugi Hoshi was almost over. This area would be a good place to settle and start his own family. He had already spoken to Tasuke about it. "I will tell you," the sensei said to the daimyō. "In Ikoma there is a woman, maybe just a little plump, but she has many years to go and many babies yet inside her. I will bring her here. My next students will come from her."

"I thought you had enough with Jujiro and myself," said Tasuke.

"Hai, I will admit that," said the sensei. "But you both were spoiled before you came to me. This time I shall not have so much trouble. I will yet produce the greatest swordsmen." He laughed.

"Keisuke, what if they are all female?" asked Tasuke, grinning.

"You had better hope not," returned Keisuke. "The first-born I will name Tasuke, after you. Can you imagine a female Tasuke, with a kogatana in one hand and a fan in the other?" The daimyō and the sensei had laughed together.

Keisuke forced his horse to follow the stream again. He left the road, bending his head to avoid the low branches that hid his land. Now he thought of his two friends at the mura of Mina. Keisuke had known both the prince and Tasuke since the two were born. The sensei had fretted over them even before they were six years old, but Okei would have none of it. On their sixth birthday, the prince and the gokarō's son were handed over to the sensei. At first, it had seemed an impossible job, but Keisuke taught them everything he knew of the sword and then gave them to other sensei. Keisuke had taken charge of the last phase of Jujiro's and Tasuke's training. Now their training was over and soon Keisuke must leave them. A part of his life would be gone.

Keisuke Shishido owed it to himself to have a new life. He could not teach the sword again; the sensei knew that no other student could compare to his last two—especially to Prince Jujiro. Keisuke remembered their last lesson together in the dōjō at Ikoma. Jujiro had beaten him, unarmed. The prince had been swift, his movements between positions undetectable. Keisuke felt there were sensei who could learn from his protégé Jujiro. Keisuke was bound by the oath of junshi to the prince by Yasumori's command. This was easy, but not letting the prince become aware of it was most difficult.

The horse beneath the sensei whinnied. Keisuke looked to the animal's ears, then in the direction they were turned. He saw only the trees and brush. The movement of a bush bird caught his eye, nothing more.

Someone called close to Keisuke. He turned. The sound of rushing air was relayed to his brain and at that moment a tremendous force cut into his body. Keisuke toppled from his horse. The released animal raced for home. As he collapsed to the ground, Keisuke pulled at his kogatana. He relaxed, limp, as a wave of nausea swept over him, but he remained conscious. The sensei heard the scuff of zōri in the dirt at his left. He tried to turn his head toward his assailant. When the second arrow hit Keisuke, it hit with a much greater force. There was no pain left for this second arrow.

Keisuke was amazed when, from inside his body, he could feel the movement as the arrow shaft vibrated before his eyes. He lay still, fighting the ringing sensation in his head. The tree trunk in front of his eyes swept in and out of focus. He fought unconsciousness as it tried to cover him. Finally the tree came back into focus and stayed.

The footsteps were at Keisuke's side. The sensei felt the clothing at his chest being pulled as his assailant tried to roll him over. Keisuke tightened his fingers on the handle of the kogatana. Suddenly he swung it upward and felt the resistance as it tore through flesh. Keisuke tried to move, but he could not keep the body of the yatō from falling on him. Again he tried to move, but he no longer had the strength. He rested. The pain in his chest changed to a numbness that engulfed his whole body. The blood of the man whom Keisuke had killed mixed with his own. At least, thought the sensei, I have avenged my— The ringing sensations in his head were stronger now. He drifted with them, then relaxed into nothingness.

Prince Jujiro fixed his own tea. He picked the hot kettle from the irori, then filled his bowl. The tea leaves floated, then curled and settled to the bottom. It was strong tea, but he needed it. Tonight he would take it easy. Each night after the long day, he and Koan talked. Tonight the oisha-san had bowed out. "I am going to the village to see whether I can shake up a good woman." Jujiro smiled. Koan, it seemed, never tired.

Prince Jujiro toyed with the small comb tied to his wrist. The leather that held it was getting worn. Soon he would have to change it. He turned the comb over. There was his own name. He had not noticed that before. Aki must have marked it the very night they met. Jujiro closed his eyes and saw Aki through the haze of time. He heard her low, sweet voice in his mind again. He saw her full lips as they formed the last words she had spoken to him: "Until we meet again. Sayonara, my samurai. I shall wait here for you."

Jujiro's mind was made up. He would return to Ikoma. His work here was done. Who but Tasuke should stay in charge here? The question answered itself. Tasuke was not yet ready to leave, his leg needed more time to heal. Hai, Tasuke could leave whenever he felt he must. If Tasuke wanted to remain as daimyō of Mina, so much the better. Yasumori and the gokarō would consider Tasuke a good choice. He, the prince, would leave for Ikoma in the morning.

Jujiro turned to the shōji to call the servant. She was already there, a wide-eyed look of fear on her face.

"What is it?" the prince asked.

"It is Keisuke Shishido. They have just brought him in. You must hurry, he is hurt badly."

"Where is he?"

"In the armory, sire."

Jujiro crashed out of the room, the low ozen upset in his wake. Steam sizzled upward as the water spilled into the sunken fireplace.

The pennant of the Red Triangle fluttered and popped in the wind. The long column of soldiers rode south out of Takata. Their halfway point to Mina was now behind them, and they moved at a steadier pace than before. They would have to make up the two days the rest in Takata had cost them.

The lead rider pulled his horse to a stop and shouted back to his officers. At the same time, he pointed to the horsemen riding toward them. "Soldiers ahead! They carry the Imperial flag!"

The Red Triangle column came to a halt and their mission leader rode forward to meet the twelve approaching horsemen.

"Ohayō gozaimasu, my lord." The Red Triangle leader bowed his head slightly to the important-looking official.

Prince Sayada Hojo nodded back, then spoke. "Your pennant is unfamiliar to me. Where are you from?"

"Ikoma, sire. We are en route to our mura at Mina. It is many days to the south."

Sayada looked down the long line of Red Triangle soldiers and noted the loaded wagons that were part of the column. This was a stroke of luck, an army already fully equipped. The prince turned back to the officer: "Who is your daimyō? What orders do you carry?"

"Sire, he is Daimyō Kumahatchi Murata, a great samurai. My orders are to reinforce our mura at Mina. Here are my papers." The leader produced them from the inrō at his side.

The prince glanced at the papers, but did not read them. He handed them back to the leader. "Ah, these matter no more. Pay close attention to what I say to you. I now countermand Samurai Murata's orders by decree of His Imperial Majesty and of the Bakufu. I am Prince Sayada Hojo, son of our living god and goddess. We war with the Mongols in the far south, at a place called Kyūshū, the land of the kuma. You and your troops will make all haste there. On your way, you will join with many others. All stores and supplies that you carry or that you see are the property of the Empire. You are cautioned against any waste." Sayada signaled to one of his aides and the man handed him a paper. Sayada continued. "This is an edict that is being spread throughout the land. Officers of His majesty are now being stationed in every village of size. They will see to your needs and issue further orders. Am I understood?"

"Hai, my lord. May I send word to my daimyō?"

"Is he at Ikoma?" asked the prince.

"Hai."

"It will not be necessary for you to send a message. I must see all the daimyō of the north. I will deliver any message you might have. You and your men will go at once to Kyūshū. But, before we part, I must ask you to dismount and kneel before me. You must swear the oath of junshi to His Imperial Majesty and the land of Dai-Yamato. You will exist only to serve the Emperor and to slay the barbarians."

The leader dismounted and knelt before the prince. Holding his palms flat before him, the Red Triangle leader kissed the earth. He looked up at the still-mounted prince and spoke. "Your highness, the oath I speak now I intone for myself and for all under my command. I am but dust to His holiness, your father. As he has let me breathe, I will die happily for the sanctity of his land. I am honored my sword can be used."

"Dōmo," said Sayada. "I now empower you to solicit the oath of junshi from those you come across who are yet ignorant of this crisis. You must make haste. Sayonara."

The prince waved his party forward. And as he passed the troops, Sayada's flag bearer waved the Imperial pennant back and forth. The Red Triangle troops cheered.

Later the hundreds that made up the Red Triangle troops knelt in the dust as their leader had done. They listened to their leader's words: "Those at Mina are no longer our enemies. All of Yamato is united. Together, we will engage the Mongol barbarians."

R*eflectors,* made from mirrors and white screens, directed the lamplight to the table where the inert form of Keisuke Shishido lay. He was stripped to the waist, and a patch of cloth covered an area of his right chest, leaving the bruised area exposed.

Prince Jujiro and Isha Koan had been working steadily, yet there was still much to do. "He should be dead," said the isha. "His kimono was saturated. But he fights to live. The point of the arrow that remains in him is much too close to his heart, I hesitate to remove it. The first arrow was not deep. This second one—I do not know. The bruise shows that it entered with great force. I doubt if I can remove it, that he will live through the operation."

"With the point in him, can he live?"

"Iie," Koan said, shaking his head. "If we try to remove it, he will die that much quicker."

"What chance is there? Can we hope for his life at all?" Jujiro clutched the oishasan's shoulders with both hands, searching Koan's eyes for an answer.

"My lord," said the isha, "he can live only if the arrow

point is removed. But his chance is slight, at that. My hands no longer have the sureness of youth, my eyes are not good enough. My lord, I do not want to be the one who kills him."

"Then either way he will die, is that what you tell me? Iie, Keisuke will not die. He must not die. We will remove the point. I will do it. I will be your eyes and your hands. Keisuke must not die. I know now that he has sworn the oath of junshi to me, yet I feel almost as though it is the other way around. We will remove the point."

"Hai."

The isha called for scalding water. While Jujiro and Koan rearranged the lamps for maximum efficiency, Koan explained what must be done. "Your hands must be scalded, but not until we are ready. I will describe first how everything must be done and what to watch for. Each movement of your hand must be slow and sure, very steady. We must cut the flesh, but there are parts that the blade must not touch. I will show you. First we must wash around the wound with boiling water."

"But," interrupted the prince, "won't that burn him?"

"Hai," answered the isha. "But there is a reason for it. The burn will call forth the healing powers that are in him. I have done this before. Where it was burned, the wound healed first. The point must be removed without more loss of blood; only that will keep him alive. We will cut a line from the wound, like so." He pointed with a tool. "Then we will spread the cut open with these two splints. Now this tool will evacuate the blood. With this bamboo clamp, you will position the shaft end of the point between its blades. Then you will slide the ring down on the clamp. It will lock the blades to the point." Koan demonstrated the tool, then continued. "This must be done steadily and surely. After the clamp is attached, the point must be drawn out slowly. The rest I will do. If we do not err, your friend will live. The main thing is the steady and sure hand. Can you do it?"

"I must," said Jujiro.

Preparations were made. Powders and bandages were set nearby. The tools to be used were placed close at hand. Once again, the lamps were more precisely placed. The men were ready.

Koan plunged his hands into the steaming water. He winced. Jujiro followed suit. He did not expect the pain, but he forced himself to bear it. A second later he thought no more about it.

The older man pointed to the small knife on the tray, then to the wound area of Keisuke's chest. "Cut here. Don't push the blade. Draw it so. You must be able to feel through the knife. Use two fingers on your left hand as spreaders. I will remove the blood as you work. Observe closely, your eyes are most important. Cut no strings or tubes. If you do, he is dead. Do you understand?"

"Hai." Jujiro picked up the knife and for a second felt its weight in his hand. Koan applied the scalding water to the wound. Jujiro stepped forward.

As he was instructed, the prince began to slice upward from the wound. He concentrated on trying to feel through the handle of the knife.

"That's enough," Koan whispered. "Now again from the wound, this time down. Ah, good. Keep alert. You will be cutting deeper this time, past the rib. Here you will be near the tubes."

Jujiro did not answer. He began the next cut. He stopped, for a second he saw the jagged end of the broken shaft, the cavity filled with blood. Jujiro looked at Koan, and the isha removed the fluid.

"Clamp quickly!" ordered the prince. He did not use the splints. He held the incision open with his fingers. Jujiro set the clamp, then carefully pulled. He felt the resistance.

"Spread it!" Koan said.

Jujiro knew what he meant. He forced the wound to open wider still. The point came out.

Still holding the clamp, Jujiro stepped to one side. He sat down against the thin wall. Koan took over.

When Koan blew out the lamps, the light from the morning sun filled the room. "We cannot move your friend," Koan told the prince. "I feel that we have done well and Keisuke will live. His color is still good. If he dies, it will be because of the blood he lost before he came to us. He needs much rest now."

"Keisuke must not die," said Jujiro. "He cannot die."

The isha looked at the prince and felt a fatherly pride. "You, too, need rest, my son. You have done what very few have ever done. Because of you, he lives. We must let him sleep now. Come."

Outside, a samurai who waited for the prince bowed. "My lord, the runner Hetomi Tajimi has returned. He awaits you at your apartment."

"Dōmo." Jujiro hastened away.

Prince Jujiro was smiling when he entered the room, but his friend Hetomi did not return the smile. The runner knelt on the tatami before his leader.

"My prince, the news I bring is heavy on my heart. Please kneel with me, for what I must tell you may cause you to fall."

Jujiro looked questioningly at the runner, but knelt as he was asked.

Hetomi continued. "My prince, it grieves me to tell you

that your parents are dead. Ikoma has fallen and all within have been put to the sword. I am sorry. I have questioned many in the town, and they all say the same thing: the force of the Red Triangle numbers in the thousands. Even now, they are riding toward us. They will attack in nine days."

The prince was stunned. He did not even hear Hetomi's last sentences. "There can be no doubt?" he asked.

"I am sorry. It is so," replied the runner.

Prince Jujiro tried to compose himself. His body quaked with stifled sobs. "This cannot be," he finally said. "And the girl Aki Taizo," he asked hopefully, "what of her?"

"I am sorry, my lord, I was told by all I questioned, no one in the mura survived. I am sorry."

Jujiro motioned the runner out of the room. He could no longer hold back his tears.

"My lord," a female voice called. "Oishasan wishes to talk to you. Shall I ask him to come in?"

There was no response from Jujiro.

The servant looked to Koan, to Jujiro, then back to Koan. The old man walked past her into the room.

"Tomosama," said the isha, "your friend Keisuke Shishido is gone. We did all there was to do. The great loss of blood . . ."

Jujiro just stared at the isha. His head ached, his mind would not let him understand anything more. Who was this old man before him? Why was he moving his mouth?

Isha Koan Tachibana knelt before the daimyō Tasuke. "My lord," said Koan, "the mental shocks that the great prince has been dealt have erased all reality from his brain.

He knows no one, he does not speak, he obeys every command as though in a dream. You have told me that you are preparing to battle with the yatō. It would be better for me to remove him from Mina and his sorrows. I will return him to you when the world becomes real to him again."

Tasuke thought for a moment before answering. "I know, sensei, that you are not without talents, for you have worked wonders with myself and the others. I know that you will take good care of him. But I will tell you something else that you must know; Prince Jujiro Fugita is the last leader of the Jugi Hoshi. His head is wanted by the Red Triangle, they are coming for it now. I am placing him in your safekeeping. You will care for him as a god and bring him back to me when he is well. But listen carefully: No one must ever suspect who he is. His identity must be kept hidden at all times. Do you understand?"

"Hai, great daimyō," answered Koan. "As I live, no one will know he is of the Jugi Hoshi. I will take him far from the land of the Red Triangle."

"Go now," said Tasuke. "Whatever you ask for will be given you. My runners can always find you if need be."

The isha bowed again to the daimyō, then backed out of the room.

The young man sat on Koan's traveling box. He wore the fudangi of an oishasan with the small red spot near one shoulder. His hair was not fixed atop his head as a samurai but hung down straight. Around his forehead he wore a white band. His head was bent as he stared with troubled eyes at the earth.

Koan Tachibana patted the young man on the shoulder. "Come," the old man said, "we will go now." Taking the young man by the arm, the isha led him away.

Prince Sayada Hojo was glad to leave the saddle, if only for the brief time it would take to deliver the edicts he carried. Then he must be on his way.

Sayada saw that the man bowing before him was a swordsman first, anything else second. The scars that were visible told of the many contacts this man must have had. The prince nodded to the swordsman.

"My lord," said Kogashira Kozo to the dignitary. "We here at Ikoma welcome you. Our daimyō makes ready for you at the court. Please follow me. I am the gokarō Kozo." He bowed to the prince once more, hoping that he had said the proper words to this royal messenger.

Prince Sayada thanked the gokarō, then walked with him to the manor. Sayada noted the burned-out, partially destroyed buildings. Now he understood the new gates he had just entered. Samurai Murata was a new daimyō. Ikoma seemed to have more than its share of soldiers. There were as many here in the mura as he had met on the road. But then most new daimyōs kept large armies at the ready.

For the first time, the prince took note of the new manor. It was different, with a strange sort of beauty.

Daimyō Kumahatchi Murata sat on the polished floor. The heavy robes he wore completely covered his crossed legs; the large square sleeves of the kimono hid his clasped hands. He had the appearance of a broad triangle which pointed to a face of dignity. Through the opened shōji, the daimyō observed intently the small group that approached his court. He smiled when he thought how fitting it was that the first visitor to his new manor should be a messenger from the shōgun. This visiting prince should feel at home here. If taxes were the reason for his visit, it was no matter. There was enough money in the treasury of the Red Triangle, and a tax system would more than replace what he would have to give to the shogunate.

Princess Sakura entered from the side, pleased to see her father sitting in his finest robes. She went to him and knelt at his side. "Otōsan," she whispered, "I am so proud. You look like a shōgun. Indeed, I am a princess now. May I stay with you when they come?"

"Hai, by all means. Your beauty will impress them all the more. Chotto! They arrive now."

Sakura looked toward the open wall where the newcomers were removing their zōri. She recognized the massive form of Kozo, but surely this other was not the Imperial prince that Oumi said was here. His face and hands were too dark and he wore the ordinary fudangi. But the band around his head was purple. Yes, he was a prince.

Kozo bowed low to the daimyō, though the prince did not. His bow was little more than a nod.

Kumahatchi shifted to his knees and touched his forehead to the floor.

The gokarō broke the silence. "Your majesty, I present to you our daimyō, Kumahatchi Murata, and these are members of his court." Kozo turned to the daimyō, then continued. "Sire, we are honored with the visit of Prince Sayada Hojo. He says that the message he brings is of the greatest urgency."

All eyes focused on the prince.

Sayada looked at the people around him. He nodded as if greeting them all at once. "I am sorry, gentlemen," he began. "I can stay with you only a moment. First, let me say that I am pleased to meet you, Daimyō Murata." Sayada hesitated. "I bring an edict that will change all ways of life in Yamato. We are at war with Kublai Khan's Mongols." The prince removed a roll from his inrō and handed it to Kumahatchi. "This edict commands all arms under you to leave immediately for the south. These are the direct orders to you from my father, the Emperor, and the Bakufu. You must note that time is essential. Your good gokarō has already given orders to supply us with new horses, and I will leave now, so that you and your court can digest this information."

"It shall be taken care of immediately," said the daimyō. He turned to a retainer. "Indicate a call to quarters. See to all the able-bodied in the village, now. Hayaku!"

The retainer forgot to bow as he burst from the room.

"Thank you," said the prince. "Some time ago, I encountered an army marching under your orders. I rescinded those orders, and the soldiers are under forced march to Kyūshū. They have sworn, as each of you must, their spilled blood for the holy earth of this land. I demand the oath of junshi this instant."

The daimyō uncovered his hands and put them on the floor before him, then spoke slowly and deliberately. "Your highness, I and all those of Ikoma will die for the Emperor. It must be said, I know, but it is fact without uttering it; to die for our Emperor is only natural to our existence."

"Dōmo arigatō," said Sayada. "Those papers will instruct you as to the wishes of the Bakufu." This time, the prince bowed to the daimyō, then to Kozo. Noticing the woman, Sayada bowed a third time, but this bow was purposefully slower. The prince looked inquiringly at the daimyō.

Kumahatchi anticipated his question. "Your highness,

before you leave, may I introduce you to my daughter. She is Sakura Murata."

Sakura held her head low in a bow, but she tried to watch the prince through her eyelashes.

"Your daughter is lovely, Daimyō Murata." Sayada turned to the woman. "Today is a good day because I have met you. I have traveled many miles these last weeks and I have learned why the gods chose Yamato as theirs. There is beauty wherever I look. It pleases me to meet you, yet I must say sayonara."

Sakura looked up and smiled, but the prince had already turned and was gone. Kumahatchi and Kozo followed him to the porch. As the prince replaced his zōri, he spoke again to the daimyō. "I think I know you, Daimyō Murata. Weren't you at one time an Imperial guard at Heian-Kyō?"

Kumahatchi nodded and smiled. "Hai."

"Ah, I thought so," said Sayada. "I was a boy then, but I remember. It is good to see you again. I only wish that I had time to stay and talk, but, Daimyō, I will keep in touch with you."

"Dōmo arigatō gozaimasu. I remember you. I was your first sensei, nē? Is it possible that we will fight the Mongols together in the south?"

Prince Sayada shook his head. "Iie, Daimyō, almost all of us will have to fight for our holy land in the south. Still, by necessity, some must stay behind to govern. It is my order that you remain here to become the link in the command chain to Hokkaido in the north. In time, runners will inform you of the wishes of Heian-Kyō and Kamakura. We must have someone we can depend on here."

"Everything that I can do for you and Yamato will be done. My gokarō, Kogashira Kozo, will leave with the troops at once. I will stay and await any orders."

"Good. Your gokarō has seen to our needs. I will leave now." Sayada smiled, and bowed to Sakura.

The prince's horse was held as he mounted. The rest of his group already stood at attention. Sayada raised his hand and signaled for them to mount. The Imperial group rode across the compound toward the gate.

The leaders of Ikoma returned to the court room. All their attention centered on the scroll that Sayada had left for them.

But Sakura Murata did not return to the manor. Unnoticed, she walked to the still-open gate of the mura and watched the departing riders until they were gone from view.

To the subjects of Dai-Nippon:

The Emperor Hojo II, descendant of the god Ninigi, conveys this matter of grave concern to your first attention.

Be it known that the Mongol Emperor Kublai Khan will dare to send fleets of warriors to this holy land again. Also know that at this time five thousand ships are preparing to sail from Chōsen and China. Their soldiers will be numerous, but they will all die in this land of the Rising Sun.

The gods, this Divine House, and the Bakufu command your entire efforts to the fulfillments of these edicts.

Samurai, soldiers, all tools of war and supplies, will gather in Kyūshū to confront and destroy the Mongols. Only the aged, the infirm, the females, and the young will remain behind, with the fewest keepers necessary.

Each contingent of soldiers will move to the south at once. They will each be commanded by their daimyō or gokarō.

All are reminded that they are bound in allegiance to the Regency and this soil underfoot. The oath of junshi is required of every citizen.

It is now.
(Stamped) The Imperial Majesty Tenshi Basho Hojo II
(Stamped) The Bakufu

The road carried much traffic today, all moving south. The dirt roadbed had been ground into loose powder, which made travel by foot tiring. Clouds of dust rose above the marchers to settle quickly once they passed. This army was unlike all others who had traveled the road before or those who would follow.

Tasuke Ito, still dressed in purple, led this rōnin army. His soldiers carried no pennants, nor did they wear the insignia of any daimyōdom. Even Tasuke had removed the monshō of the Jugi Hoshi from his tunic. Tasuke Ito wore the helmet with the black oxen horns. It told all he passed that he was the leader of these unattached bushi. His army had grown as he marched; samurai and other soldiers joined when they noted the lack of pennants or insignia.

On either side of the leader rode two black-clad runners, behind them soldiers and supply wagons. Tasuke spoke to one of the runners. "We cannot be far. See there, the masts of ships. Go forward and see what accommodations there are for us. Tell whoever is in charge that we come with one hundred samurai and with as many horses, and all are hungry."

"Hai." The runner galloped ahead.

"Ah, Hetomi," the leader said to the second runner, "we are here. I am weary of this forced march. The men are all tired. We must rest well tonight."

"Kimi," said Hetomi, "it will still be one more day

before we see the Mongols. We must cross the water before we get to Kyūshū."

"Always the delay, nē?" said Tasuke.

"What do you mean?" asked the runner.

"It is something Jujiro always said. Always the delay. Then it comes too quickly, and it is over. His words are beginning to make sense. Pass the orders, we will camp here. Sleep will speed the passage of time."

The army pulled off the road. Soon fires were built, the camp settled down. The moon rose and dipped. Only the sounds of those still traveling the road remained. Tasuke Ito lay sleepless in his futon and listened.

Daimyō Ito remembered his journey from Ikoma to Mina. It had been much the same as this, except Jujiro had been with them. Where was he now? Were he here, the prince would be awake, talking excitedly of the ensuing battle with the Mongols. There would be a bright look in the prince's eyes, the unsheathing and checking of the edges of his swords, the waxing of his armor. Instead, Prince Jujiro was lost in the clouds of bewilderment. He had not improved, a messenger told Tasuke, he stayed close to the oishasan like a faithful dog. He would probably be that way until he died.

Tears welled in Tasuke's eyes. My every stroke at the enemy will be for Jujiro! Hai, first kill the Mongols, then the Red Triangle. "I swear it!" Tasuke said aloud. The sound of his voice disturbed Hetomi, sleeping nearby.

"What is it?" Hetomi asked.

The leader looked at the runner. After a moment, Tasuke spoke. "You have sworn the oath of junshi to Prince Jujiro."

"That is so," returned Hetomi, sitting up now and looking at his leader.

Tasuke looked into the runner's eyes and spoke in a low voice. "Prince Jujiro Fugita is dead now. His body still moves, but he is dead just the same."

For a brief instant, a vision of Somiko flashed through Hetomi's mind and, with it, a stab of fear. He waited for Tasuke to speak again. A half minute passed before the runner broke the silence. "It is up to you," Hetomi said. "I have lived by the Bushidō and I am sworn to die under its dictates. I am ready for seppuku."

"Iie," said Tasuke. "It is not yet your turn to die, nor is it mine. I will speak to you of another oath of junshi. It is this: the house of Fugita is no more. Those who sired me were named Ito. My father and his father before him three times were always of the Jugi Hoshi. It is no more, and this cannot be. Your name is Tajimi. You have always been alone. Tell me, why did you swear the oath of junshi to the name Fugita? I am curious."

"What you say is true. But those in my family before me did not know of the Jugi Hoshi. I came to Ikoma with my sensei Keisuke Shishido when you and the prince were six years old. The sensei and I swore the oath on the same day. He lived and died for the Jugi Hoshi, and I will do the same. We are one."

"Then," began Tasuke, "hear what I say. The Red Triangle are hunting us, and they will try to exterminate us. We are but a handful. I swear to spill all blood from them."

"You are not alone. I will show my blood now and swear by it that the Jugi Hoshi will survive the Red Triangle." As he spoke, Hetomi gashed his cheek with the point of his kogatana. Immediately blood flowed onto his neck, staining his robe, the red brilliant on the black. "I do it here on my face so that I cannot be doubted."

"Dōmo arigatō, Hetomi. But first the Mongols, nē?

It does no good for you to bleed to death for nothing." Tasuke handed his friend a cloth as he talked. "As you say, we are one. And now we have our goal. We must sleep."

The following morning, the army boarded the ships and barges which would carry them from the mainland of Honshū across the narrow strait to Kyūshū.

Tasuke Ito stood alone near the bow of the barge, looking far in the distance. Hai, he could see them: the masts of ships, and those little sticks on the horizon were the enemy. Tasuke turned to see Yawata, a small fishing town. This town could barely hold one tenth of the people and horses that poured into it. Behind Tasuke, his men rowed and paddled with the crewmen of the barge. Others tried to calm the frightened horses.

The wind, steady from the north, sped the ships with sails past the barge. Tasuke looked at them as they came abreast. Along the rails of the ships stood samurai, shoulder to shoulder. Most of the men carried traveling boxes on their backs. As the ship pulled ahead of the barge, another took its place, this time much closer, close enough so that men from both vessels could exchange shouts.

Tasuke, the leader of the rōnin army, noticed the helmeted leader on the sailing ship. Their eyes met, and Tasuke saw the other man smile and raise his arm in salute. The rōnin leader responded. But Tasuke did not notice the Red Triangle monshō on the kimono of the other. The sailing ship pulled ahead, and as it did, its sails came down. Both vessels had reached Kyūshū.

The black piece of cloth on the post in front of the little house was soaked. Even so, the cloth fluttered in the wind. The wind blew the rain almost horizontally, driving it under the eaves and through the walls of the slatted thatched house.

Inside, two women worked. The younger woman stuffed strips of cloth and paper into openings where the drafts were greatest. The older woman knelt over the irori. Here was the warmest part of the room, and the only part where the tatami was still dry.

Somiko Sei looked up from her cooking. "Come, Aki, it is ready. We must eat while it is hot."

The younger woman stopped what she was doing and joined her friend. "If it were not for the wind, I would not care," she said. "The roof is good, but we must close up the walls. Any minute, I expect fish to swim through."

Somiko laughed. "Hai, the wind comes through with no effort at all. Maybe we should find another house." Somiko filled a bowl and placed it before Aki. "What do you think, Aki?"

"Well, we are not poor. Why don't we just have the house repaired?"

"Hai, that is a good thought. There is an old man in Takata. Tomorrow I will see him. He will fix these walls."

Aki looked at the food before her. She picked at it with her ohashi sticks. "Somiko, you will keep your man Hetomi happy. This food looks and smells good. Did you notice that I never waste it?"

"Dōmo, Aki-san. It is good-tasting but meager. When the soldiers came to this village, they took everything. It has all gone to war, even the horses. It is no wonder that you do not waste any food." Both women laughed.

"We have much pebble coin and some silver," said Aki. "We could spend some to keep out the wind and the cold. As you say, there is little to buy here in Takata."

"That is so," replied Somiko. "In two days we will go

to the coast. There we can buy food, food that will keep for a long time."

"But Hetomi," asked Aki, "what if he comes while we are gone?"

"Do not worry," said the other. "If Hetomi finds the cloth marker, he will know, and he will wait. It has been a long time since twenty days passed. I'm sure he is in Kyūshū. I do not expect him soon. I have seen no samurai or soldier here in the north. When we start seeing them again, then I know that he will be here soon."

Aki had a thought. Her face lit up. "It will be good to go to the coast. There, at the port, we can get the latest news of the war."

"Hai, you're right. Maybe we will learn something."

Outside, the wind died down. The sounds of the water dripping from the roof gradually decreased in tempo. Somiko dropped a fagot on the charcoal. When the stick ignited, she blew out the oil lamp.

With the wind gone, the room warmed, and the two women continued talking in the coziness of the flickering firelight.

"Aki-san, I feel that your Jujiro is at Kyūshū, too." Somiko paused. "If only you could have found Hetomi and me before he left that day. Then Jujiro would know that you are still alive. I have a thought. When we reach the coast, maybe we can arrange for a message to be delivered. It is not hopeless."

It was a good idea, Aki considered; it was something, at any rate. "Dōmo arigatō, your thought pleases me. I do not know what else to do. There is no Ikoma for me. My father is dead. We do not even know for sure whether there is still a Mina. The yatō sent too many soldiers." Tears were in Aki's eyes.

"Aki-san, you must not worry. I will tell you something that will ease your fears. Hetomi Tajimi has sworn the oath of junshi to your prince. Were anything wrong, Hetomi would let me know first, somehow. We talked of this. And if he still lives, so must your Jujiro. Do you understand?"

"Iie," replied Aki. "What you say still leaves questions. It makes me sad to think about this—but what happened at Mina after both you and Hetomi left there? What of the yatō army that left Ikoma for Mina? I hope, almost as much as you, to hear from your Hetomi. Maybe he can answer my questions."

Somiko felt pity for the younger woman and tried again to reassure her. She spoke slowly, soothingly. "I have not told you of this either, but I see I must. My Hetomi Tajimi is like no other. He is a god. He talks to me though he is not here, and I understand what he says. He fights now with the Mongols, but he will return here. This you must believe: that, as he lives, so must Prince Jujiro. I have one more thing to tell you. This god Hetomi tells me that inside I carry a child. His and mine."

"Oh, Somiko-san, is this true? I am so happy for you. It is good, as everything will be one day. Now we must go to the coast to get better food for you. For both of you." Aki laughed.

Now that Aki shared her secret, Somiko felt better. She could see that the news of the child took Aki out of her depression. She touched Aki's arm. "We should sleep now. It is growing late."

"Will it be a man child?" Aki asked.

Somiko smiled. "This, Hetomi did not tell me."

The futons were unfolded, the headrests set. A short time later, both women were asleep.

When Aki awoke, the room was bright. The storm had passed. The sound of boiling water roused her; before Somiko had left, she had thoughtfully put the water on for breakfast. Aki fixed her tea, set more water to heat, then removed her kimono. The room was warm, she would bathe.

Folded up in the small wooden tub, Aki rubbed her stomach. Jujiro's son would come from here. He would be a beautiful son, just like his father. Oh, she would take such good care of him. Aki felt her breasts. Were they too small? Iie, they would fill out and Jujiro's son would grow strong because of them. Aki felt better than she had in months. Somiko was with child, and she would need Aki. This, Aki needed.

After her bath, Aki dressed and opened the shōji. She looked toward the village. Reflecting the still low sun, the puddles in the road looked like slabs of polished silver. In the distance, Aki saw three figures walking toward the house. One, she knew, was Somiko. The old man, she had never seen before. And the other? Iie, he was not a samurai; no sword, the hair was wrong. But what was it about him? Ah, they were coming to fix the walls. Quickly Aki closed the shōji. She began to remove the bath and to put the house in order.

"Aki-san," Somiko called as she removed her footwear. "Are you awake?"

"Hai," replied Aki, opening the shōji.

Somiko entered. "It is done," began the older woman. "The old man and the other will fix the walls. They are oishasan. While we travel to the coast, they will use the house and fix it for us. It will cost nothing."

"Where are they now?" asked the young woman.

"They are walking around the house, looking at the walls. Tomorrow, when we are gone, they will start the work. They are a strange pair," continued Somiko. "The old man talks a great deal, but I have not heard the other speak. On our way here, they stopped and tended a farmer's horse that had fallen. I watched while they worked. The young oishasan sewed the wound and stopped the bleeding very quickly. The old oishasan told me that they will stay here in Takata for three more days, then they travel north. He told me they sleep in the woods at night. Imagine, in this rain. I told him of the work that is needed and also that the house would be empty. Soon we had an agreement. What do you think?"

Before Aki could answer, there was a light knock at the door. "Gomen kudasai," the old man called.

Somiko slid open the shōji. "So?" she asked.

"It will be no problem," the man said to her. "It will be as we agreed. We will come back here tomorrow after you are gone. When you return from Niigata, the walls will be closed." The old man turned and called to his companion. "Come, kimi, we are leaving! Sayonara, young ladies." He bowed, as did Somiko.

From within the house Aki observed the old man, then the other as he walked into view. The young man caused her to clutch her breast with a shock of fright. "Who are you?" Aki called.

The young man looked at her, but he did not speak. Seconds passed, and finally it was the old man who answered. "I am Isha Koan Tachibana, and he"—pointing to his companion—"is Kenichi Ueida. He, too, is an isha."

"Oh," said Aki, "I thought for a minute that I knew him."

The old man smiled at the young woman. "Had he ever known beauty like yours," he said, "I don't think he would have forgotten you. Sayonara. We will do a good job on your house." Koan joined his friend, and together they walked toward the village.

Somiko closed the shōji. She started to speak, but stopped herself when she saw Aki's expression. Her face was white, her eyes glassy, her head bowed, and she held her arms tightly folded across her chest. She stood motionless.

"Aki! What is the matter? Are you ill?" Somiko put her arms around the young woman's shoulders. "What is it?" she asked again.

"Nothing—nothing," Aki said. "I guess I'm too nervous. I'll be all right." Weakly, Aki smiled at her friend.

T*he* wind blew in strong gusts through the narrow streets of Ikoma. Bits of weeds rolled along the ground or were flung through the air by the wind's blasts. The few people who were about pulled their noragi close and walked bent over. The monban at the gate of the mura braced himself tightly against the wall. An upright timber blocked some of the wind for him. He watched a dog following scents along the wall, unmindful of the cold wind. At the gate, the dog looked up and sniffed, then resumed its search.

The village of Ikoma was almost a ghost town. If there were people, the cold wind kept them indoors. In the mura, it was no different. Absent were the usual hollow bangs and shouts of laughter from the dōjō. Only the incessant moan or whistle of the wind prevailed.

Within the manor, Sakura Murata stirred the hot coals in the hibachi. Her father, sitting cross-legged, looked at the black-and-white brush paintings she had just handed him. Near the shōji, Oumi, the servant, knelt with folded arms. She was impassive and oblivious to the conversation of the daimyō and his daughter.

"My princess," Kumahatchi was saying, "these pictures prove your talents even more. They are too good to be kept hidden in a portfolio. They should be hung in a toko-no-ma."

Sakura turned to her father. "Dōmo, otōsan, but there are others who are more adept than I. Theirs is the art that should be displayed. Take, for example, the pictures that are on these tea bowls. Are they not real? Can't you almost hear the breath of the men as they carry the heavy shika?"

Kumahatchi glanced at the tea bowls, then replied, "Hai, but do not underestimate your own talents. I know of no other building that can equal this manor or your garden out there with the small rock mountain and falling water."

Sakura studied her father's face. Then she spoke. "Hai, the design for the manor is mine. But I cannot take credit for the garden. I could not change or improve it in any way. It was here, as you see it, before we came." Sakura hesitated, then added, "And it shall remain as it is after we are gone."

"Ah, Sakura, we are not going anywhere. This is our home. True, almost all of Ikoma, and all other places for that matter, are empty. But this is only because of the great war in the south. It cannot last forever. Don't think that we will ever leave here. Nothing can happen to cause us to leave. Even the Mongols could never conquer this land. The gods would not allow it. Do not worry, my child."

"I know, otōsan, but our soldiers have been gone so long, almost a month. We have heard very little. Your go-karō, has he ever sent a runner?"

Kumahatchi noticed a cloud of worry on his daughter's face. He tried to dispel it. "It is nothing, my pretty one.

Kozo leads many warriors. He is busy. In time, he will be back with the soldiers. The village outside the wall will grow again and there will be much to do. You worry for nothing."

"Oh, it is not the war that troubles me, otōsan. It is just that I have not been outside these walls since the day we arrived. And, with the exception of Prince Sayada, no one new has come to Ikoma. It has been much too quiet here."

Kumahatchi took one of Sakura's hands into both of his. This little girl of his was, in reality, a woman. The natural process was pushing that fact into view, but the daimyō was not ready for it. "Sakura-san, were it not for the war and the sickness that is everywhere, I would take you to Heian-Kyō or Kamakura. There is much to see and do at these places. This promise I make to you. As soon as all is settled again, you and I will travel to these great cities. Would you like that?"

Now she was smiling at him. "Oh yes, I would. Believe me, I was not complaining. It is that I only have you to talk with. I feel that I should not take your time."

"My time is for you first, Sakura-san. In a short while we will go places. I will want some of your art for my court. And, if I keep talking to you, I will never get it." He smiled at her.

"Go now," she told him. "I will do a whole series of landscapes for your court screens. It will be a good project."

"Dōmo, my pretty one. We will talk some more later. Sayonara." The daimyō rose to his feet and left the room. This time, he left Sakura smiling. May it always be so, he thought.

Sakura unrolled a new sheet of rice paper. She used ink plates to hold it flat on the exposed floor. She sat for a moment, then started to paint. But her thoughts suddenly darted away. Dropping her brush, Sakura removed the ink plates, and the paper coiled back to the form of a tube. She looked at the servant who was still kneeling at her place. "Oumi," Sakura said, "it amazes me how you can kneel in one place for so long. I have no need for you. You may go."

"Hai," said the servant, rising to her feet. She stayed in a bowed position, her hands on her knees. She made no effort to leave.

"What is it?" asked the princess.

"My lady, if it pleases you, your hair, I have not attended to it yet."

The princess waved her away. "It will not be necessary today. I see no one any more. Just the daimyō and yourself. It would be a waste of time. If I went out, the wind would tangle it."

"As you say, my lady. I will listen for your call should you need me." Oumi backed from the room.

Sakura turned to the hibachi. Taking the teakettle, she filled one of the tea bowls. She took a sip of tea, then studied more closely the picture fired on the bowl's smooth surface. Hai, this was good art. There was roundness and fullness to the picture. Sakura examined a second bowl, and a third. The pictures differed, but the people were the same, as though models were used. Oh, but the one in white was handsome. Sakura looked more closely: the monshō on the kimono of the figure was small, so small as to be unreadable. It must be the crossed star of the Jugi Hoshi. Sakura remembered the woman she had helped, Aki. Could the prince in this picture have been her relative? Her brother, perhaps? The one in purple was also handsome. Hai, these two were beautiful samurai. Too bad they were no more. There was still Prince Sayada, though . . . Sakura touched the white-clad figure on one of the bowls with her index finger. "If I had my pick of the three of you," she said aloud, "I'd pick you." There was a sound at the shōji.

"My lady." It was Oumi.

"Hai," said Sakura.

"My lady, the daimyō calls. He says we have visitors."

"Do you know who it is?"

"Iie, but he carries the Imperial banner."

Sakura jumped to her feet. "Hayaku, Oumi, my hair!"

A single messenger was seated before Sakura's father when Sakura reached the court. The messenger wore a purple band around his head, reminding the princess of Prince Sayada.

The daimyō spoke to Sakura. "This is Baron Kamo. He brings us tidings from Prince Sayada." Kumahatchi turned to the baron. "This is Sakura Murata, my daughter and my princess."

Lord Kamo smiled and bowed to Sakura. "I am charmed. In the dispatches that came to us from the south, this was ordered by the prince to be delivered to you." He handed the woman a bamboo cylinder.

"Dōmo arigatō gozaimasu." Sakura bowed, accepting the cylinder. She held it in both hands and noted the white markings on it. These marks told her this was a personal message. She would not open it here. Instead, she dropped it into the sleeve of her kimono. Bowing slightly, she remained motionless.

"What of the war?" asked the daimyō. "What is happening?"

"We have just received the latest reports. It seems the

Khan's armies are massive. But the samurai of Yamato will not budge. Prince Sayada is there, getting our armies in order. Soon I, too, will be there. I have been assigned to command the armies defending the wall at Hakata."

"How long do you think the war will last?" asked Kumahatchi.

"It is hard to say," answered Kamo. "I can only suggest this to you: they cannot number as many as us. They cannot win."

Kumahatchi Murata waved Sakura out of the room. She bowed to the two men, then departed.

Baron Kamo continued. "Nearly one fourth of the enemy are women—"

"Women?" broke in the daimyō.

"Hai," returned the baron. "And their weapons are horizontal—"

Kumahatchi looked startled, then smiled. "What do you mean?"

"Hai, they are crossways. The bow they use is not like ours. An extension at the shoulder holds the arrow. The bow itself is horizontal. It is said to be very accurate."

The daimyō was grinning. "Forgive me, Baron. For a moment I thought you were talking of the women's weapons."

They both laughed.

In her room, Sakura heard the men laughing. The war can't be going too badly, she thought.

The princess held the bamboo cylinder. Finally she broke the seal and pulled the paper from it. Unrolling it, she read:

The wind breaks up the pond's surface,
The sun replaces it with jewels.

Sayada Hojo II

Sakura closed her eyes and envisioned the picture that the prince had sent her. She looked into the cylinder, then turned the paper over. There was no other message. She closed her eyes again and pictured the poem once more. She smiled and opened her eyes. The picture of the white-clad samurai came to mind, and the smile left Sakura's face. Dropping the paper, she reached for the tea bowl.

Gokarō Kogashira Kozo, unmindful of the arrows and rocks that flew near him, guided his mount with his knees. Unlike any other mounted samurai, Kozo fought with the long sword. Kozo's soldiers used the kogatana.

As a reaper in the field, Kozo swung his sword effectively, despite its considerable weight—upward on one side of the horse, just missing the animal's ears, and downward on the other side. Because of this, Kozo fought by himself. The Mongols before him shrank back from the onslaught. Kozo's shouts and screams underlined his mad charge. Some of the Mongols whom Kozo reached did not even fight back, simply staring in disbelief at the sight of the frightful demon, only to be chopped down as so much grass.

A Mongol sword struck Kozo's leg, but his mind refused to acknowledge that he had been wounded. He continued swinging. When he cleared a path to the water, he turned to one side to widen it.

Red Triangle soldiers suddenly found their horses falling beneath them. The Mongols were concentrating their crossbows on the charging horses, trying to turn or stop the charge. Here and there, along the battle line, some samurai reached the Mongols. The invaders were forced to use their broadswords. More gaps opened to the water, but for only a moment. Systematically, the Mongols closed those gaps, trapping those who thought they had broken through.

Kozo screamed orders to those of his men who were nearby. Together, desperately, they fought their way back to the beach. The Mongol pincers did not close in on them.

More samurai charged down from the dunes until, at last, the Mongols were outnumbered. Minutes later, the beach was clear of standing Mongols. The shouted cheers of the victors of this skirmish mingled with the sound of the pounding surf. No prisoners were taken by the samurai. The Mongol soldiers who were unable to escape to the water were slaughtered without mercy. The waves that washed the splattered sands turned crimson. Farther out in the water, amid the confusion of the swimming Mongols, sharks, attracted by the blood, began their carnage.

Kozo's eyes were glassy, his arms hung on either side of the horse he rode. He still held his long sword. It cut a trail in the sand as his unreined horse walked slowly toward the dunes. The horse stopped when its rider shifted in the saddle. Kozo slipped back and fell to the sand. The horse glanced back at Kozo, then continued walking up the rise.

Isha Kenichi Ueida reached back and adjusted the large traveling box on his back. His companion noticed that he walked with ease today. Isha Koan Tachibana looked at Kenichi and smiled. Yes, he was better now. Each day, the young man talked more and more, and today he seemed almost happy. "Kimi, why do we run?" the old man asked. "It is early. We will be in Shinjo before it is dark. Even then, it will be nothing to hurry to. I'm sure the rations will be scant there also."

Kenichi stopped, unslung the bands from his arms, and set his traveling box in the shade of the tall cryptomeria near the road. "If you are old, oishasan, and cannot keep up, then we must stop so you can rest your old bones." Kenichi laughed.

"Don't make me angry," returned Koan. "Remember, even in my old age, you don't see unhappy women around me in the villages. They all have that satisfied look after they meet me." The isha set his bag near the box, then continued. "I do not need a rest, but it would not hurt. Tell me, Kenichi, what do you think of your life as an isha?"

Kenichi looked straight into Koan's eyes. "I know who I am, if that's what you mean. But, to be honest with you, I will tell you this. I do enjoy being an isha, especially when I am successful. I owe you much, and so I will tell you now what I think." The young man sat down in the shade, facing the old man, and continued talking. "I know you want to know how I am, now I feel I can tell you.

"At first, everything was muddled. Nothing made any sense to me. Worst of all were the dreams that came to me during the day when I was wide awake. They were dreams that were not dreams. I kept seeing faces on disembodied heads moving about me. They were the faces of the daimyō, my father, my mother, the gokarō, and hai, Aki, the woman I loved. One terrified me. It was Keisuke Shishido. He had a body, just enough to show the wounds of a knife, the knife was still there and it was still cutting, the hand that held the knife was mine. I recognized it by a comb that was tied to the wrist.

"The day I saw Keisuke, it was raining. The dream of the sensei was clear. He pointed to his wounds while the blood poured from him. I ran into the house, into the darkness to hide. I tore the comb from my wrist and hid it. In the darkness, when I slept, I would not see these dead people. But I could not always sleep. The day I saw Keisuke Shishido, we were in Takata. The day before that, it had not rained. That day, I saw the woman Aki in a dream, only this time she was not headless, she had a body. I dared not speak to her or she would turn into a disembodied head again. But you spoke to her and she remained whole.

"The next day, it rained. That day I hid the comb in the house. I tried to reason with myself and could only reason that I was a madman. I became aware then that you were caring for me. I knew that you had taken care of me for a long time. I knew it was you who cured me.

"I have nothing to give you but my love. I am an isha now because that is what you wanted. I am well now. I know who I am and what I must do. You, Koan, also share this knowledge. I know also that you will help me."

The old man studied the other man's eyes before speaking. "Kenichi, tell me, who are you?"

"I am not Kenichi Ueida. I am Prince Jujiro Fugita, the last of my line. I know that I am not far from my home. I must go there. Why, I do not know. There is no one I loved left for me. There is nothing except to see my home once more. Do you understand?" He looked inquiringly at the oishasan.

"Hai! I know, Kenichi. Pardon me if I insist on calling you Kenichi, but that is who you are for me. I knew weeks ago that your memory had returned. I noticed it first when we stayed in Takata. I knew what you were going through, so I added something to your food to help you sleep. Each day I took you farther from Mina, even now it is a month south of here—"

Kenichi interrupted Koan. "Mina is not my home. I know what happened there, but it is no more. Past Shinjo, a few miles from here, is Ikoma. There is my home. I will see it, then I will head south to join the war." He paused. "Koan, we will be needed there. What do you say?"

"I agree," answered the older man. "As isha we will enter Ikoma. When you are ready, I will go with you to Kyūshū. Ne?"

"Dōmo arigatō, sensei. For the time being, I will remain Kenichi Ueida. I know there are those near here who do not love me." He smiled, and the old isha smiled back.

The men became silent as they both watched a single horseman ride toward them from the north. The rider drew abreast and slowed to a stop. He looked carefully at the two men sitting against the tree.

"Ohayō gozaimasu," Kenichi said, waving.

The rider waved back. Then, turning his horse, he sped again toward Shinjo.

"What is it?" asked Koan. "Did he recognize you?"

"Iie, I have never seen him before. He does not know me. Don't worry about him. But I had the impression that he was afraid of us. Let's eat. I am hungry."

The traveling box was opened, and the two fixed themselves cold soup and ate in silence. When they were finished, Kenichi busied himself repacking the box. The old man made himself more comfortable against the tree and closed his eyes in sleep.

The sun was overhead when the horseman returned. This time, he was not alone. Three others rode with him. The horses were pulled to a stop before the resting men.

"You are both oishasan?" one of the horsemen asked.

"Hai," answered Koan.

"Good!" returned the soldier. "You will both come with me. You are needed at the mura of Ikoma. You"—he pointed to one of the other horsemen—"ride back and bring a wagon for their baggage. You two others stay here with the baggage. The oishasan will use your horses." The leader turned to the isha. "I am sorry, but we must hurry."

Koan and the soldier rode ahead. Kenichi followed closely behind. He could hear them talking, but paid no attention to them. It was good to be on horseback again. The only thing missing was the feel of the kogatana at his side and the long sword on his back.

Suddenly a red triangle on the back of the rider in front of him danced into view. The insignia held his eyes hypnotically. Kenichi experienced the sinking sensation of looking at the living proof that Ikoma no longer belonged to the Jugi Hoshi. No Okei, no Yasumori, no Aki—all of them gone. By what reasoning of the gods should he himself still be alive?

The Red Triangle monshō drew nearer. The rider in front of Kenichi had slowed down. Koan was talking. "Ahead is Ikoma. Things are bad there. For no reason, people in the town are dying. Now it has spread into the mura. They call it the bloodless death, it is bad." Koan pointed to the soldier. "He says it would be better for us if we did not enter Ikoma. He is willing to run away with us to the south. Soon, he says, most will be dead at Ikoma."

The old man's clipped phrases filtered into Kenichi's brain, where he tried to assess them. At first, Kenichi smiled. But the smile soon left his face. He began to feel cheated. "You can do as you like," Kenichi told Koan, "but I will do as I planned. I will enter Ikoma. Death has taken much from me, maybe it is just as well that I die there."

The soldier's worried look moved from Kenichi to Koan as the old man spoke. "I will stay with you, but it is bad. I have seen it before and I have lived through it. With luck, we will survive it."

"You mean, you are both going ahead?" said the yatō. "Then—then you both will die. You cannot miss the mura, just follow the dead. I will not go back with you." The soldier shook his head.

Kenichi pointed to the east. "That way is the closest coast," he said to the man. "But you wear the fudangi of a soldier and yet you look like a samurai—at least, your hair is fixed that way. You wear the monshō of the Red Triangle. There are no rōnin walking the roads. They are far to the south at war. If you leave here, you must hurry to the south."

"I do not plan to go to war. Nor do I plan to return to the mura and take my chances with death," said the soldier.

Kenichi laughed. "Tell me, do you have a surname?"

The soldier did not answer. He looked with hate at the young isha. Now the worried look was on Koan's face.

"I doubt that you even know what the Bushidō is," added Kenichi.

Koan tried to signal his friend to stop. Why was he goading the man? Koan caught the movement of the soldier's hand to his kogatana. He wondered if Kenichi noticed it, too. There was no way to tell.

Kenichi sat at ease on his horse, as though expecting an answer from the yatō.

The hand hesitated inches from the handle of the kogatana. What was it about this mere otoko no ko? Had he no fear of dying? He could not be a bushi, he wore no arms, his head was not shaved, there were no scars. He would kill both of them. Maybe they carried silver or pebble coin.

The sound of the wagon returning from the mura caused the three men to look away. The yatō waved the wagon past, then turned again to the isha. "I do not have a surname," the soldier lied. "I will change my clothes and I will whiten my hair, and I will live. You two can go to Ikoma and to your death."

By now, the wagon had vanished around a turn in the

road to the south. The yatō's hand still toyed with the hilt of the short sword.

Koan saw the bright flash of reflected sunlight as the blade arced upward in his direction. He brought up his arm as though to ward off the blow. What seemed like minutes were only the barest particles of a second.

The kogatana was at its zenith when Kenichi's horse charged into the horse of the soldier. The impact caused the sword to plummet from the man's hand, over the head of Koan. The sword flew across the road and into the bushes. The yatō's horse spun around and tried to kick Kenichi's attacking horse. The soldier fell to the ground, rolling backward. The long sword tore free from his back. He landed in a sitting position, with the sword at his feet.

The yatō looked up and saw the young isha standing on the saddle of the horse that had sent him to the ground. The soldier clutched at the long sword, scrambled backward and upward to his feet.

The isha was in the air, coming toward him.

With both hands, the soldier swung the sword, its lacquered case flying off the blade and hitting the horses. Frightened, the horses sought escape and together they charged around the swordsman. Koan desperately hung on and tried to control his excited animal.

Before Kenichi stood the motionless vision of Keisuke holding his bamboo sword straight up with both hands. The sword threatened to turn Kenichi's hands into searing pain. The student waited feet apart for the sensei's first movement.

With the sword still up, like a dancer in slow motion, the yatō swordsman circled to his right. His eyes locked with those of the young isha. The yatō was still not sure of his unarmed man. The isha's total lack of fear made him cautious. He must take no chances. He would kill the isha with the ichi-no-do. The yatō shifted his sword to the proper position for the start of this stroke.

Kenichi followed the soldier's movement, keeping the yatō in the same position in relation to himself. If the swordsman was successful, he would hit Kenichi above the waist at his left side, and cut horizontally. He would cut where there were the fewest bones.

Kenichi waited until the sword was almost horizontal. The isha's last step to the right was with his right foot. He seemed to fall over it. At the same time, his left foot flew to the unprotected left side of the soldier. The soldier's sword was swinging, and Kenichi felt it tug harmlessly through his hair. The isha's foot made contact with the yatō just below his armpit. The solid impact pushed the yatō swordsman away, though he managed to stay on his feet.

The yatō held the sword overhead again. He did not move. He would let the isha attack. Surely, the isha must know the sword. How else could he have escaped that first swing? Hai, he would let the isha make the next move. The soldier held the sword now in the defensive position, daring the isha forward.

Kenichi studied the man and noted that the eyes of the soldier were watering. He had hurt the yatō. He must get him before he recovered.

The swordsman was prepared for the attack, but he was not prepared for the speed of it. Again the yatō swung too late.

This time Kenichi sidestepped to the left, then, turning, hit with his palm's edge into the man's side. The sword dug into the earth.

Again the isha hit, but now with hooked fingers at the indent behind the man's right ear. The force of the blow twisted the yatō's head to the left, the body followed too late. His neck broken, the soldier slumped to the ground.

Tasuke Ito raised his clenched fist, and his army of rōnin stopped. Before them was the wall, and just beyond that, the beach. Everywhere Tasuke looked along the dunes, he saw tents and crude lean-tos—wagons, carts, even palanquins had been converted into shelters.

A messenger appeared from out of the chaos and bowed before the mounted samurai leader. "My lord," said the messenger, "the commander of the forces has asked me to welcome you and help you find a site that will be comfortable for you and your soldiers." The messenger pointed. "The west end of the wall is where the Mongols hit us the hardest. The commander asks that you make your camp quickly and be prepared to stand by there. He hopes your men will be ready to meet the Mongols in two hours."

"We will be ready sooner than that. Tell me, why is it that I do not see the enemy. Where are they?"

The messenger pointed. "My lord, they are there, beyond the rise of the dunes. They come ashore at odd hours. At first, we could not stop them, but now we are holding. Come, I will show you where you can set up your camp."

The small army bivouacked in a depression of the sand dunes. Daimyō Ito climbed atop a wagon and shouted to his men for order. "Those of you whom I have appointed to be leaders will come with me now. The rest, be ready to do battle in one hour. Eat, rest, and pray to the gods for strength."

Tasuke Ito climbed the great dune to the beach with his

officers. When they topped the rise, the wind from the sea brought them the sounds of war: the clash of metal mixed with the shouts of many voices; the screams of animals and of men in continuous waves. Tasuke and his companions looked at the scene, noticing the ships first. Visible as far as the horizon line, they littered the sea side of the breakers like fallen leaves on a pond.

A battle raged below, on the beach and in the surf. The Mongol line was a human wall that paralleled the stone wall of Hakata. This Mongol wall was fashioned of large bamboo shields, side by side, each shield held by a single soldier, all marching as a unit from the water. Behind the shield bearers, other Mongol soldiers followed; archers, swordsmen, and throwers waited their turn.

Samurai charged from the stone wall, on horseback and on foot. The bamboo fence caught the first arrows before it was pushed to the ground by the pressing Mongols. The fire power of the invaders was released as the two forces clashed. The first to give ground were the soldiers of Yamato, but other samurai troops charged from the dunes, and soon the Mongol advance was checked.

Tasuke Ito shook his head as he watched. It was a shock to see so many horses and men die at one time. He motioned his officers back. They returned to their camp and prepared for battle.

This time, when Daimyō Tasuke Ito reached the top of the rise, he was fully armored. His officers stood in a line behind him, widely spaced. Behind them were the troops. Tasuke spoke first to his leaders.

"We will charge to the beach and then stop when I give the signal. We must relieve those already in battle and allow them to retreat through us. Now listen carefully to what I say. We will feint a charge in a line as we are now. We will cover for the others while they retreat. Then, at my signal, we will turn and charge in a phalanx. If we reach the water, we will split to widen the breach. Does everyone understand?"

The officers nodded.

Spreading his arms to the sky, he called: "Then we will go forward, and the gods will be with us."

Tasuke felt his horse strain and pull at the bit. The run began. "With the gods! With the gods!" The shout was repeated in unison as the column raced to the Mongols.

As his horse took him forward, Tasuke saw those samurai already fighting fall back in retreat. A cloud of arrows filled the air from the many small landing craft that had suddenly crossed the breakers. The Mongols were preparing to make another landing.

His rōnin had covered half the distance to the battle line when Tasuke noticed the color of the water that washed the sand; it was red. Bodies littered the beach, almost all were soldiers of Yamato.

Tasuke gave the signal, then pulled his horse to a halt. He prepared his bow. The battered samurai he and his rōnin were trying to rescue had to be coaxed with shouts before they would begin their retreat. Meanwhile, the Mongols disembarked.

The enemy looked strange to Tasuke, reminding him of the kuma of the forest. Even the weapons they carried were strange.

Tasuke urged his men forward. As the fresh samurai forces charged toward them, the Mongols spread into a dotted line, a line that became thicker as more craft landed and waited for the enemy that raced forward.

Tasuke's rōnin had not yet reached their bows' effective range when the Mongols fired their weapons. As they did, the Mongol line looked like waving grass to Tasuke. The projectiles of the crossbows were accurate. The line of rōnin thinned as, along its length, both horses and men tumbled to the reddened sand.

Tasuke released his first arrow, reached for another, then saw the uselessness of it. He signaled for retreat. When his army turned, the Mongol line advanced to the sand. They held again, waiting for the samurai's second attack.

"We will follow the plan," Tasuke shouted to his officers. "We will charge in file, retreat, then phalanx." As he spoke, the rōnin leader saw another file of samurai topping the rise behind his men. He signaled to these new samurai, urging them forward. Tasuke held his men until the opportune moment, then charged with them into the Mongols.

Again, as before, the Mongols hit with their arrows first. Tasuke spurred his army on into firing range, sensing that his men were dropping beside him. He fired, and again gave the retreat signal. His timing had to be perfect. Tasuke gave the next signal and his army phalanxed before the file of the new samurai army. Together, they hit the Mongol line.

Tasuke released one arrow after another, not daring to look sideways. A horse went down beside him. Still, Tasuke kept his eyes on the targets before him.

All at once, there were only Mongols around him. He dropped his bow, using his kogatana to cut at the heads of the enemy that pressed upon him. Tasuke's horse could go no farther. Tasuke circled, still chopping at the furclad invaders. When he surged forward again, he was in the water. He saw only empty boats. Tasuke swung his horse around.

The Mongol line had collapsed. The long swords and the kogatana of the samurai finished off those Mongols that could not escape. More samurai raced from the dunes, eager to be part of the victory. They massed on the beach and began ripping trophies of war from the bodies of the Mongols.

Kogashira Kozo sat on a nearby hillside and witnessed the battle. His wounded lay around him. Even those who tended the wounded wore slings and red-soaked bandages. Kozo was angry. He wanted to get up and run down to the beach to join the fighting, but he could not. So he sat where he was, and fumed. He had almost laughed when he first saw the young leader of the rōnin. Now Kozo knew that he envied the young man's brilliant tactics. Kozo knew that he himself would not have been capable of the thought, or even the timing. True, the young leader's ploy had cost him dearly, he had lost many samurai. But the number of rōnin slain by the Mongols did not compare with those lost by Kozo. He watched the rōnin army climb up from the beach, carrying their casualties. The army still looked fresh, it did not have the battered look of his own soldiers. Kozo's own army had tripled that of the rōnin, they had fought against lesser odds, but they had come out in worse shape. Kozo looked at his soldiers. Almost all of them were wounded. He, Kozo, was cut, not able to stand on his own two feet without help. Tears of anger rolled down his scarred face.

Kozo noticed that the Mongols were massing again. A small number of strange-looking boats were approaching. As Kozo tried to guess the purpose of the odd vessels, a lever-like structure raised itself vertical on one of them and a trail of smoke arced from the lever toward the beach. It turned into a large burning ball that bounced among the defenders, scattering them. Seconds later, the dull thunder of an explosion brought panic to the samurai.

More thunderballs flew from the catapult boats, and the soldiers who had been on the beach retreated to the dunes. They watched with awe and amazement as huge craters were blown into the sand.

But the bombing of the beach did not help the Mongols; the explosions only brought more samurai from the land side to the dunes. The crest of the rise looked as though a forest had suddenly covered its sands. The landing craft did not come closer but withdrew as a unit together with the catapults. Tomorrow would be another day.

The sky was turning black when Gokarō Kozo painfully made his way down the hill. Every step of the horse beneath him sent pain through Kozo's injured leg. Kozo leaned sideways as he rode, to ease the pressure. The grimace frozen on his face was caused more by his anger than his pain. Kozo understood what had gone wrong. As soon as they had arrived, Kozo and his army had plunged into battle. As each new army of samurai had reached Hakata, they, too, went into battle immediately—but where was the collective leadership, the strategy, the communications?

Behind Gokarō Kozo were the remnants of his Red Triangle soldiers. They had been weary before their battle, now they were exhausted. Kozo chose to make his camp site near the command post. He had something to tell the generals.

When Koan Tachibana returned, he was leading the two riderless horses. He came back in time to see Kenichi dragging the body of the soldier into the shrubs. "You will never know how happy I am to see you dragging him, instead of the other way around," began the old man. "I was sure, well, I was going to keep right on going. I don't know what brought me back."

"We have no time to talk," returned Kenichi. "The others will be here any second."

The sound of an approaching wagon reached the ears of the two men. In less than a minute, the wagon would be in view.

Koan jumped from his horse. "I know how to use a kogatana," he said, reaching for it.

"It won't be necessary," said Kenichi. "Put the sword with the yatō's body. There's been an accident."

"Ah, sō desu." The old man smiled.

Kenichi picked up the long sword and felt its weight. His other hand caressed its back, then Kenichi returned it to its scabbard. Keeping the sword in line with his body, he dropped it near the dead man. The wagon drew closer.

"A hare bolted his horse," Kenichi explained. Koan was making a professional examination when the wagon stopped. "I cannot help him," he said. "His neck is broken. He is already dead."

The yatō soldiers inspected the body. They removed from it anything of value—his swords, his inrō. Then, together, the yatō rolled the dead man into the bushes alongside the road.

The three yatō soldiers argued as to who should own

which sword. Kenichi shook his head, then motioned to Koan. They would continue their trip to Ikoma without the companionship of the yatō.

Koan was surprised to hear the laughter of his friend after they had traveled a few miles. "What is it you are laughing at?" he asked.

"You, kimi, you. It is too bad you couldn't see yourself when the horses broke away. You reminded me of a loose bag of rice, the way you flopped around on the back of that horse."

"You mean you took the time to watch me while you were being measured with that long sword?" Koan shook his head.

"The sword didn't bother me," said Kenichi. "All I was worried about was whether or not you would stay with that horse."

The isha passed through Shinjo. Ahead, they saw the walls of the mura. Towering above the walls, the glistening structure of the new manor made everything seem strange. Was this Ikoma? Even the gates of the mura were new and unweathered.

The houses of the village looked dead and uninhabited. But smoke rose from some, proving otherwise. The only living person in view was the monban standing near the gate.

The smell of putrid flesh assailed the riders. Close by them, near the road, lay human bodies. Koan was saying something as Kenichi looked at him.

"I said," the old man repeated, "that is how the bloodless death multiplies." He pointed to the bodies. "They should be removed. Nature always rebels against man until man does the right thing. Things are bad here, things are bad."

When the isha reached the mura, the monban opened

the small door within the gate to allow them to enter. When they had dismounted, the guard took the lead ropes of both horses.

"How is it inside?" Koan asked.

"The sickness has started in the mura now," the guard answered. "Already, many are sick. None are dead yet. You will see." The monban pointed. "That is the dōjō; those with the bloodless death wait for you there."

Once inside the mura, Kenichi could see the full expanse of the new manor. The inside of the mura was still recognizable, though most of the buildings had been replaced, others removed altogether. Kenichi looked at the practice fields and the compound; they were the same. But smoke no longer issued from the kilns, Ikoma no longer produced any pottery. Kenichi noticed the guards at one of the kiln buildings. They had turned it into a prison.

A heavy-hewn T-shaped structure was in the center of the yard before the dōjō. It had always been beyond the kitchens, where the oxen were kept. The flushing buckets of the slaughter T lay nearby, the soil beneath it dry. It had been some time since anyone had died here.

Koan spoke to Kenichi. "We are in the lair of the Red Triangle. Are you all right?"

Kenichi managed a weak smile. "Daijōbu!" he answered. "I see now why I have lived. We are where my father and my mother and my beautiful Aki died. I will do something."

Koan understood his meaning. He stopped and faced his friend, taking hold of both of Kenichi's shoulders. "Kenichi, listen to me. Don't think about anything. It is done. The bloodless death avenges you. You need do nothing. It is simple."

"Iie, sensei, that is just it," returned the young man.

"It is too simple. It is too easy for the yatō this way. I cannot let the gods take my duty from me. I am committed, it must be me. Nothing could have kept me from here. I will work out something. In time, I will have a plan."

The crunch of gravel caused both isha to look up. A servant woman bowed before them. Koan noticed her haggard look and forced smile.

"Komban wa," the woman greeted them. "I am Oumi, please follow me." She led them the rest of the way to the open dōjō.

Inside, the isha walked among the dozen who had come down with the sickness. They were in various stages: some lay still as death but awake; others were delirious. For one, it was evident, it would be just a matter of hours before death took him.

Koan, with Kenichi at his side, looked at each sick man. At the same time, the old oishasan kept up a commentary on the sickness. "It is called the bloodless death because, not only do they die without the sword, but also, were you to cut them, no blood would flow. These men are samurai, they have their swords at their side as they die. But for them, it is a bad death. In most cases, they have been promised by their relatives that their bodies will bear the cut of the sword before they are buried. This is not an easy way to die. It is bad. See this one, he appears to sleep, but he cannot. He will stay awake until he dies, maybe two days from now. And this one, too, is beyond help. This one also—" Koan interrupted himself. "Kenichi, there are twelve men here. I doubt any of them will survive. Those that appear strong have a slight chance, but we can do no more than make them comfortable."

Kenichi listened intently to the older man. The phrase "make them comfortable" triggered something in the young isha's mind. "Sensei," he said, "I do not want to tend them." Kenichi rebelled at the thought of aiding the yatō. There was no reason for it. "We are wasting time. I have no love for them."

Oumi, the servant, stood nearby, listening. Her eyes widened when she heard Kenichi's statements.

Koan opened his mouth to speak to his friend, but he realized how close the woman was. He spoke to her instead. "Who is it that brings us here?"

"Sire," Oumi answered, nodding toward the manor. "The daimyō is very worried. He has been sending runners these last three days looking for an oishasan who can cure these men. In the village, already, many are dead. The daimyō fears it will happen within the mura. You will be expected to cure these men." Oumi motioned the isha away from the sick. By the dōjō door, she spoke again, this time in a low voice. "The daimyō looks for the oishasan on whom the gods smile. Many have told him such an oishasan exists." Oumi looked about her before continuing. "If either of you is this oishasan, do not make it known. It is I who must take care of the sick. I feel I may be killed because I did not keep them alive. But another from the prison will only take my place. We will all die if what you say is true. I believe that you"—Oumi pointed to Koan—"are the oishasan the daimyō seeks. I listened to every word you both spoke. You will not cure them, and you do not want the gods to cure them. Then you will be killed as I." A resigned look came into her eyes. "Come, I must bring you to the daimyō. Please follow me."

Hetomi Tajimi, clad only in a loincloth, bent over the small campfire in front of the tent. He poked at the coals with a stick, trying to coax more heat out of the fire for the suspended kettle. The breeze from the sea circled the tent and chilled his back, but the heat from the fire felt good. Every once in a while, Hetomi turned and warmed his buttocks.

Laughter came from inside the tent. "Kimi," Tasuke called to the cook. "What is it that you are cooking?"

"I'm making gohan. What's so funny?"

"I don't want any," said Tasuke, laughing. "Every time you turn around and squat, I'm not sure you're not adding unchi to the rice."

"You mean you don't like it fixed that way?" Hetomi joined his friend in laughter.

"Tomosama," a third voice said. "Excuse me."

"What do you want?" asked Hetomi as he turned and looked at the young messenger who had walked up to the fire.

"My lord, the commander of all the armies holds a council. I was sent to bring your leader."

Tasuke joined the two by the fire. "They asked for me by name?"

"Iie, my lord," the messenger answered. "I was told to find the one that leads the unmarked rōnin. Your camp is the only one that shows no pennant. I assumed this is the camp they meant."

"Where do they hold this council?" asked Daimyō Ito.

"If you follow this way"—the messenger pointed—"to

where the long wall starts, the wall that was to stop the Mongols, you will see the pennants of the Red Triangle. The command post is the next camp beyond."

"Dōmo," said Tasuke. "We will be there directly."

The command post was under a large cloth roof supported by long, guyed poles. Fires burned at all four sides of the shelter. The hum of talking ceased when Tasuke and Hetomi stepped into the light of one of the campfires.

"Komban wa," a voice said. "Please join us. I thank you for coming and I am happy you are with us. We would be honored if you and your lieutenant would be seated." The man who spoke wore a small mustache and goatee. He was one of thirty or forty samurai who sat in two rows. Many of them still wore their armor, others wore practically nothing. Before most of the soldiers already seated were saké cups. An attendant made the rounds, keeping the cups full.

Daimyō Ito and his lieutenant bowed low to those assembled. It was Tasuke who spoke to the silent crowd. "Dōmo, dōmo arigatō gozaimasu. I am Tasuke Ito, daimyō of a lesser daimyōdom in the far north, which none of you have ever heard of. My able lieutenant is Hetomi Tajimi." Tasuke and his aide bowed again, then took their places with those seated. The hum of talk resumed as more saké was poured. Finally someone called for order, and the hum subsided into silence.

Sayada sat in the center of one of the rows, flanked by two important-looking officers. He began to speak. "Gentlemen, I am Prince Sayada Hojo. I carry direct orders from the Bakufu. I have some information I must share with you. Five days ago, our island of Iki fell to Kublai Khan. His troops have landed west of Kumamoto, and all along our defense wall here, as you well know. His ships have been sighted rounding the south tip of Kyūshū. Our fleet lies in wait to the east. Many thousands of our samurai are massed all along the beaches of Kyūshū."

The prince consulted papers before going on. "Stated simply, my orders from the Bakufu amount to this: I must set up a chain of command to all areas. Baron Kamo would have been your commander here in the Hakata area, but I am sorry to tell you that he was killed this morning at the wall. He was very close to me, and I know his passing is a great loss to all of Yamato." Sayada bowed his head for a second. "Gentlemen, I must now select a deputy leader."

A commotion outside interrupted the proceedings. A man on horseback had ridden up to the very edge of the carpeted shelter. Sayada and the others looked up at the horn-helmeted rider. The rider's aides were working to extricate him from the saddle.

"I'm sorry, gentlemen, if I interrupt," said Kogashira Kozo, "but what idiot commands this fiasco?"

Complete silence answered the rider.

While Gokarō Kozo was being helped to a seat, he studied the shocked faces of the men in the shelter, surprised to see Sayada's face among the others. "My prince," Kozo burst out. "I am glad to see you again. Since we've been here, the battlefield has been a nightmare of confusion. Our soldiers are taking turns dying. Are you here to do something about it?"

Prince Sayada shook his head slowly, a faint smile on his face. He looked at the rough samurai and returned his bow. "My friend from—ah—Ikoma. Your bluntness is refreshing. I must tell all of you here, it is good not to talk from behind the kichō. Hai, it would be better if everyone spoke the words they think."

At the prince's mention of Ikoma, Tasuke Ito looked carefully at Kozo. He saw the red symbol on the man's kimono. This, then, was one of the yatō tōryō. Anger swept through Tasuke. He turned to Hetomi, who was also staring at the tōryō, his fist clenched on the handle of his kogatana. Seeing Hetomi's hate stifled Tasuke's own. He put his hand on the runner's arm. Hetomi turned and looked at his friend. They agreed with their eyes: not now.

The prince was still talking, but now it was to all the leaders. "Gentlemen, it is growing late. I have many places to go. This is what I have decided: Suenaga Takezaki will be your commander."

One of the samurai at Sayada's side bowed to the prince.

"Suenaga, I do not know where your camp is. I know your new duty will not deter you from wishing to be involved in the action, but I would prefer that your camp be centered along the wall. The ends of the walls are where the most pressure is, especially at the west end. But then that is for you to work out. Rokuro Shiraishi will be your second-in-command and responsible for all communications and liaison. Because of this, his army and those you send him will defend the east end. I don't want him to have too much to do." Sayada smiled.

The prince turned to Kozo. "Ah, Gokarō Kozo, I understand you lead many men. Even so, the west end might be a formidable task. I'm sure Suenaga will assign two other armies to work with you."

Kozo held up his hand. "Sire," he said, "since I have been here, our samurai have arrived at the front and charged into the Mongols. The organization that has been lacking no doubt will be behind us now. Too many of us have died. We do not have enough nōmin to carry and bury our dead. But this is not the point. I want to speak of battle plans and of tactics—"

"Pardon me, my good gokarō," someone broke in. It was Suenaga Takezaki. "And if you, too, will excuse me, my lord." Suenaga bowed to the prince. "I would like to keep others from jumping to conclusions." Suenaga turned to Kozo. "Battle plans are the luxuries of the aggressor, tactics are something else. Today, when Prince Sayada arrived, he sought out myself and Daimyō Rokuro Shiraishi. We were all given orders as to what must be done and how we must do it. Each of you leaders, from this moment on, will be responsible for carrying out the orders that will be assigned to you. As for tactics, for the time being we will leave them up to individual leaders as long as they are approved by this command. If the assigned orders are carried out precisely, we would hope that very soon we can enjoy the luxury of battle plans."

Kozo bowed to General Suenaga.

"There it is, gentlemen," said Prince Sayada. "It is all spelled out. As I sail north very soon, sayonara. Ah, Gokarō Kozo. Before you leave, I would like to have a word with you."

"Hai, tomosama," said Kozo.

The meeting was over. Some of the leaders left, others formed small groups and chatted.

General Suenaga walked over to Kozo, who still seemed upset. He bowed and smiled at Kozo, then he spoke. "I do not want you to leave with the wrong impression of me. Before you arrived tonight, others brought up that we must go on the offensive. Everyone here knows that my comments were not in response to your statement." He smiled again at Kozo, as though asking his pardon.

"I understand," said Kozo. "I took no offense. I am most happy that you are our commander. I will be your best officer."

"Dōmo." Suenaga bowed.

"Sire," said the gokarō, "the prince said something about the assigning of the lesser armies. I request that you assign the unpennanted rōnin army under Tasuke Ito to work with me."

"Ah, sō desu," Suenaga said. "So you, too, have heard of the brilliant charge of the unmarked daimyō. You have made an intelligent choice, Gokarō Kozo. I will take care of it for you." Suenaga turned and called out to the crowd. "I would like the rōnin leader to approach." He turned back to Kozo. "You will find that he is quite young."

"Sire." Tasuke Ito was at Suenaga's side. "I am Tasuke Ito, the leader of the rōnin. How may I be of service to you?"

General Suenaga bowed to Tasuke. "You will not have to wait until tomorrow for your assignment. This is Gokarō Kozo. You and your men will have the west end of the wall with him. I am sure you two will make an effective team."

Tasuke's face was expressionless. "Hai," he said.

"Good," said the general. "I will leave you two to make plans. I have much to attend to. Sayonara." General Suenaga departed.

Kozo started to speak, but Prince Sayada walked up to them. Tasuke and Kozo both bowed to the prince.

"I have a palanquin here for you, Gokarō. For the time being, I think it will be more comfortable than your horse." Sayada turned to Tasuke. "Ah, you must be Daimyō Ito. I must congratulate you and your men. I have heard much good talk of you today."

"Dōmo arigatō, my lord," said Tasuke. "I must congratulate you in return for your choices tonight."

"Dōmo," Sayada said. "I could not help but overhear that you and Gokarō Kozo will fight together at the west end of the wall. I pity the Mongols that try to get by you!" He laughed. "Ah, Gokarō Kozo, what is your first name?"

"Kogashira, my lord."

"Hmm, very fitting. Kogashira, I have some news for you. Before I left Kamakura, I received an answer to a letter I had sent to your daimyō at Ikoma. Daimyō Murata states that all is well there." Sayada turned to Tasuke. "Someday you will have to see Ikoma. It is a very beautiful place."

"I know, I have been told that many times. I would like to be there."

"Hai," said Kozo, "wouldn't we all? Daimyō Tasuke, you did not say where your daimyōdom is, exactly. You only said 'in the far north.' But where?"

"My daimyōdom is no more. It is sad for me to even mention it, so you will pardon me if I do not. If ever I become powerful, then I will call it home again. Now I try not to think of it."

"Ah, sō desu," said Kozo. "I know what you mean. It has happened to many."

"Hai," broke in Sayada. "You are young. I am sure that you will win it back."

Kozo put his hand on Tasuke's shoulder. "I saw you fight the enemy. I think you will get your daimyōdom back. You have my wishes that you do."

"Dōmo, dōmo arigatō." Tasuke smiled. "From you, those are good words."

"You have my good wishes also," said Sayada.

"Dōmo, tomosama," said Daimyō Ito. "I am happy to have talked with both of you." Tasuke bowed to the prince. "My lord, may I have your permission to be excused?" Sayada nodded, and Tasuke bowed again and backed away.

"You were saying of Ikoma?" asked Kozo when Daimyō Ito left.

"Hai," replied the prince. "It is that your daimyō Kumahatchi Murata has agreed that his daughter Sakura will be my bride."

Kozo was stunned. He coughed, holding his hands in front of his face so that Sayada could not see his troubled eyes.

The leaves on the forest floor were hammered to the ground by the incessant droplets of rain. Through the forest, the roofed wagon followed a wet road that was more water than earth, not much different from the nearby stream.

The horse pulling the wagon walked with its head held low, either from boredom or from fatigue. It seemed to ignore even the old man handling the reins, who also kept his head low as he tried to prevent the slanting rain from hitting his face. The mino and the sloping rice-straw hat which he wore effectively kept him dry. Every so often he laughed, overhearing snatches of the conversation of his passengers.

Aki Taizo and Somiko Sei were in good humor. The trip to Niigata on the coast had been pleasant and without incident, except for the rain. It seemed that fortune would follow them all the way back to Takata.

A goat accompanied the women in the wagon, but in the back, near the open rear end. With her legs folded and trussed, the goat had spent most of the journey looking balefully at the women and bleating.

"At least the animal is quiet, eh? Now she just stares at us," said Aki. "It will be a miracle if she lets us near her after this."

Somiko smiled. "You needn't worry. Once she learns who is feeding her, she will be happy to see us. I know."

"I am worried," Aki said. "Maybe she is not like you—I mean, maybe she isn't carrying a child."

"Oh, Aki-san," said the older woman, "you worry too much. I'll tell you how I know. The he-goat has a habit, not pleasing to you or me, but very exciting to the she-goat. When they mate, he makes certain to spread his smell all over his lover. So that the other he-goats know this female is his. They run from her even if she wants them. She chases after them, but the he-goats run faster, thinking of the male.

"She-goats do not have a smell of their own; only when she loves a buck does she carry a smell." Somiko's eyes twinkled. "Our goat smells very strongly, she had much love, and because of her, we smell just as bad. But the unfair part is—we didn't get any love at all." The old man driving the wagon again joined the women in laughter.

It was still raining when the wagon pulled to a stop in front of the house in Takata. The black pennant still hung, undisturbed. Neither of the women made any reference to it.

The house looked different, even in the dark. The wooden slats had been added, as the oishasan had promised.

The wagon was unloaded and the women bid the driver goodbye.

"Where are we going to put the animal?" asked Aki. The animal was unbound but tethered to a post. Unmindful of the rain, the goat picked at the grass along the path. "We can't leave it in this weather, and it's too late to find shelter for it now," added Aki.

Somiko laughed. "This we did not consider. Hmm. We

have no choice but to let the animal stay in the house with us tonight. Tomorrow, when it is light, we will make other arrangements. Come, let us get in out of the rain."

The goat was led into the house and tied in a corner. Somiko busied herself with lighting the lamps and the irori, while Aki unpacked the bundles. The goat lay quietly, watching the movements of the women as though it was perfectly satisfied.

Somiko surveyed the room. "The oishasan have done well for us. It is dry now, and we will not have to use so much fuel for warmth. Also, they have been honest, everything is as we had left it."

"Hai," agreed Aki. "I knew they were kind."

"Eh, I thought you were frightened of them."

"Iie, why do you say that?" asked Aki.

"Well, when you saw them, you acted strange. I thought you were frightened. Weren't you?"

Aki did not answer. She walked over to the goat, sat down by it, and stroked the animal's ears. Finally she turned to her friend. "I was nervous, I guess."

Somiko looked at Aki inquiringly.

The younger woman continued. "I thought he was Jujiro. I watched the three of you that morning from the porch. The younger one's movements were Jujiro's, only the fudangi and the hair were wrong." Aki smiled at Somiko. "Then, when they got ready to leave, I looked at him carefully. I was sure it was Jujiro. See how silly I am?"

Somiko smiled. "It is because you love him. I, too, look carefully at everyone I see. I always hope that one of them will be Hetomi coming back to me." Somiko quickly changed the subject. "I see that our new friend is comfortable and will be all right." She poured water into a container. "Here, set this before her. She may want a drink before morning."

Aki put the bowl near the goat. The animal smelled it, but did not drink. "Hai," Aki talked to the animal, "you are quiet now. If you want a drink, it is here. There is no need to cry, for we, too, are tired. Oyasumi nasai."

The women readied their futon. Soon the house was quiet.

During the night, the rain stopped. The women slept, despite the fact that the goat did not.

The sun was well up when Aki was jolted awake. The animal, now loose, had put her face near the woman's, and was baaing loudly, as if to say, "Wake up!"

Aki let out a shriek, frightening the animal, which bounded back to its corner. "Oh, no!" shouted Aki.

The older woman woke up, rubbed her eyes, and looked around, dumfounded.

The little room was a shambles: one tatami was ripped to shreds; others were still in place but had large tufts sticking out of them where the goat had nibbled; everywhere, the exposed floor was wet and littered with marbles. But the water the women had given the animal was undisturbed.

Tears welled into Aki's eyes. Somiko, too, looked ready to cry. But instead she burst out laughing, and soon Aki joined her.

With the animal tethered outside, the women began the cleanup. Aki held up a square. "These tatami are ruined. I may as well let her have the rest."

"Don't bother, she won't eat them now. She wet on them," said Somiko.

The younger woman dragged two of the squares outside toward the goat. When Aki returned, Somiko held something out to her.

"Here, this is yours. You must have lost it between the tatami. It has your mark on it."

Aki stared down at the comb in the woman's hand.

There was no doubt of it: this was the very comb she had given to Jujiro, his leather thong was still attached to it. She opened her mouth to speak, then brought her hands forward to catch herself as she collapsed to the floor.

Kogashira Kozo looked at the palanquin that Sayada had left for him. Then he looked into the darkness in the direction the prince had gone. Kozo made no effort to board the conveyance. His aide Hitari waited patiently for his leader to make up his mind. He held Kozo by the arm, helping him keep his weight off his injured leg. The four nōmin who would carry the palanquin squatted at their positions, also waiting for Kozo's orders.

The general waved the nōmin away, then spoke to Hitari. "I want to see Sayada before he leaves; we will walk."

"It is a long walk, my lord. He—they are headed for the south beach, toward the boats."

The gokarō untied his long sword. Grasping the scabbard below the hilt with his right hand, he tried using it as a cane. "I will use my sword to walk with. I do not revere it, the symbol on it is not mine. But it will serve its purpose. I do not need your help to hold me, but I want you to walk with me."

"Hai," Hitari responded. He released his grip, letting the leader stand by himself. Together they walked up the beach, following the footprints left by Sayada and his aides.

After a while, Kozo motioned the other to stop. "Do you wish to rest?" asked the aide.

"Iie, it is that I must make you aware of my intentions." Kozo would need help to carry out his plan, but he was not sure of Hitari. He would speak to him, then watch his reactions. "Tell me, Hitari, what do you expect from life?" Kozo watched the aide carefully as he waited for an answer.

Hitari looked down and thought about Kozo's question. It seemed strange to him. Why would the general care about him? Hitari had no surname; he was not a bushi. Hitari was frightened of his swords. In battle, he did not use them. Instead, he was a thrower. Even a nōmin could become an expert thrower.

"Well?" asked Kozo.

The aide looked up. "I do not know," Hitari answered truthfully.

This told the gokarō nothing. He must prod further. "How well do you know your swords?" The general was smiling. He continued. "I have never seen you use them. At Ikoma, you carried no swords, eh? You were a thrower. I admit you did well, but—"

Hitari interrupted the general. He did not like this subject. He felt he had a right to the swords, and he would tell Kozo so. "These swords I carry have the same monshō on the hilt as yours, the crossed star. I killed the man who wore them before me, with a rock. Someday I will learn to use these swords as well."

"Hmm," began Kozo. "How long have you lived?"

"Twenty-two years," Hitari answered.

"You are young, but you are also too old. Before you could learn the sword, someone much younger than you will have killed you. Those who know the sword well are already proficient by the time they are as old as you are now. I am a sensei of the sword. Believe what I say. The left-handed swordsman is the most potent of warriors. Tonight I will give you your first lesson."

This made no sense to Hitari. Did Kozo intend to kill him? Hitari stepped back, ready to run.

"Don't worry," Kozo said. "I want you to listen carefully. Come back, I do not want to have to shout. You and I are going to kill Sayada!"

"What?" gasped Hitari. The aide could not believe his ears. This man must be out of his mind. The prince was their leader. The blood that flowed through him also flowed through the gods. "You cannot be serious?" Hitari asked. "Surely, you are not serious?"

But Kozo was not smiling.

Fear swept through the aide. His fingers trembled. Hitari opened his mouth to speak again, but did not know what to say.

Kozo noticed his reaction. "We are running out of time," he said. "Now listen, I am not mad, I understand things that you do not. Sayada is selling us to the Mongols. Hai, it is true, as you will see—"

"I do not believe you," Hitari interrupted. "It would have to be proven first."

"There is no time for that. Listen: Sayada told me tonight that he will take Ikoma."

Fear was still visible on the aide's face. "I am sorry," he said, "but Ikoma means nothing to me. If we were to slay the prince, we would not see another day. I want no part of it." Hitari stepped back again.

Kozo's thoughts raced. He needed Hitari's help, the gokarō was sure he could not accomplish the deed by himself. He must convince Hitari. "Sayada cannot live, for the reasons I have given. If he lives, you will die! We will all die. But I mean to live. Ikoma belongs to me, and I will keep it. Think now, when I am daimyō of Ikoma, someone must be the gokarō. Could it be you?"

Hitari took a step toward the general. Ah, he is making

sense, after all. Hitari would hear him out. "What is your plan?" asked the aide.

"It may be too late already. You must catch him before he leaves shore. Here, where we are, there are no tents, it is dark. Run to Sayada. Speak only to him, so that no one else can hear. Tell him that I have information of the greatest importance for his ears alone."

"Then what?"

"It is imperative that you lead him to me here. Then we will kill him."

"But must we? Can we not report him? About the Mongols, I mean."

"Iie," said Kozo. "For many reasons. It would demoralize the soldiers if others found out. It is better for Yamato that Sayada die a hero—as though a Mongol spy had killed him."

"His aides will see me when I talk to the prince. I—I—" Hitari stammered.

"That is no problem. I will cover for you. I do have information for him. But go now, and cover the monshō on your kimono. His aides should not see the red triangle. Hayaku! You must run."

Hitari turned from Kozo and sprinted in the darkness toward the beach.

Kozo watched intently in the direction of the shore. At last, he could see figures approaching. Ah, good, there were only two. Hitari had succeeded.

Prince Sayada was surprised to see Kozo standing, leaning on a sword. When he got close enough, he returned the smile on Kozo's face. "It is well that you caught me. I was just leaving for my ship. What is so important?" The prince looked about them. "Where is your palanquin? You shouldn't have walked this far. You should take care of yourself."

"I could not trust the bearers, tomosama," the general said, still smiling. He shifted the long sword to his left hand, then leaned on it as before. Kozo's right hand moved to his kogatana.

Suddenly the prince sensed danger, but he wore no sword. He backed away. "What do you want?" He looked from Kozo to Hitari, whose hand was on his short sword.

Kozo spoke quietly to the aide. "I will not need your help, after all." At the same time, Kozo slashed out with his kogatana. The prince was still within reach. The force of the blow threw him to the sand. Prince Sayada Hojo made no sound as he died.

Kozo stared down at the dead man. "We must remove his head and hide it. If he had been killed by Mongols, they would have taken it. Do you understand?"

There was no answer from Hitari. The aide had disappeared.

Hitari ran blindly toward the command post. He fell when he tried to run up the slippery sand dune. Clawing his way to his feet again, he saw the four fires arranged in a square. Hitari kept his eyes focused on the fires as he ran. He did not notice the soldier who stood in his way.

Tasuke Ito heard the footsteps of a runner drawing close. He readied his short sword. Tasuke's first thought was that it must be the Mongols. Iie, it was one of ours. Tasuke waved his arms, and Hitari stopped before him. The Red Triangle monshō was visible on the aide's kimono.

Tasuke held his kogatana ready. "What is it?" Tasuke asked.

"He is dead! He is dead!" The frightened nōmin gasped. "I was there, I saw him do it. Hai, you are one of our leaders. He is dead! Prince Sayada is dead!"

"What?"

This is impossible, thought Tasuke. This man is mad. There was no way the Mongols could have gotten to the prince. Little more than an hour ago, Tasuke had been talking with him. Iie, the prince was too well guarded. The leader studied the nōmin. The man was shivering, and there were tears in his eyes.

"Calm down," Tasuke said. "Slowly, now, tell me what happened."

"It was there." Hitari pointed back into the darkness. "I took no part in it. You must believe me."

"What?" exclaimed Tasuke again. The leader had been thinking of Mongols. "What of the Mongols? Where are they?"

"There are no Mongols, just the general."

"Show me! Take me there. First, untie your swords and leave them here."

Hitari did as he was told, letting the weapons fall to the sand. Tasuke returned his kogatana to his belt and unsheathed his long sword. "Lead!" he directed.

Hitari started to walk, with Tasuke close behind.

"Tell me," said Tasuke, "his aides and his guards, are they with the prince?"

"Iie, my lord. They are waiting in the boats, but he . . . will not return." Hitari glanced back and saw the long sword in the leader's hand. The nōmin dropped to his knees. "Is it my turn to die? I—I had no part in it."

"Get up! Keep walking. Tell me about the general."

"It was he. He killed the prince," Hitari stammered.

"Who is with him?" Tasuke motioned the man to stop.

"He is alone, sire."

"Are you sure?"

"Hai. You have to believe me. I took no part in it."

"Calm down! What general is it?"

"It is our general, Kozo. There—there he is."

"Get down!" Tasuke commanded. "Lie flat on your face. Don't utter a sound."

Hitari did as he was told. Tasuke sprang quickly to one side and crouched in the sand. He was certain that Kozo had not spotted them.

Kozo seemed to be walking in circles, as though looking for something. The tōryō walked, using his long sword as a cane. What was that he carried in his other hand? A sack? Tasuke drew closer.

The clouds moved, and a bright moon illuminated the scene. The bag became something else. It was a head.

Tasuke saw the small mustache and goatee on the swinging head, he recognized the face of the prince. Tasuke screamed as he charged toward the limping man.

Sakura Murata sat beside the pond. The fish were drawn to her fingers as she played with the water. She enjoyed the gentle kisses. Water ran down the miniature moss-covered rock mountain, sparkling like emeralds in the bright sun.

Sakura had prayed to the goddess of the sun for a month. Each night, before she went to sleep, she would kneel with her head on the tatami and pray. In her first prayer, Sakura had promised Amaterasu thirty nights of indulgence if the goddess would grant her an end to her loneliness and boredom.

Deep down, Sakura believed that Amaterasu listened to her prayers. Something would happen, the princess was sure. But, whatever it was, only the Sun Goddess knew. She would tell Sakura in due time.

Sakura wore one of her best kimonos. It was black,

with large red flowers embroidered in threads of silver and gold. Two women had combed Sakura's long hair until every strand fell perfectly about the hem of her kimono.

Sakura let her mind wander. She thought of the war, and wondered whether Prince Sayada already knew of what otōsan had told her. This was frightening; there was no way of knowing how a princess should act. What was it that Aki had told her? Just be yourself, as you are. But surely there must be more to it. Ah, Aki. Had she found the baron she had sought? Undoubtedly, this baron, too, was at war in the south. It was even possible that the prince and Aki's baron had met. They might even be talking together at this very minute.

The scuffing of zōri on the courtyard side of the hedge caught Sakura's attention. The princess could hear the court monban speak. "What is it? Why did you bring these men to the manor?"

A woman replied. "One of these might be the oishasan the daimyō wants. He ordered that all oishasan were to be brought here."

Sakura recognized the voice of Oumi. The monban spoke again. "You two, kneel and bow. Stay that way until told otherwise. You, Oumi, go back to the dōjō. I will tell the daimyō myself."

Sakura heard the shōji slide open. So we have visitors. At least they will be new faces to look at, she thought. She would go to the court and see otōsan. She hadn't talked to him in days. She would bring him tea.

Daimyō Kumahatchi Murata looked down at the kneeling figures in the courtyard. He sat with legs crossed, his hands hidden in his sleeves. Kumahatchi coughed and clapped his hands. The isha raised their heads.

Hmm, that old man may be he, thought the daimyō; the other is not much older than a boy. Well, he could help with the sick. The daimyō cleared his throat. "You are Tachibana, nē?" Kumahatchi did not wait for an answer, but went on speaking. "You realize that I am a most powerful daimyō—I asked for you a few days ago and you are already here. The gods have seen fit to slay those about me with the bloodless death. First, I heard they were dying in the village. I sent my own oishasan there to find out what was happening. Three days ago, he came back to kneel where you are now. He did not speak; he fell unconscious. He was one of those you saw in the dōjō." Kumahatchi pointed to Koan. "You are Tachibana, are you not?"

Koan Tachibana bowed. Ah, they know of me even this far north. Surely, I am famous. Koan smiled at the daimyō. "Hai, I am Koan Tachibana. But we cannot help you. We cannot bring back to life those that are already so close to death."

Kumahatchi's face showed his displeasure. This was not what he had expected to hear. But the daimyō smiled; he would show patience. "Oishasan, many times I have heard of Koan Tachibana. You are called the oishasan on whom the gods smile. The gods are not angry with me. If so, you would not be here now. I do not ask any help from you, I will tell you what I want done and you will do it. What have you to say now?"

The faces of both isha showed no emotion. The daimyō had expected to see fear.

Koan spoke slowly, picking each word carefully. "Tomosama, the tales you have heard of me have been magnified many times. True, I have been successful, but they were the simple cures of simple ills, the healing of cuts and the like. The bloodless death is something else." Koan paused to let his next statement sink in. "The cure for the bloodless death can be granted only by the gods."

The daimyō's face was blank as he stared at the old man. "If what you say is so, then it is very simple. This is what I want done. Tonight you will talk to the gods for me. Tomorrow you will be here again and tell me what they say. We will see whether they smile on you." Kumahatchi was grinning. He turned to the young isha and looked at him as though seeing him for the first time. "Do the gods smile on you, too?"

Kenichi looked into the daimyō's eyes but did not speak.

"I am getting old," Koan said. "Soon I can be an isha no more. Some time ago, I took on an apprentice. He is capable, so—"

But Kumahatchi was not listening. Something about this young isha bothered him. Kumahatchi interrupted Koan. "What do they call you?" he asked the young man.

"I am Kenichi Ueida."

"So you have two names. That is interesting. You look as though you have had enough to eat most of your life. What did you do before becoming an isha?"

Kenichi did not like the daimyō's sneer, and felt his anger welling up within. But he would not lose his temper. "My parents were not unwealthy. I did not do anything special, sire."

The shōji opened behind Kumahatchi. Sakura bowed, setting an ozen before him. She whispered, "Treat them as guests, otōsan. They are almost our first since the war started."

Kumahatchi nodded to his daughter and returned her smile. Sakura poured the tea for the daimyō, then she looked at the isha. First she noted the red mark on the kimono of the old man, the symbol of an oishasan. He was impressive-looking, she thought. His white hair contrasted with his tanned face and hands. Sakura could see that this oishasan spent much time outdoors. She looked at the other oishasan, who was now watching her father. He seemed to take no interest in Sakura. She noticed that this one was young. He was tall and muscular, his kimono was tight across his chest.

Sakura looked at Kenichi's face and was startled. She felt that she almost knew him, as a lost word on the tip of her tongue. It was maddening, she could not place him.

"You both must be welcome," said the daimyō. "I, or rather we—this is my daughter, Princess Sakura Murata—we want you to feel at ease here in Ikoma. It has—"

But Kenichi was no longer listening, he was looking at the princess. It—it was Aki! Kenichi's face, expressionless, changed suddenly to a look of surprise. His mouth opened slightly, for an instant.

The daimyō broke off his sentence and looked inquiringly at the young isha. "Is there something wrong?" he asked.

"My lord?" Kenichi turned to the daimyō.

"You gave a start. I asked whether there was something wrong," repeated the daimyō. Ah, the young one jumped when he looked at Sakura, it must be her beauty. Kumahatchi smiled as he waited for the isha's reply.

"Iie, my lord, there is nothing wrong. There is a pebble under my knee."

"Then by all means remove it. You have my permission." Kumahatchi tried not to smile.

When her father introduced her, Sakura bowed first to Koan, smiling as she looked up. She bowed a second time to Kenichi. Sakura studied the oishasan's face carefully, she was now certain that she should know this man. "It is not fair," said Sakura. "You tell them who I am, but you say nothing of them."

"Ah, Sakura-san, forgive me. This is the famous oishasan, Koan Tachibana. He and his friend have come to bring an end to the bloodless death. They will be our guests until it is over." The daimyō turned to Koan. "Is that not so, oishasan?"

"Tomosama," began Koan, "as you command, we will try to do. But there is no way we can perform miracles, and you—"

Kumahatchi's smile faded as he interrupted the old man. "I do not ask for miracles." The daimyō controlled himself, then continued. "I have already made it clear to you what I want done. You"—he pointed to the young isha—"do you remember what I said?"

"Hai, my lord, it is vivid. Please forgive my sensei. He is tired. Tonight we will confer with the gods, and tomorrow we will tell you what they say." A plan took shape in Kenichi's mind. Was it really possible that this yatō believed they could talk with the gods?

The daimyō's next words proved it. "Hai, oishasan, that is correct. Tell them my name carefully: Daimyō Kumahatchi Murata. I am sure they will smile on me also." The daimyō looked about him, then clapped his hands. "Isha, you will want time to settle yourselves before dark."

A servant entered the court and bowed before the daimyō. Kumahatchi spoke to the servant in a whisper, so that the isha in the courtyard could not hear. The servant nodded, then bowed as she backed from the room.

"She will take you to the woman Oumi," said the daimyō, "who will see to your needs. Tomorrow, before the sun climbs too high, you will be here." Kumahatchi gave the signal for the shōji to the courtyard to be closed. As the panels came together, Kenichi could see Aki staring at him.

Koan and Kenichi followed the servant in silence. She led them to the small house that was once occupied by Aki and the samurai Taizo. Kenichi felt dazed, helpless.

"This will be your quarters." The servant bowed. "I will send Oumi to you. She will cook and care for you." She departed.

"It is unbelievable," Kenichi said to Koan. "I thought the young princess was Aki, but that is impossible. How could two people look so much alike? Can it be that it is Aki, but they have taken her mind away?"

Koan glanced at his friend. "She does not look like that has happened to her. You must be mistaken. I am sorry, kimi. Sometimes the mind does strange things with our memory. You have been through a great ordeal. But now we have a great problem. You led the tōryō to believe that we could talk to the gods. I know of no way to do that. What can we tell him tomorrow?"

Kenichi put his hand on Koan's shoulder. The young man's face was lit up with excitement. "Don't you see, sensei? It is perfect. The tōryō will do whatever the gods want. Good, nē?"

"Ah, sō, Kenichi, but this is no good. I am afraid that might give us away. What the gods say must indeed sound like it is the gods who have spoken."

"Daijōbu, do not worry," returned the young man. "I will do it. Tonight we will be the gods and we will make our plans." Kenichi pointed outside. The woman Oumi walked toward the isha.

When she entered, she spoke first to Koan. "You have seen the daimyō," Oumi began. "I have been given my

instructions. But you should know that I am not of these people. My home is Hokkaido, across the water to the north. I want you to trust me. I am told that I must be at your side always and report whatever is spoken." Oumi paused, and a look of fear crept over her face. "Maybe I should not have told you this. Have I erred? You are a great oishasan. The other servant told me so. I see in you my chance to stay alive, and I can be of help to you. Just before the war, many were killed on the beams." The look of fright remained on Oumi's face as she waited for Koan to speak.

"Any help we receive from you, we will be grateful. We will help you in return, however we can." Koan studied the woman. She was not unattractive. Hai, perhaps she would sleep with him tonight. He smiled at her. She smiled back. Koan was sure that she would.

Oumi paid no attention to the oishasan as she worked over the irori, fixing the food. The men talked in low whispers, but she did not care. Tomorrow she would tell the daimyō that they talked only of the work of caring for the sick. And tonight she would please Koan. The food she brought from the manor was the best. Hai, she would please this man who could talk to the gods, in any way she could.

She turned to the isha. Kenichi was talking to her. "What do you know of the daimyō's daughter? Tell me everything."

Hmm, thought Oumi, the young one has high ideas. Oumi smiled. "I have been her servant for three years now. In the forest, I cooked for her and her father. Whenever she was sick, I tended her as if she were my daughter. She is a good woman, and she is greatly loved by her father, the daimyō. He will do anything for her.

"One day she told her father she wanted to live in a splendid manor. He promised her that they would have one and that he would make her a princess. But then, when we came here to Ikoma, the manor had been destroyed. The first thing that was ordered was the building of a new manor."

"So," began Kenichi. "Is he her real father?"

"Hai," replied Oumi. "I am friends with her. She told me many stories of her life. She cannot remember her mother, but, hai, he is her father. There is no doubt of it. Why?"

"She resembles someone else," said Kenichi. "Is it possible that she has a twin?"

"Iie, no! I would surely know. I remember that she told me there was only her father. He is a samurai, and for many years he was attached as a sensei to the palace at Heian-Kyō. Ah, I remember now, her mother died of the bloodless death there in Heian-Kyō. That is why the daimyō is frightened now."

Koan broke in. "Hai, I was at Heian-Kyō when the bloodless death came. It was there I learned its secrets."

Kenichi was interested. "Obāsan, tell me more of this sickness."

"We will eat first," interrupted Oumi. "When we are through eating, you may talk all you want of your sicknesses." She served the food, setting her own dish beside Koan's. The three ate in silence. When they were finished, Oumi spoke first. "Now you can speak of your bloodless death. I am not interested."

Koan laughed. "You listen, too; it will do you good. The sickness always follows a pattern. First, there is war or famine, but in any event, many deaths. These bodies are not removed. When I was at Heian-Kyō, I discovered the two things about the sickness that are unknown to most isha: fire and water."

Kenichi looked at Koan with surprise. "Fire and water? They are the things that never come together. I do not understand."

Koan smiled. "It is the key to the bloodless death. Let me explain. You must not reveal this to anyone," he said to Oumi. "The sickness travels from one to another by way of water. It is the water that is poisoned. The well, the spring—"

Kenichi interrupted. "Are you telling me it is a poison that causes it?"

Koan held up a finger. "Not exactly, or maybe it is. Everything that touches the sick is cursed. Hai, you are right. It is a poison." The old man smiled: Kenichi was like a sponge. Koan continued. "But the poison is a powder, too small to even see. It clings to almost everything and is very potent. It loves water most."

"And the fire?" asked Kenichi.

"Fire is the only weapon against it," said Koan. "In Heian-Kyō, the sickness kept returning. But wherever we burned in the city, it did not return. It happened that way in other places, too. Hai, fire is the secret."

"I see," said the young man, "then it can be stopped. But you said those in the dōjō would die."

Koan shook his head. "There is little hope for them. Maybe one or two will live." He hesitated. "A long time ago, I told you of the power of the oishasan. Do you remember?"

"Hai, sensei, I remember."

Koan continued. "Here, then, is some power. We can control or spread this sickness. But it is potent, and its path is unpredictable."

The young man thought about this for a moment. Then: "I have one more question, my sensei. We cannot see this poison of the bloodless death. How do we keep it from us?"

Koan put his hand on Oumi's leg. "Tea, kudasai—and hot!"

Oumi reached for the kettle, poured, and placed the bowl before Koan.

The sensei pointed to his bowl, waving his fingers through the steam. "This is the only thing we will drink while we are here. Notice, it must be hot. When we are with the sick, we will touch very little. When we leave them, we will drink hot tea. We will even wash our bodies with it. But it must be hot. Remember the fire. It is the heat that nullifies the poison. Our clothes must be washed in water that has been boiled. Anything we think might have the poison, we burn." The old man looked into Kenichi's eyes. "What is it you want me to say tomorrow?" asked Koan.

"I understand," began the young man. "Especially your last statement. I do have a mission here. Already, I know some of what the gods have told me. Tomorrow you will tell the tōryō that the gods talked only to me. You, Oumi, listen to me carefully. They want to know what we speak here. Tell them only this: we spent the night talking to someone behind the kichō, you could not hear what was said, but you were very frightened of the strange voices, nē?"

Oumi bowed to the young oishasan. "Hai, it will be that way, even if my life depends on it." She forced a smile.

"It does," said Kenichi as he turned to his friend. "What I say to the tōryō tomorrow, you must swear to. What you don't know, the gods would not tell you. I have a plan. I will tell you this much of it: I do not want this poison of the bloodless death in Ikoma, and I will help you work to remove it. I am tired. Maybe I will talk to the gods while I sleep." Kenichi laughed as he left the room, closing the shōji behind him.

Hakata's commanding general, Suenaga Takezaki, sipped wine from a saucer. The three men who sat with him did the same. Rokuro Shiraishi, Tasuke Ito, and another man set down their saucers and waited for the leader to speak.

"It is indeed strange," Suenaga began. "We will follow the madman Kozo's suggestion—we will make plans for battle. Were Prince Sayada alive now, he would agree that we have been fighting on the Khan's terms too long. Each night we sleep, wondering what the Mongols will attack us with next. And each day it is something different: catapults, the bamboo fence, delayed explosions on the beach. And then there is today's surprise: a great roaring pipe that blew fire and hurled a thousand rocks at once." Suenaga waved his hand toward the fourth man, a stranger to those in the room.

"Gentlemen, this is Minoru Soga." The commander bowed to the visitor. "Sire, these two men are my ablest officers: First General Rokuro Shiraishi and General Tasuke Ito." The men exchanged bows and greetings.

Minoru Soga was not a soldier. His hair was long and tied close to his head with a broad white band. His dark complexion reminded Suenaga of his dead friend, the prince. He, too, had spent much time on the sea.

Commander Suenaga resumed talking. "Minoru Soga is captain of a ship. He has been busy transporting men and supplies from Honshū to Kyūshū since the beginning of the war. His ship is anchored now at Hirado-guchi, west of here. Earlier this evening, an unmanned Mongol boat drifted into him. Minoru made the boat fast to his and brought it in to shore. He now offers this prize to us. Minoru, will you continue?"

Soga smiled and nodded, then began, "My lords, this boat is one of those that throws fireballs. It carries pitch, straw, charcoal, and yellow-painted containers of a special black earth. It was my thought that this might be of interest to you. I want nothing more to do with it; the boat is very dangerous. My men experimented with its cargo, only a small amount, but still they were burned. The Mongols know how to handle it, perhaps you do, too. One of the missiles on the catapult was ready to be fired. From disassembling it, I can tell you how the missiles are made." Minoru sat back on his heels and waited for the commander's response.

"There you have it, gentlemen," Suenaga said to his generals. "What can we do with this weapon?" He looked first to Rokuro.

"Well," said the first general. "I know now what you meant about battle plans." Rokuro smiled. "Should we turn the catapult on the Mongol ships?"

Tasuke held up his hand. Suenaga nodded permission to speak.

"Sires," Tasuke said, "I saw the catapults when they were used on the beaches. There must have been scores of them, and they had to come quite close to the breakers for the thunderballs to reach us. The question is: how can we attack the Mongols with just one catapult?"

Rokuro broke in. "You have a point there. Tell me, Minoru, how many times can we fire the catapult? How many thunderballs are there?"

"You have a problem," began the captain. "The catapult is not operable. Maybe that is why the boat was abandoned. But it does hold nine yellow containers of the special substance. When we opened a completed missile, we saw how it was constructed: the mixture of straw, charcoal, and pitch is on the outside, and this is bound with line around the yellow container. Inside the container is the black earth. We touched fire to half of the earth in one container—the great fire it made lasted less than a second. It seriously burned two of my men. There are still nine and a half containers left."

"How are they ignited?" asked Tasuke.

"There is an iron hibachi in which a fire is kept burning, in the rear of the boat. They simply touch a torch to the missile."

Tasuke Ito turned to Suenaga. "Sire," he said, "I have it. I know of another way we can make good use of these thunderballs."

Much later that night, a slight wind swept down from the north, blocking out the stars with clouds.

A small boat, heavily laden, cleared the breakers and made its way to the Mongol fleet. Silently, the five men in the boat worked as a unit, moving the heavy boat forward. Four rowed, the fifth used his oar locked to the stern as a tiller. He stared ahead, trying to distinguish the ships in the darkness.

A light rain had begun to fall. The tillerman, Tasuke Ito, was pleased. The rain would help cover them when they started their second run.

Tasuke saw the large dark hulk of a ship. He pushed hard on the tiller and whispered orders. The oars were pulled in, but the small boat continued its course, propelled now only by the stern oar. One of the men went over the side, taking with him a pitch-smeared bundle. The small boat circled, picked up the swimmer, then moved to the next ship.

For almost half an hour, the small boat zigzagged through the Mongol fleet, delivering its deadly bundles, then turned back to make the second run. This time, they moved with greater speed. They drew abreast of the last ship they had visited moments before. The tillerman gave an order.

Suddenly the interior of the moving boat was illuminated as archers lit their heavy flaming arrows. Four arrows hit the ship in the same place at almost the same time. The steady rain had no effect on the fiercely burning arrows. Instead of dying, the flames flared up.

A Mongol shout marked the beginning of an uproar, as the small boat moved to its next loaded target. Again, flaming arrows were released. Again, the arrows struck home. The archers headed for the third Mongol ship.

Meanwhile, a tremendous explosion from the first ship ripped open the sky, the white flash creating an instant of daylight. In that brief moment, the raiders saw the enemy looking at them as they neared the third Mongol ship. A rain of arrows were shot into the darkness, aimed at the small boat.

Commander Suenaga sat on thick carpets. He tried to count the explosions, but the sound of the rain drowned them out. Suenaga shouted, and a guard entered. "Bring in the other monban, I do not want them to have to stand in the rain because of me. Send one of them for a hibachi."

"Hai." The guard bowed, and departed. A moment later he returned with another guard. They pulled off their straw capes and hats and, at the leader's signal, made themselves comfortable.

"Did either of you hear the eruptions?" Suenaga asked.

"Hai," both men answered as one.

"Did either of you count them?"

The men shook their heads. One spoke. "There must have been more than a dozen."

"That is too many," said Suenaga. "But it was surely more than seven."

A third guard entered, carrying a still burning hibachi. Thick folds of cloth protected the man's hands from the hot handles. He nodded to the general. "My lord, they have returned. General Shiraishi says they will be here presently. They are changing into dry clothes."

"Ah, dōmo. You men may return to your quarters. One monban will do."

The first guard motioned the others out.

The commander beamed when Rokuro and Tasuke entered the room. "Are you to be congratulated?" Suenaga asked.

The newcomers pulled off their outer robes. They sat down before Suenaga, their smiles his answer.

"The gods were with us every second," said Rokuro. "Our only problem was trying to land that flimsy Mongol boat. It finally broke into pieces in the waves, but all are back safe."

"Ah," said the leader, "what you say is like the sweet sound of a beautiful woman playing on the koto."

Rokuro continued. "The weapon was effective." He pointed to Tasuke. "But his plan was brilliant. It is too bad that we do not have more weapons. We must have destroyed at least five ships. What do you think, Tasuke?"

"Hai, I agree," Tasuke said. "There were many explosions on one of the ships. Hai, it was a good sound. Listen to the rain." Tasuke looked up, spreading both hands in front of him. "Minoru told me the signs indicate that the storm will become a typhoon. It is indeed the wind of the gods, the kamikaze. It will destroy the Mongols the same way it did seven years ago, nē?"

"If that is so," said Suenaga, "then we, too, will have our troubles. Tomorrow we can move our bivouac, but where can the Mongols go for shelter?"

"To the bottom of the sea," said Rokuro. The three of them laughed.

"Gentlemen," said the commander, "I have preparations for tea here, or a stronger drink if you prefer. Today has been a long one for us all. But it has been a good one, nē?" He turned and set saucers before him.

"It is too much trouble to prepare tea." Rokuro grinned. "Saké is easier. Then I need to run for my futon."

"General Ito," said Suenaga, "I have some information that concerns you. Two weeks ago, when Prince Sayada died, I sent dispatches north by sail to Kamakura. At the same time I returned the effects of the madman Kozo to his daimyō at Ikoma and informed them of what had happened. Today, or rather tonight, a ship returned with messages from both places. I am proud to tell you, Tasuke Ito, that the seii-taishōgun, Lord Hakoi, has approved your appointment as general. When the war is over, there will be a place for you at the Samurai Dokoro."

"I am pleased this has happened to you, Tasuke," Rokuro added. "I am proud to be at your side."

"Dōmo arigatō, gentlemen," said the new general. "I can find no words. It is I who is most proud to be among soldiers such as you. Dōmo arigatō gozaimasu."

Suenaga tilted his head as he smiled at Tasuke. "I received a second message from Kumahatchi Murata, the powerful daimyō of Ikoma. Rokuro, pour the saké. I must read exactly what the man wrote." Suenaga unrolled a paper. For a moment he studied it. "Ah, here it is: 'You say that this samurai, Tasuke Ito, has lost his daimyōdom? Please tell him that he has served Dai-Yamato and myself well, and because of this, he will receive double koku—his own pay as my new general, and the money due the traitor Kozo. I hope he will take command of my samurai immediately. I look forward to meeting him when the Mongols are defeated.'"

Sakura Murata readied the court room. She arranged the new screens and placed the cushions the daimyō would use slightly in front of hers. She positioned the cushions for the visitors so that she would have an unhindered view of both oishasan. The ozen between the cushions was not bare, but held a dish of sweet cakes and four tea bowls. To one side of the hibachi, a kettle sent a slight trail of vapor toward the ceiling. The water was ready for tea, and Sakura moved it away from the hot coals.

Today Sakura was dressed in a bright-blue kimono. The gold obi which bound her waist sparkled in the morning light and matched the gold ribbon which loosely held back her hair. Her feet were bare, but only her toes were visible when she moved, the nails a golden gilt. She felt beautiful.

Hearing a scuff of feet in the corridor, Sakura knelt by her cushion, waiting.

"The oishasan are here," a voice said.

"Ask them to enter," said the princess. She looked up when she heard the sound of the shōji sliding. The young oishasan entered first and bowed. Sakura smiled, then pointed to the cushions across from her.

"Ohayō gozaimasu, please make yourselves comfortable. The daimyō will be here presently."

Both isha returned the greeting and moved to their cushions.

"Are your quarters satisfactory? Do you have any complaints?" Sakura asked Koan.

Koan smiled. "We are happy, my lady. Everything is satisfactory. Dōmo."

Sakura finally looked at Kenichi. She bowed her head just a little. "I know who he is"—she pointed to the old man—"I am sorry, but the daimyō did not tell me your name." She smiled.

Kenichi met Sakura's gaze and saw Aki's smile. Sakura's voice was Aki's voice. He shifted uneasily. This was Aki, yet it was not. If he were still sick, he would understand his confusion. But Kenichi knew he was well now. The dreams that frightened him had not returned since he had gotten rid of Aki's comb. Aki Taizo was dead. Hetomi, the runner, had told him so. Now all of them were dead. Even Hetomi and Tasuke. Mina was not strong enough to survive the hundreds of yatō that had been sent to attack them. Still, this woman before him was so much like Aki. Kenichi shifted again, felt his knees rub against the smooth ribbing of the tatami. Aki spoke once more.

"I am sorry I did not speak clearly," said Sakura. "I said the daimyō did not tell me your name."

"I am Kenichi Ueida, my lady." Kenichi bowed his head and stared at the tatami between them. He did not want to look at her any more. Where was the tōryō? The yatō—hai, this false Aki is also a yatō, Kenichi would not let himself forget this. Aki was dead, and the dead cannot live again. This woman was only a yatō bitch. He looked up. Aki was still smiling at him.

"The woman, Oumi, who serves you, has cared for me

for many years. She is also skilled in tending the sick. I miss her already." Sakura was making small talk now, she wanted the young oishasan to talk. Who was he? Why did he bother her so? She must know about him. Sakura would think of something to bait him into the conversation. Ah. She spoke to Koan. "Tell me, sire, where are you from? Where is it you call home?"

Koan thought before answering. "To be honest with you, my home is the forest. I spend most of the year living under the trees, since I am always traveling. I think I prefer it now."

Sakura nodded and smiled at the old man, then she turned to Kenichi. "And you?"

Kenichi did not answer. Instead, he turned to the shōji; the daimyō had arrived.

The others in the room bowed while Kumahatchi adjusted his pillows.

"Ohayō gozaimasu." The daimyō nodded to the isha, then to his daughter. "Hai, it is much nicer to welcome you here in the manor as guests, to talk as friends. I meant to be here earlier, but I received messages from the front that had to be attended to immediately. Our samurai are holding the Mongols with no effort, it is just a matter of time." The daimyō covered his hands with his sleeves. "It is hoped that all of your wants are being cared for."

"Hai," replied Koan.

"If not," continued Kumahatchi, "I will give the necessary orders. Do not hesitate to speak." The daimyō looked questioningly at his guests.

"Otōsan, I will look after them," Sakura said. "My own Oumi tends them, and her orders come from me. I am interested in the work of the oishasan. It is different, it will give me something to do. As it is, I am bored."

The daimyō chuckled. "If it pleases you, hai. I think

you will find their work drab but, as I say, I will leave it in your hands." Kumahatchi turned to the isha. "Well, Isha Tachibana, I trust you have carried out my wishes?"

Koan looked at Kenichi as if expecting him to speak in his place. He did not. Kenichi's eyes were fixed on the ozen. The tea bowls fascinated him.

Sitting slightly behind the daimyō, Sakura stared at the young man.

"Come," said the daimyō, "you should have no fear. We will talk as friends. Remember, I said you were my guests."

Finally Koan said, "My lord, I spoke to the gods for only a moment, and they would not answer my questions. I—" Koan hesitated. "They spoke mostly to him."

This time Kenichi's head was up. "It is true, my lord. The gods would not confer with Koan Tachibana. Instead, the goddess Kannon talked with me."

"Ah, sō." Kumahatchi put his hands on the tatami in front of him and leaned forward. "And what did she say?"

Was it fear that Kenichi detected in the daimyō's voice? The isha would have to be sure. "Kannon is the one who can stop this sickness that turns its victims gray, dries up their blood, and keeps them awake to suffer until they are dead." As he talked, Kenichi watched the reactions of the yatō tōryō. His words seemed to have the right effect on him. "I told Kannon who you were, as you commanded—"

"And?" broke in the daimyō.

"Please forgive me, my lord. The goddess laughed."

Kumahatchi sat back on his heels, there was no doubting the fear in his eyes.

"Kannon is displeased. She says she does not look with favor on Ikoma."

The daimyō's eyes widened expectantly. Kenichi continued. "She told me that those in the dōjō will die, and more will follow. Maybe even yourself—"

"Why is this?" interrupted the tōryō. "Tell me now."

Sakura gazed straight at the young oishasan. Kenichi noticed this, also that there was a hint of fear in her face.

"Kannon thinks you keep too many soldiers and too many prisoners. The goddess lives only for mercy. She says you do not know what mercy is. She wants the prisoners freed, and she does not want too many soldiers."

Kumahatchi held up his hand. "That is wrong. My soldiers are at war, there are fewer than fifty here now. And the prisoners were to be freed tomorrow. Kannon should not be angry. I do know what mercy is."

"My lord, I told her that you had but thirty soldiers. She said that was too many."

"I will cut my samurai to ten, the prisoners will be freed today. What then?"

Koan moved. He, too, was frightened. He felt that Kenichi was going too far. The daimyō was not stupid. Koan looked down at the tatami and prayed silently.

Kenichi answered the daimyō. "If what you say will be, then there will be no worry. Kannon demands very little more."

"Ah," said Kumahatchi. "She demands. Tell me, oishasan, what else does she demand?"

Both isha caught the first hint of anger.

"This," said Kenichi. "Wherever there is water, you will not use it. Every building where the bloodless death has struck must be burned. No one, except those we pick, must tend the sick. No harm must come to us or to the woman Oumi. She has heard us talk to the goddess."

"But we will die without water!" Sakura broke in, the fear unmistakable in her voice.

Koan looked up. He would take over from here. "My lord and lady," he began. "The water you will drink from now on will be hot tea. Very hot. The water you use to bathe must be very hot also. You can use water, but it must always be hot. Those that die must be burned with everything they owned. If these demands are followed precisely, the bloodless death will leave Ikoma."

"Is that all?" asked Kumahatchi.

"Hai, that is all," replied Kenichi. "No more than ten soldiers, free all prisoners, and stay away from cold water."

The daimyō relaxed. This was much less than he had expected. But what assurances did he have? "If I follow the wishes of Kannon, I expect that those in the dōjō will live. At least they should live."

"Iie, no, my lord," said Kenichi. "It is too late for that. They will die, and maybe others will follow. But you must do only as Kannon demands."

"Hai." The daimyō resigned himself. "We will see what happens." Kumahatchi turned to his daughter. "Tea, kudasai, I feel that I need it."

Sakura reached for the hot kettle. She poured tea into all four bowls. As she handed the first bowl to Kenichi, she noticed the picture on it. Sakura looked at Kenichi, then at the bowl. Heavens—it was he! Her hand shook, some of the tea spilled on the ozen. Her face turned ashen.

"What is it, Sakura-san? Are you ill?" asked her father.

"I will be all right, otōsan," said the princess. "If the oishasan will be kind enough to take me into the garden. I think I need a little air. Really, I am all right." Sakura stumbled toward the young isha.

Kenichi took Sakura's arm and led her outside. "My lady, I am sorry you do not feel well."

When they neared the pond, Sakura spoke. "Save your sorrow. There is nothing wrong with me. I brought you here so that we could talk."

"Hai."

"I know who you are, Kenichi Ueida." There was a half smile on her face.

Kenichi stared at the woman without expression.

"Who do you think I am?" he finally ventured.

"You are a samurai that pretends to be an oishasan."

Kenichi felt his body begin to sweat under his kimono. He turned his back to her so that she couldn't read any signs on his face.

"Why do you turn from me, samurai?"

"Because I no longer wish to look at you."

"Do you know that I, too, talk with the gods?"

"So?"

"The goddess Amaterasu told me you were coming." Sakura walked around Kenichi to face him. "You do not believe me, do you?"

"What else did she tell you?"

"Very little. But I know you to be a friend. I will speak to the daimyō tonight. He does not trust either of you. I will see to it that he does." She smiled at Kenichi. "Come, we should go back or they will come looking for us."

Sakura Murata was happy. Amaterasu had fulfilled her part of the bargain. As they walked back to the court room, the princess studied Kenichi, trying to picture him as a samurai with the proper haircut.

The leader of the small army that made its way north paid no attention to the villagers who cheered him as he passed. Tasuke Ito was tired of their ovations. But the soldiers who preceded General Tasuke's army continued to brag of the exploits of the leaders—Takezaki, Shiraishi, and Ito. And here, marching before the villagers, was one of these leaders: General Ito.

"Ito! Ito! Ito!" The villagers shouted the name in unison. At first, Tasuke had accepted the flowers that the women and children brought to him, but now he was tired of it and paid no attention. Whenever he could, he avoided the villages.

One village Tasuke bypassed was Mina. There, two of his unmarked rōnin left the column. At Takata, the last other Jugi Hoshi, Hetomi, said goodbye to General Ito.

Tasuke Ito was now marching alone with the Red Triangle soldiers. He would return to Ikoma with them and be their leader under the daimyō.

In two weeks, Hetomi Tajimi would lead other Jugi Hoshi samurai to join Tasuke at Ikoma. It was good the way things were working out. Together, they would produce the now hidden symbol, the monshō of honor. Hai, they were prepared to die wearing the large and vivid monshō of the Jugi Hoshi.

A voice nearby caught Tasuke's attention. Another horse had pulled alongside the general's. Tasuke looked at the messenger and saw the mark of the Red Triangle.

"General Ito," the man said, "I am from Ikoma. I have a dispatch for you from our daimyō. It is important that you read it before you reach the mura." The runner fumbled in his inrō, finally producing a folded paper. He handed it to the general.

The leader held up his hand, stopping the small army behind him. Slowly, he unfolded and read the paper. "There is no answer," Tasuke told the man, "except to say that those of us who want to will arrive after dark. Dōmo."

"Hai." The runner spurred his mount onward.

Tasuke Ito gazed in the direction the rider had taken, then he turned his horse around to face his men. He spoke so that all could hear. "You sixteen men are the remnants of a mighty army that left Ikoma more than three months ago to help defeat the barbarians in the south. I must say sayonara to some of you now. I have just received word from your daimyō. It is his wish that I tell you that a great sickness has eliminated the village of Ikoma. Only the mura remains. Even now, if you look to the north, you will see fires still burning there. This sickness that wastes Ikoma is the bloodless death. Only those of you who have families will be welcomed at the mura." Tasuke paused, then added, "I'm sorry, some of you no longer have families at all."

A murmur rose from the soldiers. Tasuke waited until they were quiet.

"I myself am alone. But I will go there to receive my koku, that which is due me. All of you men have fought under my command those last days after the kamikaze. We have fought well together. At Mina, two samurai who had been with me for years left to seek employment there. At Takata, another, the runner Hetomi Tajimi, deserted me. I am the last among you who does not wear the Red Triangle. I go to Ikoma for one reason only. And I will not be there long."

"General," a soldier called to him. Tasuke nodded. "Is it true that you will take a post at the Samurai Dokoro?"

"I do not know," replied the general. "We are but cherry blossoms blown before the wind." He held up his hand to forestall any other questions. "Those of you who choose to continue to Ikoma, let us go." Tasuke pulled on the reins to turn his horse, then stopped when the nōmin Hitari rode to him.

"My lord," said Hitari, "there is nothing for me at

Ikoma, I have no family. But your aide is gone, and I will go where you go."

Tasuke looked at the man without smiling. He lowered his voice so that only Hitari could hear. "I said I would not be at Ikoma long. I go there only to die. Do you still wish to follow me?" The general did not wait for the nōmin's answer, he waved his army forward.

For a moment Hitari stayed behind, considering his general's words, but finally he joined the end of the column. Only two had turned their horses to the south.

It was dark by the time the army approached the gates of the mura. The village was truly gone. Where once there were buildings, blackened squares of ash and rubble waited to be cleared. Only stacks of new-cut lumber proved that the village of Ikoma had not been completely abandoned.

Tasuke signaled his followers. The massive gates of the mura swung open. The army marched in and the portals closed behind them. When Tasuke saw the manor and the Red Triangle pennant, he felt a twinge of pain and anger.

Two samurai on the path before Tasuke bowed. One of them spoke. "Sire, the daimyō sends his greetings. He is aware that you are tired. So he will not bother you tonight. This building to your right will be your quarters. It has been made ready for you. He hopes you will be comfortable." The samurai bowed again to the general. "You others," the samurai continued, "can find shelter in the kiln area. We are most happy to welcome you home."

Tasuke nodded to the man, then dismounted. He held the reins of his horse and looked helplessly about. Hitari bowed before the general. "May I serve you?" the nōmin asked. "I will take care of your things. I know my way around here very well."

"Dōmo arigatō," replied the general. "After you put

up the animal, bring me my saddlebags and the other things. I will want to talk with you."

"Hai."

When he entered the guesthouse, Tasuke found the oil lamps already lit. A drawn hot bath, set in the center of the room, looked inviting.

"Tadaima!" No one answered Tasuke's call. He was alone in the building. He stripped, then climbed into the vat. It was good. He closed his eyes and enjoyed the luxury. With a sponge, he squeezed hot water on his head. Above the sound of the water, he heard the shōji slide. He paid no attention. It would be Hitari with his things. But there was more than one set of footsteps. Strange, the visitors had not removed their zōri. Tasuke wiped the water from his eyes, then turned.

Two bowmen, with weapons taut, stood at his back, pointing the lethal tips of the arrows straight at Tasuke. The general had not seen these samurai before.

"Iie, General Ito," one of the bowmen snarled. "You will not sleep here tonight. There is a pallet waiting for you at the kiln."

A third soldier entered. He passed the archers, at the same time drawing his kogatana. He pressed the sword's point to the nape of Tasuke's neck. "Now stand up!" he commanded. "Step very calmly from the tub."

Tasuke did as he was told. The bowmen were too far from him and the blade at his neck made no signs of leaving. One of the guards lowered his bow. The other held its position. The archer's face was sober, deadly-looking. Just one movement and it would be over.

The other archer joined the swordsman behind Tasuke. The general's arms were grabbed, pulled back, and tied behind him. Tasuke felt his feet being hobbled with leather bands. Only then was the second bow lowered. The kogatana still jabbed at his neck.

"You will walk now," said the swordsman. "We three will accompany you to the kilns." The man laughed. "Ah, you are new here, nē? Don't worry, the kogatana will show you the way."

Kumahatchi Murata held the special weighted sword over his head. His eyes stared straight ahead at no enemy. He practiced the okesa, the robe-of-the-priest swing which produced a cut from the shoulder down across the body. Kumahatchi would combine this, one of the simplest swings to execute, with the more difficult suritsuke, a shallow cut made horizontally below the chest. The two movements must be performed as one, in the space of an instant. If Kumahatchi missed with the first, he would not with the second.

The daimyō was practicing in the garden, wearing only a loincloth. When Kumahatchi moved, he made no sound. He had mastered the art of not expelling his breath with each strenuous effort. Sanda, his sensei, had taught him this, and it was different from the method taught by the other teachers of kendō. Sanda maintained that, though the sudden evacuation of air from the lungs added to the force of the blow, there were two drawbacks: first, it robbed the body of a reserve of oxygen necessary for the next quick effort; and second, it warned the opponent of the start of a swing.

In actual encounters, Kumahatchi found that Sanda was correct. Hai, controlling his breath and combining two different swings into one would make him invincible.

Kumahatchi tried the swing again. This time, he

started the thrust with the suritsuke, and finished with the okesa. But he was not fast enough, he lost all the force of the blow. He tried it again. Ah, good.

"My lord!" someone called.

The daimyō lowered his sword and turned. "Ah, Isha Kenichi." Kumahatchi smiled. "Ohayō gozaimasu. Have I been practicing too long? But I have been enjoying my workout." Kumahatchi reached for a towel and rubbed his face with it. Then he continued. "You are a young man. You should train with the sword. I have made many swordsmen. If you wish, I would be happy to work with you. Or—or do you already know the sword?"

"Hai," Kenichi answered. "I have devoted some study to it."

"Ah," the daimyō returned. "I was sure you had. I could tell by the way you move. And you know the Bushidō, nē?"

"Hai, I am a samurai. Now I practice the arts of the isha."

As the daimyō rubbed his body with a towel, he looked at the young man. Finally he spoke. "This is good news to me, important news. Come, we will talk more while I bathe. And we will drink some of that hot tea the gods prescribed."

Kenichi followed the daimyō into the manor. A steaming vat of water had already been prepared. The isha sat on the tatami and waited while Kumahatchi disrobed and climbed into the bath.

"Sakura!" The daimyō suddenly called. "Tea, here in my room." Through the thin walls came Sakura's "Hai."

Kumahatchi slid forward until just his head protruded from the water. He closed his eyes and enjoyed the sensation of the hot water melting into his body.

Kenichi still waited, his arms folded across his chest.

His hands, in tight fists, were pressed against his body. Kenichi stared at the head before him. Kenichi knew that in time it would all work out according to his plan. Hadn't he already stripped this daimyō of most of his samurai? He, Kenichi, had cut their number to ten, and the bloodless death had taken some of these. He had no idea how many samurai had returned from the war. Since the bloodless death had abated, the isha were kept confined to their quarters and the manor. Today Kenichi would ask questions.

The head in the tub opened its eyes and began to speak. "The reason I have asked you here today, Isha Kenichi, is that I have come to respect you and trust you these past few weeks. A little more than a week ago, what is left of my samurai returned from Kyūshū. I tried to keep this information from you. But I remember now that it is the gods I must deal with—"

The sound of the shōji opening interrupted Kumahatchi. Sakura entered and pushed an ozen across the tatami. "Ohayō gozaimasu, Kenichi. I will stay and prepare tea for you, nē?"

Sakura's father replied, "Hai, but this time you shall only listen. What we are discussing now is most important."

"Hai, otōsan." Sakura smiled, then poured the tea. The tea bowls were plain.

"As I was saying," Kumahatchi continued, "we now have twenty-five samurai. That is very far from the fifteen hundred I used to feed here." He reached from the tub for his tea bowl. He sipped. "I am beginning to forget what a cool drink of water tastes like," Kumahatchi said, setting the bowl down.

"My lord," said the isha, "it is no longer necessary to

avoid the water. It has rained a great deal these past few days, and now there is ample for both the gods and us." Kenichi hesitated, then added, "If you are thinking of adding more soldiers to the mura, I would advise against it. It is true the bloodless death is no longer with us and until now you have followed the rules and the plague has disappeared. But you are the daimyō and you will do what you will. Koan's and my job here is at an end. Are we going to be allowed to leave?"

Sakura looked up at this question. Her father caught the look of concern in her eyes. "You sound as though you cannot get away fast enough. Iie, I will not hold you here against your will. But before you make up your mind, weigh carefully what I have to say to you." Kumahatchi turned to Sakura. "My towels and kimono, kudasai."

Sakura put a towel on the tatami and held another for him as he stepped from the vat. After he was dry, and clothed with the kimono, he continued. "Kenichi Ueida, we do not want you to leave—neither you nor Tachibana your friend. I offer you this to keep you here at Ikoma with us: From now on, you will be the gokarō of Ikoma. The fact that you are bushi has confirmed it. Tell me, Kenichi Ueida, what have you to say?"

Both the daimyō and the princess looked smilingly at the isha and waited for his reply.

Kenichi fumbled with his bowl. He had not been prepared for this. What if he were the gokarō? Would it make his task easier? Kenichi looked at Sakura and knew the answer. He must do as he planned. It would be easier to follow the singing arrow into the mura with the war drums behind him. He had grown to love Sakura, and this love would not let him become an assassin. "I—" Kenichi began, "I—Koan Tachibana cannot stay in any one place.

We have been here well over a month, and this is not his way of life, he grows older too fast because of it. I, on the other hand, am deeply indebted to him."

The smile faded from Sakura's face.

Kenichi continued. "He has brought me back to life and he has given me his secrets. I am sorry, but I must leave with him." Kenichi would not look at Sakura now. He knew her eyes would be filled with tears.

"Surely," said Kumahatchi, "you will reconsider. Ikoma is nothing now, but already the village is beginning to rise again. The fields are yellow with heavy crops. Remember, Kenichi Ueida, as gokarō of Ikoma you will be a rich man. It will all be yours after I am gone. It will be Sakura's and yours."

"I thank you, my lord." Kenichi spoke quietly. "I have done what was needed here." Kenichi looked into Sakura's eyes. "I cannot do more. Until this moment I did not realize that you did not have a gokarō. Who leads your soldiers? Haven't your leaders returned from war?"

"Iie, they did not," answered the daimyō. "And because of that, I have another problem. Sakura, I want you to leave us alone. What I want to say to Kenichi is not for your ears."

"Hai, otōsan, but call me when you are finished, please."

"I will," he promised. Sakura bowed to each of them, then departed. Kenichi saw her put a handkerchief to her eyes.

Kumahatchi waited until he heard Sakura's footsteps go down the hall, then he spoke. "My gokarō led my troops to war and died there. But he did not die at the hands of the Mongols. I did not learn the exact details of his death until my samurai returned. Among those who returned was the nōmin Hitari. He is a good man who has fought alongside me. He was present at my gokarō's killing. The man who murdered my general was a leader of samurai with no monshō. Hitari watched this man carve the monshō of my enemy on my gokarō's stomach before he killed him. This murderer, the leader of my enemy, became famous because of the war. His talents would have been sought by many daimyōs, but luckily, I hired him first. He is here now. He will not work for me, though. Instead, he will die." Kumahatchi rose to his feet. "Wait, I have something to show you," he said. He held up his hand as he left the room. When he returned, he carried a small lacquered box. Setting it down, he drew a paper from it.

"I want you to know this, Kenichi Ueida. I still need your help. Ikoma has enemies—not the yatō, they do not bother us, but another, the clan that called Ikoma their home for many years. For a long time, they harassed and killed my samurai until I defeated them. Since then, I have been eliminating them one by one. I keep this list of the names of those few I have not yet accounted for. I know them to be at Mina, a town far to the south. Now, this is why I need your help. When my samurai passed Mina on their way from war, their leader sent two of his samurai there. Hitari listened while this general talked to them. They plan to storm these walls. I know not when, but it will be soon. I need someone to help me prepare Ikoma for war. I hoped that you would do it with the help of the gods."

Kenichi's head spun. The revelations were almost too much for his mind to grasp. Kenichi was sure of only one thing: he would accept Kumahatchi's offer. He would be Ikoma's gokarō.

"My lord," Kenichi said. "I will be your gokarō. But first grant me this: allow Isha Koan to leave Ikoma. Also, the woman Oumi, whom he has become attached to."

"Done!" complied the daimyō. "Hai, that Oumi is a

good-looking woman. I'll do even better than you ask. They will not leave poor." Kumahatchi was pleased. He had achieved what he wanted most. With the gods on his side, he would have no need of a large army.

"My lord," said Kenichi. "You were going to show me that paper." He reached for it, but the daimyō returned it to the box.

"It is not important, the names on it will all be crossed off soon."

"The leader of the rōnin, this general, who is he?" asked the new gokarō.

"He is General Tasuke Ito of the house of Fugita. He has come here to slay me. Thanks to Hitari, we can send this Jugi Hoshi to my slaughter T. As my new gokarō, Kenichi Ueida, I will let his execution be your first amusement, nē?"

Aki whipped the reins up and down once more. The old horse pulling the wagon eyed the green clump of grass to one side of the road and edged his way toward it. The quick motion of the reins distracted the animal and brought him back to the center of the road.

"Iie!" shouted the driver. "You will stop soon enough. For now, we want you to keep going."

Somiko sat at Aki's side. "It seems the animal understands what you say. Even the goat in back is quiet since you scolded her."

The wagon the women rode in was small. Its two large, solid wheels thumped from every pebble or rut, but the wagon was sturdy. It was built for rougher roads than this. The seat the women sat on was well padded, so that the occasional bounce of the wagon did not bother them. The trussed goat in the back of the wagon was not so fortunate.

"We have done well today," Aki said. "And it is still early. We will reach Ikoma before dark. I have a good friend there in the mura. She will—" Aki cut herself off. Iie, she could not be sure that Sakura was even alive any more.

"You were saying about your friend?" asked Somiko.

"Oh, Somiko, I don't know. Much has happened since I was at Ikoma. In Shinjo they said a plague had all but wiped out the village. I am not sure what we will find."

"Don't worry about it," returned the older woman. "Hetomi has not failed us yet. He is there now, and everything will be fine."

"I know," said Aki. "If I worry, it is because I feel that you should be resting on a tatami, not being jolted on a wagon."

"It is not that bad, Aki-san. I am enjoying the trip. We have been sitting in Takata too long; this is nicer. My Hetomi has come back to me. Soon our baby will arrive. I am very happy, Aki. I feel as though we are very wealthy."

The horse moved to one side, and again Aki whipped the reins. A wagon was approaching from the north. The couple who drove it leaned together and were close in conversation. They seemed to take no notice of the wagon coming from the south. As the wagons passed each other, Aki and Somiko waved to the other couple. The old man nodded at the two women, then resumed his smiling conversation with his female companion.

"See," said Somiko, "they, too, are happy. Did you notice? She still wears the white headpiece. They are newly married. That man, I'm sure I know him from somewhere. Oh, I guess it would be cruel to stop them. He has no time to talk to us." Somiko giggled.

Another rider drew toward them from the north.

"Ah, it is my Hetomi," Somiko said to Aki.

"I am sorry," Hetomi said when he stopped at the wagon. "We must camp again tonight. The village of Ikoma has been destroyed by fire. They are just starting to rebuild. I doubt that even fifty people live there now. The gates of the mura are closed, no one is allowed in. I did not try to enter just yet. Tonight we will camp on the hill."

"What of the oishasan?" asked Aki. "Have they been there?"

"Hai, I inquired of them," Hetomi answered. "They were there during the sickness. No one has seen them since." He saw the disappointment on Aki's face, then added: "Only in the mura would they know for sure of the isha. Tonight I will go in. If they are there, I will find them." Hetomi smiled reassuringly at Somiko. "Daijōbu, they know me as friendly. Remember, General Tasuke is there. I am supposed to be his aide. The gate will be opened for me."

Near Ikoma, the wagon pulled off the road and circled a small hill as it climbed. Finally they reached their campsite. Pines enclosed the small clearing just below the hilltop.

Aki caught sight of a shika watching them as the women dismounted from the wagon. "This camp is beautiful and well chosen," Aki said to Somiko.

"You have been here before," returned the older woman. "Perhaps you do not recognize the place because the season has changed the colors. Listen to the sound of the stream. Good, nē?"

Night enveloped the clearing. Aki, in a lean-to of her own, tried to sleep. Ikoma was less than an hour away. Amaterasu, her goddess, had not yet let her down. Aki knew that Jujiro was near, and she felt that she would see him soon, but Aki could not sleep. Would tomorrow ever come? Only sleep would speed up the hours. She closed her eyes and tried to relax.

When Hetomi Tajimi walked to the gates of the mura, he did not try to conceal himself. Now and then, he scuffed his zōri. He knew that the monban on the other side of the door would hear him. "Gomen kudasai," Hetomi called into the gate.

"Who is it?"

"I am Hetomi Tajimi, the runner and aide for General Ito. He expects me."

After a moment, the guard called back. "You will have to wait. I will tell him you are here."

Ten minutes later, Hetomi saw a light from a torch reflecting on the posts of the mura's walls. The small door within the gate opened.

"Come in," called the monban.

Hetomi smiled at the guard as he stepped through the doorway. The guard closed and latched the door behind the runner.

"You will stand. You will not move," the monban commanded.

Hetomi turned to face four bowmen. At that instant, he felt the pressure of a kogatana's point bite into his back.

"We have been waiting for you," said the swordsman. "Preparations have already been made for you. General Ito awaits your company. Go!"

Tasuke Ito strained his eyes in the wavering torchlight, as he tried to make out the figures entering the cell block. In the dim light, the newcomers were only forms. But Tasuke could see that the new prisoner was bound and hobbled as he himself had been over a week before. The light of the torch came closer. Tasuke Ito pulled forward on the rope that held his neck, following the progress of the guards.

"Put him in the cell across from Ito. It should make them both feel good," said the leader of the guards, laughing.

Tasuke watched as the prisoner was tied, and realized why he himself was so helpless to escape. A long rope tied to one corner of the cell made one loop around the prisoner's neck. The free end of the rope was tied to the next corner. A second line bound the loop behind the neck, then down to tie the prisoner's hands behind him. This, in turn, was fixed to his hobbled feet. Just barely enough slack was left in the first rope to allow the prisoner to sit. Before the final adjustments of the ropes were made, the prisoner was knocked unconscious by a blow to the head. The door to the cell was closed and the guards left the building.

In the darkness, Tasuke listened intently for any movement or signs of life from the other prisoner. Only the soft scurry of a rat came to him. He drifted back into his half sleep.

"Tasuke! Kimi!"

"Hai." Tasuke opened his eyes. It was morning. He focused his eyes on the prisoner across from him.

Tasuke's heart sank when he realized that the other prisoner was Hetomi.

"Don't talk so loud; the monban will hear. What has happened?"

"Nothing, kimi, except I walked into this like a fool. I should have waited for the others. Are you all right?"

"Hai, as well as can be expected," answered Tasuke. "At least, my head no longer hurts." He smiled weakly at the runner. "I am sorry, Hetomi, were you wounded?"

"Iie, the guards were kind to me, they did not stick me. There was no way for me to resist, so I just went along."

Tasuke laughed. "Kimi, you have a new experience waiting for you. Wait until they feed you. To the right of your head—that shelf there—from it, somehow, with no hands, you must feed yourself from the bowl. You must learn to fight off the rats with your nose. Twice, I have been bitten. But if you learn to spill some on the floor for them, you can eat."

"How did you end up in here?" asked the runner.

"Much the same as you," answered the general. "At least, they had the graciousness to allow me a bath first. It was their gratitude for bringing their soldiers home."

"Do we have any help here?"

Tasuke did not answer right away. "I am counting on one of them," he said. "It is the thrower, Hitari. But there is only a slight chance. I know none of our guards. Because Hitari is a nōmin, one day I am sure he will take his turn as our monban."

"There is one more possibility," Hetomi said. "The woman Aki is near. She says she knows that Prince Jujiro is here. Could it be?"

"Hmm, I doubt it," returned the other. "If it were so, I don't think he could help. He would be in here with us. What makes her think that he might be here?"

"The women saw him with an isha in Takata. They were told by the isha that the two were on their way here."

"She talked to Jujiro?"

"Iie, she did not realize it was he," replied the runner. "Now she says she is sure of it."

"It could be," said Tasuke. "Jujiro was with an isha. But if Jujiro came here, he is already dead. All we can do is wait—either for help or for death."

On the hilltop near Ikoma, two women talked. Both of them had been avoiding the subject of Hetomi, and it was Aki who finally brought up the subject. "Two days is no time at all. I am sure that he will return by tonight. If he does not, I have a plan, I have been thinking of it all day. Somiko, don't say anything until you hear all of what I have to say. I know of two ways that I could get into the mura—"

"Impossible!" broke in Somiko. "I will not allow it. Iie, forget about it."

"If you will not listen," said Aki, "then I must show you something." She drew a small packet from her sleeve. "This is a pass that will allow me to enter the mura as a friend of the Red Triangle. It bears the marks of the tōryō and his princess. I cannot disturb the string that ties it, but believe me, it is what I say it is."

"Granted that the pass gets you in, but what then? Do you dare ask questions about a missing Jugi Hoshi? It is too much of a risk, Aki. It is better to stay here until Hetomi returns. I have waited for him before, and he returned. I don't care how many days pass, I will wait here as he asked. He is still alive. I would know if it were otherwise."

"Somiko-san, I love you. To see you distressed hurts me also. You are right, to enter the gates would be a dangerous mistake. But I have another plan that would involve no risk at all."

"Are you sure? What is your plan?"

"I will tell you, and you think about it. If you do not agree, then I will forget about it."

"Tell me," said Somiko.

Aki smiled, she felt her friend would agree. "There is a way into the mura known only to me, through a passage hidden and covered and impossible to detect. Twice, I have left the mura in secret this way. Now listen. This path leads to a person who was a great friend to me at one time. I am sure she will help us in any way she can. She will tell me what we must know."

"But what if someone else should see you?"

"It is impossible. I will wait in the hiding place until I see my friend. She always visits the garden. What do you think?"

"How long will you be gone?"

"Just as long as it takes," replied Aki. "The only problem is that I might have to wait all day. But I promise you I will take no chances."

Somiko thought about it. Then: "Hai, I agree. You must try it. But only on one condition."

"Hai?"

"You must wear Hetomi's dark clothes and you must take a weapon. Then I will let you go."

"I have my small knife," said Aki. "And to please you, I will wear Hetomi's clothes."

K*enichi* went to see Kumahatchi to continue their conversation. Now that the isha was safe, Kenichi would follow his plan.

"This general, General Ito, where is he now?" asked Kenichi.

"He is quite secure in our cell block. We can deal with him any time, and incidentally, we also have his aide. Hitari, the nōmin, has just told me this. Now the two Jugi Hoshi can die together."

His aide? thought Kenichi. Who was Tasuke's aide? "The general's aide, do you have his name on your list?"

"Iie," said Kumahatchi. "But he is Jugi Hoshi. The

weapons he wore—I have them here—are all marked with the crossed star. Sakura!" he shouted. "Bring the swords that rest in the hall."

"Hai," Sakura called back. In a moment, she was in the room.

"Take a look," pointed the daimyō, "at the hilts of the kogatana and of the long sword. See, they bear the monshō of the Jugi Hoshi. Here, I make you a present of them. You have no swords, and these are quite exceptional. I know of only three other sets like them." He placed the weapons in Kenichi's hands, and continued talking. "I told you of my sensei, Sanda. His swords were the match of these." Kumahatchi looked at Sakura, then added, "Someday, my princess, I must tell you of him. Remind me."

"You have always said that, otōsan," said the daimyō's daughter. "You have referred to Sanda many times. Tell me now."

"First things first, Sakura-san. Right now I have something else I wish to tell you. Kenichi has agreed to become our gokarō. He did not leave with Tachibana. And he is a samurai."

"I have always known he was," Sakura stated. She smiled at Kenichi. "I always sensed that he was someone important. How did you persuade him?"

"I did not have to," replied the daimyō. "And I suppose I am revealing something I shouldn't when I say that I think you are the true reason for his acceptance." Kumahatchi looked at the new gokarō, then added, "Nē?"

Kenichi's face reddened. "My intentions, my daimyō, are ever honorable."

"Well said," returned Kumahatchi with a laugh. He noticed that both young people looked embarrassed, and so he changed the subject. "Kimi, now that you have the proper swords, you should know about them. Both of these blades are marked with the kanji Masamune. As I said, I know of only four sets of Masamune swords in existence, and three of them are here. Masamune was the greatest swordsmith that ever lived. It is told that even the lightest touch of Masamune's blades would cleave a thing into two. This set I have given you is one of Masamune's. My sensei, Sanda, also had a set. The nōmin Hitari has it now, the swords help him feel important. In time, I will take them from him." Kumahatchi laughed. "Another set of Masamune swords is carried by the sensei Keisuke Shishido. Remind me to speak of him later. The fourth set is the one I carry. It is fitting that the best swords in all Yamato should rest each night at Ikoma. I expect the only set that is not here will become our prize very soon."

"What of the sensei Keisuke Shishido?" asked the gokarō.

"Ah yes, Keisuke. He is our enemy. He is the one I expect to be knocking at our gates soon, bringing his Masamune swords to us. Throughout Yamato there was always the argument as to which sensei, Keisuke or Sanda, was the greatest swordsman. Have you heard of either, Kenichi?"

"Only Keisuke, my lord. I have heard the name Sanda mentioned rarely."

"That is because Sanda no longer lives. He died within these walls. It is ironic that our greatest swordsman was killed with a stone. Now Hitari carries his swords. He was the one who killed Sanda."

"It sounds as though you had no love for your sensei," said Kenichi.

"On the contrary," returned the daimyō. "He was my closest friend. I would have died for him. Had I reached his side in time, Sanda would be my gokarō now. When I saw him last, he was fighting seven samurai at one time and had defeated them all. But he would wear no helmet, it maddened his opponents to see a naked neck they could not touch with their blades. Sanda was my sensei, and now I look forward to matching my sword with Keisuke, for the sake of his memory. When I defeat Keisuke, it will settle once and for all the old argument."

"Ah, that will never happen," said the gokarō. "Keisuke Shishido is dead. He died at the hands of robbers."

"What! When? How do you know?" asked the startled daimyō.

"Far to the south, near a small mura. The isha Koan and myself tried to keep him alive. He was ambushed by a bowman just before the war."

"You say you were there?"

"Hai," answered Kenichi. "We traveled all over in those days. Many times we were summoned when an isha was needed."

"Ah, the mura was Mina, nē? By chance, do you know how many soldiers they feed there?"

"It was night when we worked on the sensei. He died in the morning. We left the mura that day."

Kumahatchi reached into his lacquered box. He crossed another name off his list. "Here, you wanted to see this." He handed the paper to the gokarō. "See, already you have taken care of one of them for us."

Kenichi looked at the paper. Only one name remained—his own.

"Enough of this," Sakura said. "We talk only of the dead. Today is not the day for it. Today we should celebrate, it is a happy day." She put her hand on her father's shoulder. "Please, otōsan?"

"Hai," Kumahatchi agreed. "The three of us will celebrate together."

But Kenichi wanted only to get to the kilns and make sure that Tasuke and Hetomi were all right. Together, the three Jugi Hoshi would work out what needed to be done. "I have a few things that I must tend to," said the gokarō.

"They will have to wait," said Sakura. "Instead, you will come with me. I will be your kamiyui. I know exactly how your hair must be cut and fixed. Come now." She pulled on his arm.

"Go ahead," said the daimyō. "You may as well give up. I will wait here to witness your transformation." Kumahatchi clapped his hands, a servant entered.

"Bring saké, sweet cakes, and tea," the daimyō told the servant. "Bring the best of everything."

Gokarō Kenichi Ueida sat back on his heels as Sakura pulled his long hair forward over his face. She divided his hair crossways on the top of his head, twisting the forward part in ropes, then cutting them off. She spiraled the hair in back and on the sides into a bun, which she tied with string. That finished, Sakura prepared to shave the forward part of the gokarō's head.

"Ah, Kenichi-san, this is easy. I can see how it was cut and shaved before you let it grow. I have just to follow where the hair was shorter. Hai, the work of the kamiyui is easy."

"Sakura, it does not matter how my hair is fixed. We could do this some other time. There are things that I must do, and there are things that I must say to you."

"I am here and I am listening," said the woman. "Your hair will not take much longer."

"To begin with," Kenichi said, "I have sent Isha Koan away. He was not happy. I feel that I have let him down."

"It was not necessary to send him away," Sakura said. "No harm would have come to him here."

"But I felt I had broken a promise to him," returned the gokarō.

"You worry for nothing, Kenichi. He is happy. I heard that the holy man of Ikoma performed the marriage ceremony for him and Oumi. I don't think that he needs or wants you with him now."

The gokarō smiled. "I suppose you are right. It is love that hides everything sad. Hai, he will not miss me."

"You are wanted here, Kenichi-san. You know that, nē? Hold still, I am almost finished. I do not want to cut you."

"Tell me, Sakura, why must you love me?"

"I will tell you," Sakura answered. "You were sent to me by the gods. Do not smile, it is true. I asked for you and they did as I asked."

"It was only a coincidence," said Kenichi.

"Iie, it was not a coincidence. Before you came, I knew the precise day you would arrive and exactly how you would look. I knew this hairline on your head. Iie, it cannot be a coincidence. Ah, I am finished now. Indeed, I have fixed your hair perfectly. Oh, Kenichi-san, I do love you." She put her arms on his shoulders, and he drew her to him and kissed her.

"Sakura, I have tried to keep away from you, I did not seek your love—"

"It is the Kamiwaza, Kenichi-san, the act of the gods. You had no choice. Hai, it was meant to be." Sakura pulled away. "I must not hang on to you so, or you will tire of me quickly and go to other women. I have a kimono for you. I had the servants make it as it should be. When you are dressed and wear your swords, you will be a samurai again. I already know how you will look."

Kenichi turned his head as he rubbed the back of his neck.

"It is the cut hairs, Kenichi-san. I will see to your bath in my apartment. We must hurry, though; the daimyō is waiting for us. I will wear my blue kimono with the gold obi. My servant will ready your clothes—"

"Sakura-san," Kenichi interrupted, "you are going too fast. I have been trying to tell you something."

"What is it?"

"I will not stay in Ikoma long. I will be here only a short time longer—"

"You are not serious?" Sakura's face clouded. The woman waited for Kenichi to speak again. When he did not, she added, "But you are needed here, and you have no one else. If you must leave, then I will leave with you. There is some trouble, isn't there? What is it?"

"I cannot tell you. But there are things that I must do. If you love me now, I am sure the gods will help you understand after I am gone."

There were tears in Sakura's eyes. "That would be impossible," she said. "Hai, even for the gods, it would be impossible. They could not stop my love. I will leave with you, Kenichi-san." Sakura knelt before him.

"Iie, I will only hurt you, Sakura. I cannot love you."

Sakura looked into his eyes and shook her head. "Iie, that is a lie. I know that cannot be the truth. You do love me. The daimyō thought he was the first to know two weeks ago, but I told him that you loved me the first day that you and Koan came. I told my father that the gods had sent you to me." Sakura glared at Kenichi, then continued. "You tell us that you talk to the gods, but I know you do not. You do not know how to talk to them. I do, and I have done it. And, Kenichi-san, they have listened to me. Isn't it true, Kenichi, that you have never talked to them?"

"You are guessing!" Kenichi spat out.

"Iie, I do not guess," Sakura returned. "I do not have to guess. Oumi was my friend, she told me everything. My father did not trust you, but he did after I talked to him. I did not betray you because I love you. Now can you say that I talk too much?" Sakura rose and ran out into the hall.

Seconds later, a knock.

"Hai!" Kenichi barked.

"My lord, the water in your bath is hot. The daimyō is waiting."

"Hai." Kenichi followed the servant. Minutes later, he was in the vat. He motioned the woman to open the outside shōji. He looked out into the garden of his boyhood. It had not changed. For a few moments, Kenichi was in the old manor. Instead of the silence that came to him now, he tried to imagine the bustle of the caravan preparing to depart.

The servant's voice brought him back to reality. "My lord, your clothes and your swords are here. If there is nothing more I can do for you, I will go to the princess, she will need my help."

Kenichi waved her out, then closed his eyes again. This time he thought of the present. All day he had been occupied in the manor. How long must he be entertained by the daimyō? Tasuke and Hetomi needed him now. Hai, Kenichi made up his mind. He would see to his friends first. The daimyō could wait.

Through the thin wall behind him, Kenichi heard Sakura dismiss the servant. Minutes later he could hear the faint whispers of two women. Who could be with her? He dismissed the thought from his mind, concentrating on what he must say to Sakura before he left.

After Sakura left Kenichi, she ran back to her room to cry in private. Soon she became aware of a strange noise. The sound outside her room became insistent. She turned to the open shōji, but saw no one. She heard the noise again. She rose and entered the garden, walking to the pond and looking about her. The shōji to the bath was open. It must have been Kenichi who made the noise, but if he wanted her, he would have to call her. Sakura had nothing to say to him right now.

Sakura sat on the pond's edge and smiled as the koi swam toward her. The sound came again. Iie, it did not come from Kenichi. Sakura looked at the little mountain, then walked to it and listened.

"It is Aki," a voice said quietly. "Are you alone?"

"Hai," the princess said. "But wait, I will dismiss the servants. In a minute, I will come back for you."

Sakura looked toward the bath. She could see only Kenichi's elbow. His view could not take in this end of the garden. It would be no problem getting her friend to her room.

"We must whisper," Sakura said to Aki when they were in the building. Sakura pointed to the other room. "There is someone nearby."

"I am glad that you finally heard me," said Aki. "I was getting worried."

The friends hugged each other.

"It is good to see you again, Aki-san. Much has happened since you left. Why are you wearing such strange clothes?"

"So that I could not be seen in the darkness," Aki whispered.

"But in the meantime you will give yourself away by tripping on the pants. Oh, Aki-san, I have much to tell you." Sakura hesitated. "What is the reason for your visit?"

"Hai," said her friend. "I am looking for my man, I know he is here."

"It is impossible—" Then Sakura remembered the prisoners in the cell block. "Oh, Aki-san, I am so sorry. Hai, he is here. He is a prisoner, and I have just learned he was joined by his aide, Heromi."

"Hetomi," corrected Aki. There was fear on her face.

"Hai, Hetomi. Do not worry, Aki-san. Maybe I can help, I will think of something. The daimyō is my father. He will do as I say in almost everything. Then there is the gokarō, but he will marry me soon. Tell me, Aki-san, is your man—is he stubborn?"

"Iie, Sakura-san. His name is Jujiro. He is far from being stubborn. He is more like a little boy who must always play with his own swords, only in that way is he stubborn."

"Ah, then he is different from my Kenichi. He had no swords until they were forced on him. Oh, he is beautiful." Sakura pointed. "It is he who bathes in the next room. I wish that you could meet him. Hmm, maybe we can arrange it."

"Iie, Sakura. I could not take the chance. I promised my friend, Hetomi's woman, who cares for me, that I would take no risks. Besides, in these clothes—never. It was she who insisted that I wear these clothes. She knew that I would never let myself be seen wearing them. Hai, Somiko is very smart."

Sakura smiled, then her face became serious again. "Aki-san," she whispered, "I have made up my mind. I will talk to the gokarō, my Kenichi, about your friends. I cannot promise anything, but their treatment will be more lenient, Kenichi will see to that. But first there is something that I must know. I have heard rumors that your clan plans to storm these walls soon. You must understand, Aki-san, I am not asking you for secrets. I ask only for your honesty as my friend. If your man and Hetomi are set free and then these walls are stormed, I would be a traitor. This is one possibility. The other is—if the prisoners are well treated, then released much later, unharmed, and the walls are not stormed, then all would be taken care of. You must make the decision. I will speak to the daimyō and the gokarō. Because we are friends."

Aki did not reply right away. Her eyes watered, then: "Sakura-san, I would owe you much if you would see that the prisoners are well treated, I cannot ask you to release them. We both know what is going to happen." Aki started to sob.

The princess put her arm around her friend. "I have an idea, Aki-san. You must smile. Put on these clothes here, the blue kimono with gold. I will arrange for you to see your Jujiro, but you must wait here until I return. No one will bother you, I have dismissed all the servants. Hai, you will see your man. Iie, you won't be taking any chances. Being my friend does not brand you a Jugi Hoshi in everyone's eyes. I—"

"Sakura-san!" The call came from the bath.

Sakura held her finger to her lips, then whispered again to Aki, "Go ahead, get dressed. We cannot do it while you are in those clothes, they even have the Jugi Hoshi monshō on them." She pointed to the bath. "There is the gokarō, I will talk to him now. And to my father, if necessary. I will arrange it, nē."

"Dōmo arigatō, Sakura-san, I will wait here for you."

"It is getting dark," said the princess, "but do not light

the lamp." She closed the shōji to the garden, then crossed the room to depart by way of the hall. Sakura waved to Aki, then closed the shōji behind her.

Kenichi Ueida stepped from the vat when Sakura entered the room. "Say nothing at all," he told her, "until you hear what I have to say. I have thought much about us while I bathed. First, I will tell you this: I do love you. Without you, there is no reason for me to live. If it were not so, I would have left with my friend."

Sakura smiled as she threw herself into his arms.

"Back off, woman!" Kenichi said, laughing. "Can't you see that I am not dressed?"

Sakura giggled. "But that is the way I want you."

"Too bad, there is no time for that," returned Kenichi. "I have something that I must do." His face became serious. "I am going to the cell block. I do not believe that Ikoma should hold prisoners again. I am going to free them."

Sakura was taken aback. Her eyes widened in amazement. It did not make sense to her, then it did. "Kenichi-san, I love you so much. The gods are still working for me. It was the very reason I came back to talk to you."

"I don't understand," said the gokarō.

"Just do this for me, Kenichi-san. Go to the cell block, see that they are well cared for. But wait until I talk to the daimyō before you release them."

The puzzlement dissolved from Kenichi's face. Ah, this woman was surely Aki reincarnated. Sakura, also, did not like war, she could not bear to see the prisoners suffer. Kenichi gathered her to him again. "I must hurry," Kenichi said after he kissed her. "I do not know how much patience your father has, but he must wait a little bit longer. Here, help me with my kimono."

When Sakura Murata left her room, Aki Taizo stripped off Hetomi's kimono. From her inrō, she took her comb and she fixed her hair the best she could in the darkness. She donned Sakura's kimono and tied the gold obi around her.

Aki could hear the voices in the next room. She listened and smiled when the man told Sakura of his love. But something was strange. It was the man's voice, his choice of words. Aki's heart suddenly beat faster. She edged toward the shōji that separated the bath from the room she was in. Now she could almost see them through the paper walls. The voices from the bath were clear now.

"But that is the way I want you," Aki heard Sakura say.

Carefully, Aki hooked her fingers on the edge of the sliding door. Soundlessly, she pushed it open enough so that she could see. Aki's head swam when she saw Jujiro. She closed her eyes, then opened them again. He was still there.

The name Kenichi was a fraud. There was no doubt in Aki's mind that this was Prince Jujiro Fugita. The white kimono was his, his swords with the Jugi Hoshi monshō lay on the floor near enough for Aki to see.

Aki closed her eyes again. Amaterasu, is my debt to you so great that this is how it must end? When Aki opened her eyes, she saw Sakura's look of love as Jujiro kissed her.

Aki Taizo pushed the shōji closed as she backed from the scene. "Oh, Sakura-san, I owe you so much," Aki said, sighing. Tears ran down her cheeks. She reached into her inrō and withdrew the wood-covered knife from it.

Aki did not tie her ankles. She had no reason to care how anyone found her. She dropped the sheath of the tantō to the floor. The side with the crossed-star symbol faced up.

One quick jab and the knife's point was in her neck. It took both hands to pull the blade through her jugular vein. The blue kimono turned crimson. Aki slumped over backwards, making no sound.

But where is the gokarō?" asked the daimyō.

"He will be here soon," said Princess Sakura. "I have just been with him and he is beautiful."

"I am sure he is," replied her father. "I have been sitting here waiting almost two hours. I expected you both would be here any minute."

"Otōsan, we have all the time in the world, and besides, I am not dressed. Kenichi said he had something he must attend to. I wanted to talk to you alone."

"What is it that is so important?" Kumahatchi asked.

"It is that I will marry Kenichi," Sakura answered simply.

He smiled down at her. "So this is what you are worried about? Hai, you will marry him, I have already concluded that."

"And there is another thing. You have spoken many times of your sensei, Sanda. Then you always say you must tell me of him. Why? Now you must tell me." Sakura would keep her father talking, giving Kenichi enough time to finish what he was doing and return from the cell block. She would not ask her father about the prisoners right now.

Kumahatchi smiled at his daughter. "Hai, it is time. Otherwise, you will pester me without end.

"Sanda was my sensei and closest friend. Years before

you were born, I found employment as a monban at the palace in Heian-Kyō. Because of an incident there, only the most efficient swordsmen were allowed to be guards around the Empress's living quarters.

"Those that guarded the Empress were paid double koku, and it was a mark of prestige to be one of them. I sought the best sensei to tutor me. This was Sanda. Together, we were assigned as the Empress's guards and soon we became close friends.

"One day we saw the most beautiful woman in the garden. It turned out that she was companion and confidante to Her highness. Her name was Sakura, the same as yours. 'Sakura' is a word always associated with the samurai.

"Sanda and myself spoke of her and argued together over which of us would court her. I had been with Sakura many times, but she had said she would not marry me. I had never mentioned this to Sanda, but now I did and he admitted it was the same with him. In time, Sakura was heavy with child.

"No rain fell for many days. The bloodless death struck the capital. Your mother was one of the first to fall sick.

"The day your mother died, her twins were born, you and another. But there was no room in the palace for girl babies, and you were to be destroyed. Sanda and I stepped forward to save you. We went to the Empress, each of us claiming to be the father.

"Her solution was to award to each of us a child and, to avoid any scandal, she banished us from the capital.

"So you see, Sakura-san, it is possible that I am not your blood father."

"It makes no difference to me," said Sakura. "You are my father. Was Sanda a nōmin?" she asked. "He had only one name."

"Iie, he had two names. He was Sanda Taizo, and I loved him." Kumahatchi's eyes watered.

Sakura felt great pity for her father. She threw her arms around him. "No one but you could be my father." She kissed him.

"There it is," Kumahatchi said. "Go now, get dressed. Wear your gold and blue kimono. You look exactly like your mother in it."

Sakura felt good when she left the room. She thought of what her father told her, and it made her proud. And it meant that Aki was her lost twin. No wonder they had drawn together instinctively. Hai, it was the gods who had brought Aki to her. But Aki's name was wrong, it should be Taizo, not Fugita. If Aki had been married, she would have told her. When she got back to her room, Sakura would ask Aki about Sanda. Oh, they would have so much to talk about.

What was keeping Kenichi? He should have been back by now, even though the kilns were a long way. Sakura stopped at the shōji to her room, her hand an inch from the door. She turned. She would see if she could find Kenichi. Aki would be all right, no one would bother her. The servants were gone.

In the darkness, Sakura could see the square forms of the kilns. A single torch gave out feeble light before one of them. This must be the cell block. There was no monban. Had Kenichi already freed the prisoners?

Sakura would not enter the building. She was on foreign ground. She did not even want to think about this part of Ikoma.

The low murmur of voices came to Sakura. Kenichi was still there. "Gomen kudasai," Sakura called.

"Hai." It was the gokarō who answered from within. A moment later he stood in front of the princess.

"You should not have come here," Kenichi said.

"But I thought I must, the daimyō is impatient. Iie, it was I who was worried. If you want me to return to the manor, I will, or I will wait for you."

For a moment, the gokarō gave no answer. Then: "Go back to the manor. Tell the daimyō that General Ito is dead. The rope tightened on his neck and strangled him. Also tell him this: Prince Jujiro Fugita is here. Tell the daimyō to prepare himself to meet him."

"What has happened, Kenichi?" asked Sakura.

"I am not Kenichi. I am Jujiro Fugita, Prince of the Jugi Hoshi, the last name on your father's list. If you do not leave now, I will reach the manor before you can warn your father."

D*aimyō Kumahatchi Murata* stared at the painted tea bowl before him. The pictures of the two samurai fascinated him. He picked up the bowl for a closer look. He realized it had been done by one who knew the art form nise-e, recreating a picture from life, in perfect detail. It was an art which Sakura sometimes experimented with. Hai, whoever painted these was a true artist.

Kumahatchi turned the bowl upside down. The kanji words—Okei and Aki—circled around the bold monshō of the Jugi Hoshi on the bowl's bottom. He looked at the picture of the samurai again. My God! It was General Ito. He recognized his purple karaginu. There was no doubt of it. Kumahatchi had visited the cell block the night Ito was brought there.

The other figure on the bowl was familiar also, it bore a resemblance to . . . Hai! It was Kenichi Ueida.

The daimyō set down the bowl and picked up another. The picture was different, but each face held true. He put his thumb over the white-clad figure's hair. It was Kenichi Ueida.

"Sakura!" Kumahatchi shouted.

There was no answer.

"Sakura!" the daimyō called again. He clapped his hands, but no servants appeared. Kumahatchi rose to his feet. What could be wrong? He felt a cold chill on his neck. He clapped his hands once more, then listened. The only sound he heard was the soft rustle of his own kimono as he moved.

Leaving the room, Kumahatchi stepped into the hall. There was a light coming from Sakura's bath. She should have heard him.

"Sakura, do you hear me?" Still, only silence answered him.

Kumahatchi opened the shōji to the bath. No one was there. He felt the water in the vat. It was cold.

There was no light in Sakura's room, but the shōji to it was slightly ajar. Kumahatchi slammed the shōji open, flooding the scene before him with light.

Kumahatchi saw the blood first. The tatami near the dead woman's head was saturated. Her legs were wide apart, her blue kimono above her knees. Now he saw the wood sheath of the knife. Its symbol burned into Kumahatchi's eyes.

"Iie!" the daimyō screamed. "Iie! Iie! I am too late. Iie, this cannot be. His revenge is too great." Kumahatchi fell to his knees and gathered the dead woman to him. He whispered in her ear between sobs. "Oh, my Sakura-san, forgive me. I did not know. I have failed to protect you. My gods, my gods, do not do this to me."

Tears flowed freely down Kumahatchi's cheeks as he

fixed Sakura's futon. He placed the dead woman on it and covered her with the blanket up to her chin. A strand of hair was out of place on her head, carefully he straightened it.

Kumahatchi Murata knelt down by his sleeping daughter, his princess. He held her hand in his, as he had done so many times before.

Jujiro Fugita stood near the door of the cell block, watching Sakura walk away from him. She was outlined in the darkness by a light farther on. He saw her stop, then look back.

She has no part in this, Jujiro reminded himself. He should not have sent her to the manor. That was the last place he wanted her.

"Hetomi," the prince called into the cell block.

"Hai," answered the runner, as he stepped from the prison.

"That woman"—Jujiro pointed to Sakura—"bring her back!"

Hetomi hurried toward the woman as fast as his weak legs could go. Moments later, Hetomi and the woman were back at the kiln.

"Leave us," Jujiro told Hetomi. "See to Tasuke."

"Sakura-san, you will only listen. I do not wish you to speak."

The woman nodded. Her eyes were wet and red from crying.

"I ask you, Sakura, to forgive me for what I am about to try to do. I came back to Ikoma for a purpose, but because of you, I forgot it for a while. Now that is changed. Yes, I love you and want you with me always. But know this: the gods never reveal their plans to us. We drift in the winds, like the fragile cherry blossom, with no set course. We do not know where we stop. This is called sakuran.

"Yes, I am Prince Jujiro Fugita, son of Yasumori Fugita, the daimyō of Ikoma. My mother was Okei Fugita, an artist like yourself. Sakura, my closest friend lies dead in that cell block. He is Tasuke Ito, son of the gokarō of Ikoma. There was Shishido, Taizo, many others you have never heard of. All were a part of me, and now all of them are gone. Again, I say that I am sorry I must hurt you by what I must do, but—"

"Kenichi!" Sakura broke in.

"Silence. I am not Kenichi, I am a Jugi Hoshi samurai. I must challenge your father, he must answer for all those I have just named. The honor of my family is beyond even the love I feel for you. Hetomi, lock her in a cell. She will be safe there, whatever happens."

Jujiro and Hetomi walked to the manor in silence. The prince held the long sword ready in his hand. As the two men neared the building, Hetomi finally spoke. "What is your plan, my lord? He is not unguarded."

Jujiro did not look at the runner. He stared straight ahead as he walked. "I have no plan," he said. "It is only that this tōryō must die before the next sun rises."

"Where are his guards? I will take care of them."

"I have no idea," returned the prince. "They cannot stop me."

"I beg you, my lord. Wait a bit while I check his monban's positions. They will not see me."

"Do as you like. Go ahead, but it is not necessary. I do not plan to ambush him. He told me once he had a point to prove."

Hetomi sprinted ahead of the prince.

The manor was in darkness when Jujiro reached it. He did not enter. Instead, he circled around until he saw the only light, the one coming from Sakura's apartment.

"Yatō Murata! Do you hear me?" Jujiro shouted.

Something struck the bushes close to the prince's head. Jujiro spun down and away, trying to blend with the shadows. He knew the pale silk kimono he wore would not let him hide. Again, something whooshed the air past his ear. An archer? No, Jujiro did not hear the string.

Jujiro's eyes swept the garden. He spotted the man who drew back his left hand to throw again.

The prince moved quickly to avoid Hitari's missile. In a split second, Jujiro was at the man's side. He did not hesitate, but swung his sword hand, feeling it bite through the body of the nōmin with no resistance.

Jujiro looked down at the dead man. The hilts of the useless swords the nōmin wore had the Jugi Hoshi symbols on them. The prince pulled out both of the nōmin's swords and plunged them hard into Hitari's chest. The long sword swung back and forth, the kogatana did not.

"Yatō Murata, do you hear me?" Jujiro shouted again.

"Hai, I hear you, rapist of little children. Hai, I am here. I am here to see that you die slowly."

The shōji burst from Sakura's room as Kumahatchi kicked it before him.

Jujiro Fugita held his sword over his head. His feet were apart in the defensive stance, as training and instinct had taught him.

The two swordsmen drew together in slow motion.

Jujiro checked the position of the daimyō's elbows in relation to his feet, and the angle of the sword, trying to guess the direction of the daimyō's first swing. Quickly, the prince shifted, he had read the clues properly. His sword blocked Kumahatchi's as it swung upward. The tōryō was trying the more difficult swings first. The prince remembered Keisuke and how much he had suffered from the blows of his sensei's wooden sword.

When the daimyō readied for his next charge, Jujiro was already moving. His sword swung up from the last block, hitting Kumahatchi's wrists with the flat top edge. Jujiro had almost succeeded in disarming the tōryō, but he realized the daimyō knew how to lock his grip to the handle. Jujiro would not waste time trying this again. With each swing you should learn, Keisuke had said. If you do not, you are dead.

"So you know the sword?" Kumahatchi leered. "Then I will not play with you, rapist. I will cut you quickly." The daimyō charged, this time using the okesa, the robe-of-the-priest swing. But he missed, the Jugi Hoshi was not there, he was on the other side of Kumahatchi.

Jujiro held his sword straight before him, as though pointing at the daimyō. "You should know who I am, yatō. I am he, the last name on your list, the one you have waited for."

"I know who you are, Jugi Hoshi. Save your breath, you will need it to die easier."

Kumahatchi circled to his right. In a moment, he would attempt the swing he had practiced for so long. No sensei taught its defense. This Jugi Hoshi would have the honor of being the first to die from it. Take your time, Kumahatchi told himself. This youngster is much too quick. Easy, easy, wait, he is not on the defense, the youngster readies for his own swing.

The daimyō's mouth moved as he talked to himself. Easy, easy. Unconsciously, the daimyō shifted his sword to the defensive. He did not even see the start of the young man's swing, yet somehow he was able to block it. He heard the swords clang together.

Kumahatchi retreated, then pushed forward with the simple attacks that were noted for their speed in execution.

The prince blocked them all.

The daimyō was soaked now. He tightened both hands firmly on the handle, interlocking the little finger of one hand with those of the other. He would not allow his sweat to loosen his sword.

The two men circled again, both held their swords up high, each invited the other. Both weapons swung and met, the daimyō backed away, but the gokarō's sword was preparing to swing again.

This time, the young man's blade tore through Kumahatchi's sleeve. The daimyō felt the sharp point slice across his wrists. The daimyō's mouth moved again. Iie, iie! he attempts sodesuri, the removing of the hands, the most difficult cut of all. Iie, he could not do it, his try had been an accident.

Kumahatchi feinted at Jujiro, driving him back. The daimyō could afford no error, he must end this duel soon. Kumahatchi must watch for the opportunity of striking with the double swing. His mouth moved again. Ah, it comes now . . . Get ready . . . When the Jugi Hoshi makes his next move, it will put him in the right position. Easy . . . Easy . . .

The two moved together in slow motion. Each antagonist sensed that the battle's end was near.

Jujiro's eyes swept up and down his opponent. He must not miss any hints. Hai, let the tōryō swing, then Jujiro could hit with the sodesuri again.

Kumahatchi's sword moved, then changed direction at mid-point. With surprise, Jujiro felt the tōryō's blade cut across his chest. It did not hurt. Jujiro twisted on his left foot, avoiding the blade as it crisscrossed his body the second time. Suddenly the prince remembered Kumahatchi at practice, and shifted his weight to get under the daimyō's sword. Jujiro knifed his blade up and felt the hesitation of the sword as it cut through bone. He achieved the sodesuri in reverse.

The daimyō's sword fell to the ground, his fingers still locked around the handle. Kumahatchi dropped to his knees. His glassy eyes could not believe what had just happened.

"Do you hear me, tōryō?" asked Jujiro.

The wounded man did not answer. He closed his eyes, as though trying to keep everything out.

"Tōryō, do you hear me?" This time, Jujiro spoke in a lower voice.

Kumahatchi opened his eyes and looked at his gokarō. Shock and pain had driven all hate from the daimyō's eyes.

"Hai," Kumahatchi whispered. "Hai, I hear."

"Before I kill you," said the prince in an even voice, "I must tell you this one last thing. Keisuke Shishido was my sensei."

The daimyō shook his head. "Iie—it was not because of Keisuke. I—I had to fight against the gods. Kenichi—you are fading. I am fainting now—kudasai, my swords—my swords must stay with me."

Sorrow suddenly overwhelmed Jujiro. Helplessly, he looked at the watered eyes that could not see him. "Hai," said the prince. "You are a samurai. Hai, they will stay with you."

Kumahatchi's mouth moved once more, with gratitude. The daimyō dropped his head to his chest, swayed, but steadied himself once again in his kneeling position.

"Dōmo. Hayaku. Now!" It was a low whisper, but the gokarō heard it as a shout.

Prince Jujiro screamed as he swung his sword once more.

The gokarō let the point of his sword rest on the ground. The sorrow he felt now was no different from the sorrow he had felt before, at Mina when he had heard of the death of his parents and of Aki.

"Ah, it is done," Jujiro told himself. He turned to walk away, dragging his sword on the path. "My gods, it is no more," Jujiro said aloud. "It is over."

Suddenly Jujiro felt cold. A faint gust of wind seared his body with pain. Remembering his wound, he reached to his chest, a picture flashing before him, a picture of Keisuke Shishido lying helpless on the table.

Jujiro's fear increased when he realized he could no longer hold his sword. It tipped to the ground, and the sudden weakness of his legs threatened to bring him down as well. Wildly, Prince Jujiro fought against it and reached out for support, to find Hetomi at his side.

The charging horses pounded the turf of the practice fields, sending sounds of thunder to the manor. The daimyō listened, remembering when he had aimed carefully with the bulb-nosed spear and shot at the target with the bow from horseback.

The kilns of Ikoma were smoking again. Though there were few wagons that left the mura now, in time there would be enough for caravans again. The daimyō had once wanted to be part of the caravans, but now he had no time. He looked at the hills of Ikoma and marveled again at the varied colors of the rice paddies. These rice paddies were stepping stones to the hilltop where he and Tasuke Ito had hunted the shika with the bow. Hai, the daimyō had too much to do now. The first pottery shipments were leaving; when the wagons returned, the manufacture would be doubled.

The harsh sound of the wooden clapper erased the sound of the hoofbeats for a moment. The daimyō rose and made his way to the small, austere room. When he entered, Daimyō Jujiro Fugita nodded to his wife as she smiled and bowed before him.

"The gokarō will not come," the daimyō's wife told him. "He is awaiting the birth of his second son. It will be any minute."

"Suppose it is not a boy," said the daimyō. "He would be so disappointed."

"I am sure it will be a boy," replied Sakura. "I tell you that now, before it is born, so that you cannot say it is a coincidence. Hai, it will be a boy."

"Have you been talking to the gods again?" asked Jujiro, smiling.

"You do not believe me, so I will speak no more about it." She whipped the tea, first in the large bowl in front of her husband, then in her own bowl. They sipped the tea in silence. Sakura spoke when she set her bowl down. "Someone is coming. Hetomi's son must have been born."

"I hear nothing," said Jujiro. He listened carefully. A moment later, he heard the footsteps.

Hetomi entered the tearoom. Sakura pushed a bowl toward him. She poured the hot water on the powdered tea, then mixed it with the whisk. "Well, are you not going to tell us?" she asked.

Hetomi broke into a grin. "Kimi, my son is born. He lies beside Somiko now, and he will be big."

"What did I tell you, Kenichi-san?" Sakura asked the daimyō, her eyes laughing at him.

Jujiro smiled back, but spoke to Hetomi. "What name have you picked for the new samurai?"

"Why, he is Tasuke, of course," said the gokarō. "Tasuke's swords are in his crib. They are almost five times his length, but he will grow to use them and become the greatest warrior of all. And he will laugh at what we have done in our lives."

"Is that right, Sakura-san?" asked Jujiro.

"Of course, Kenichi-san." Sakura laughed also.

The woman fixed more tea, and for a while the three friends were silent. Finally Jujiro spoke.

"Have I told you, Sakura, that you are the most beautiful woman in the world?" Jujiro paused, as Sakura twinkled. "But you have held back our child for too long a time. Do you always want to be fat in the middle?"

"I do it on purpose, Kenichi-san. His time with me is much too short. In six years, your son and Hetomi's will be given to you both. But for this short time they are ours, Somiko's and mine."

"Sakura, I have a thought. Six years is too long a time. I think it should be cut to one. Do you agree, Hetomi?"

The laughter in the room was part of the peaceful sounds of Ikoma.

DOMAIN OF
KUBLAI KHAN
Sea of Japan
Yellow Sea
CHŌSEN
Seishin
Fu
Fusan
Kaike
Yonago
Mina
O
Heian-
H
Kure
Tsushima
Iki
Yawata
Hakata
SHIKOKU
Kochi
Torosko
Hirado
KYŪSHŪ
East China Sea
GREA